MURDER
ON THE
ZENITH EXPRESS

MURDER
ON THE
ZENITH EXPRESS

Gordon Mamon
THE ~~GRODON MAMMAL~~ COLLECTION

SIMON PETRIE

Typeset in Adobe Garamond Pro / Century Gothic
Cover artwork by Shauna O'Meara

National Library of Australia Cataloguing-in-Publication entry

Title: Murder on the Zenith Express: the Gordon Mamon collection
                / Simon Petrie.
ISBN: 9780648322887 (pbk.)
Subjects: Science fiction, Australian.
                Short stories, Australian.
Other Authors / Contributors:
                O'Meara, Shauna, cover artist.
Dewey Number: A823.4

Table of Contents

Books by Simon Petrie

(The Titan Sequence)

Matters Arising from the Identification of the Body

Wide Brown Land

A Reappraisal of the Circumstances Resulting in Death (forthcoming)

Flight 404

Murder on the Zenith Express: the Gordon Mamon collection

80,000 Totally Secure Passwords That No Hacker Would Ever Guess

To some editor

Preface

I have a definite fondness for Gordon Mamon, who (for good or ill) has been a formative influence on my writing in several ways. My first Gordon Mamon story, 'Murder on the Zenith Express', written during the last weeks of 2006, was also my first SF story sale; my first published story of more than five thousand words (written at a time when two thousand words was a major threshold for me); and the first story I started without already knowing the ending. The Gordon Mamon stories are also my earliest series: by 2009, I had written three of them. I've added to that total over the years.

One of the aspects of the Gordon stories that I find most appealing – and I'm speaking only for myself here, since I suspect there is a very sizeable sector of the community for whom such a notion is anathema – is that a Gordon Mamon story doesn't just permit puns, it requires them. (They're not, as a rule, my most outrageous puns – I think my story 'Hare Redux' might sweep the pool on that score – but there are quite a few of them. I pity the narrator, in the remote chance that this volume is ever converted into audiobook format.) I mention this now (hopefully after the point of purchase) as fair warning that the seriously pun-averse might wish to just put the book down and quietly walk away.

I should note that this collection of six Gordon Mamon stories – the first four of which have previously appeared in an electronic collection, *The Gordon Mamon Casebook*, now out of print – is, in a sense, intentionally incomplete. I have omitted the story 'A Night To Remember' on the grounds that I now consider it (a) non-canonical and (2) written in undue haste, since it was speedily drafted and published online during one week in September 2012, as one of the online events associated with SpecFicNZ's 'speculative fiction blogging week'. Though I retain a certain fondness for the story, it has always seemed to me to be a bit of an ugly duckling alongside the others, and so I've withheld it from this collection.

The total wordcount on my significantly more serious Titan stories now substantially exceeds Gordon's wordcount, and that gap seems likely to increase; but the world of Gordon Mamon, with its freakish nominative determinism, its fickle technology, and its propensity for fiendishly-motivated murder is one to which I've returned repeatedly, after having told myself several times that, no, this was the last one I'd write. Will there be more? As the oxymoronic axiom has it, never say never...

As always, there are others I must ~~implicate~~ thank for their involvement in these stories. Several were fed through the Canberra Speculative Fiction Guild's short story critiquing group; additional improvement has been variously effected by the editorial intervention of Dirk Flinthart, Fred Coppersmith, Gillian Polack, Scott Hopkins, and Edwina Harvey. I'm grateful, also, to Jacob Edwards, Kim Gaal, and Rob Porteous for their insight and suggestions on various of the longer stories. And, of course, I am indebted to the sublimely-talented Shauna O'Meara (no relation) for her stunning cover art.

Simon Petrie
May 2018

Murder on the Zenith Express

Gordon Mamon was the lift operator in a hotel that didn't have a lift.

The hotel, the "Skyward Suites 270", *was* the lift.

Skyward was an organisation that had taken the concept of multi-tasking, and embraced it so firmly as to hold it in a virtual death-grip. As well as lift operator, Gordon's job description encompassed first aid officer, complaints officer, janitor, dishwasher, room service, security officer and house detective. In his spare moments, which were few and far between, Gordon was also a crossword and trivia buff.

Gordon's life was full of wardrobe changes, since he was a firm believer in always being dressed appropriately for the duty at hand. Right now he was wondering just where he'd left his "detective" hat. He couldn't recall having needed it before today.

He'd been called to the bathroom of a guest's suite to attend to a problem of some errant plumbing, but his knock hadn't been answered and he had had to override the door's biometric scanners to let himself in. Now he pocketed his master glass eyeball and plastic thumb, and gazed around the bathroom. There was a problem, sure enough, but it didn't look like the plumbing.

The suite's occupant, Neil B. Formey, was dressed ready for a bath, but wasn't going to be taking it anytime soon. Formey was clad only in a hotel bathtowel two sizes too small for him; and Formey was dead.

Gordon reviewed what he knew of Formey, which was reasonably superficial. He'd only met the man a few hours ago when the hotel was beginning its ascent. Formey was famous, an egotistical financier and ruthless industry heavyweight from the thriving colonies of Proxima Centauri, but had kept out of the public eye as much as possible. A generous tipper (Gordon had received a C-credit for showing Formey to his room), but you felt that he expected much for that tip, and that the service delivered was just the beginning: the hotel tip as Faustian bargain. A busy man, brash; a man with his fingers in a hundred pies. A man, too, who apparently always licked those fingers: he was a heavyweight in a literal as well as metaphoric sense.

Gordon gingerly adjusted the corpse's bathtowel for the sake of modesty, and ran an autopsy scan of the body using his handheld. The scanner's immediate diagnosis was "*dead*", but hopefully it would come up with something more useful after it had completed its analysis. Still, that could take hours.

There was nothing to indicate how the guest had met his end. No visible marks on the body (though Gordon wasn't game to lift that towel again just yet), no blood, no discarded weapons or misplaced items. Nevertheless, Gordon was reasonably sure it was murder. Men like Formey just didn't die a natural death, they'd made too many enemies.

The Skyward Suites was a *distributed* hotel, partitioned into five hundred and sixty self-contained, airtight, independent units. Each unit alternated between a five-day "sessile" cycle, when it was incorporated into the hivelike conglomerate of the Skytop Plaza (a mega-hotel in geostationary orbit which served as one of Earth's principal gateways for interstellar travel and in-system space tourism); and a six-day "motile" cycle when individual units were detached from the larger structure, slotted into the massive descending drive chains of the Plaza's dedicated space elevator tower, and propelled on the long return journey to Earth's surface. The Plaza was rated as a five-star hotel;

the individual units lacked some of the diversity of facilities and services accessible to the parent body, but still rated four stars and a brown dwarf. Not bad for a glorified elevator cubicle.

Gordon was seated in Formey's loungeroom. He'd sealed off the bathroom and its occupant, and had decided that the loungeroom was as good as any place to set up as his headquarters for the investigation. The surroundings, so close to the scene of the crime, might well yield some subliminal clue to the murder, if only through the suspects' reactions. Besides, the chairs were much more comfortable than those in his own quarters.

He checked the guest register. Aside from Formey, there were three other guests: Hostij, O'Meara, and Taybill. He'd have to interview each of them in turn.

Frida Hostij was a noted police negotiator from the North New South Carolina police force on Mars. She was a shapely, athletic-looking brunette who was dressed well, in good quality off-the-rack garments: Gordon, who considered himself a snappy dresser, tended to notice details of other peoples' outfits. Still, he couldn't help thinking that the trim short-sleeve top was, for her, a mistake, since it gave prominence to an incompletely erased tattoo on her left forearm. Gordon couldn't keep from stealing glances at her forearm while he questioned her, but the partially-eradicated tattoo remained stubbornly indecipherable.

Hostij had been assigned the suite next to Formey's, and there was a connecting door between the rooms. This allocation, Gordon learnt, had not been accidental: the two were romantically involved. Furthermore, they'd apparently been talking together in Formey's suite not half an hour before he'd met his end.

'—can't *believe* it!' she complained. 'We – we were going to start a new life, at Colony 337 around Barnard's Star! He was going to leave his wives for me! I'll – I'll kill him!'

'He's already dead,' Gordon observed.

'No, I mean – whoever did this!' She breathed deeply, and steepled her hands atop the bridge of her nose before burying her face in her hands. Gordon waited a minute, and then offered a handkerchief which was disdainfully waved away. Hostij gave a healthy snort, replaced her hands in her lap, and lifted her gaze back to meet his. Her eyes were rimmed with red, and with stray moisture. 'Thanks, I'm fine now,' she said. 'It's just such a *waste!*'

'Ms Hostij,' Gordon asked. 'My condolences: this must be a difficult time for you.' (She snorted again, more derisively this time.) 'However, I need to ask. Do you have any evidence to support your assertion that Mr Formey was going to leave all the trappings of a highly successful career, all his family ties, to embark on a… romantic adventure with you? In a colony which, from all the media reports, is – shall we say – rustic to say the least?'

'*Rustic?*' she snapped. 'Listen, Mr Mammoth, or whatever your name is! I don't have what it takes for your amateur skepticism right now. I'm telling you straight. I… didn't… kill… Neil! I could *never* do that!'

'Yes, you could,' Gordon protested, bristling at the "mammoth" slur. 'You're trained to kill in the line of duty.'

She sighed, as if dealing with a child. 'Yes, alright, I'm a *cop,* I'm trained in the use of deadly force. But that doesn't mean I could kill Neil. I would *never* kill Neil! And no, I don't have any *proof* that he was going to leave them, he just told me so. But he was telling the *truth*. And *I'm* telling the truth!' She sounded exasperated: Gordon supposed he could hardly blame her. She reached into her purse for a make-up mirror.

Gordon persisted. 'Nonetheless, Ms Hostij, you have to admit it doesn't look good.'

'What doesn't look good?' she asked, glancing up from the mirror, and back again.

'Your story, I mean. You might have just found out that, in fact, he wasn't going to leave his wives for you. We have only your word for it that he didn't tell you such a thing. You're in an adjoining room, with ready access to his suite, *and* you're trained in the use of lethal force. Means, motive, and opportunity. Plus, you don't have an alibi.'

She clenched her fists. The look that she shot him could skin a small animal. 'Arrrgh! But I DO have an alibi! Honestly, you don't know the first thing about interrogation!' She took a calming breath. 'Listen, I told you at the beginning! All the time I was in here talking to Neil, the other guy was in here too! He wouldn't leave! Eventually I got called to reception to deal with some irregularity with my baggage. They other guy was still in here when I left.'

'What other guy?'

'Look, I don't know what his flicking name is! The wrestler.'

'What wrestler?'

She adopted the tone normally used by primary school teachers when talking to slow learners. 'How many wrestlers do you have in this place?'

'Yes, I suppose you're right. I should be able to find that out through my enquiries. Thank you.'

She stood to leave.

He called her back at the door. 'Before you go, Ms Hostij, do you mind telling me what the tattoo says? Said?'

'Look, it's not important.'

'Nonetheless…'

She sighed. 'Very well. It's a membership badge. Was. *Indecisives Anonymous.*'

One Ton O'Meara, the champion Mexican-Irish sumo wrestler, settled himself awkwardly into the chair across from Gordon. O'Meara, dressed in a short-sleeved open-necked leisure suit, appeared rather more liberally endowed with body hair than Gordon had expected for one of his profession. In other respects, however, he fitted the mould.

Gordon asked how he was connected to Formey.

'He's my new manager,' O'Meara answered. 'Was my new manager. Suppose I'm between managers at the moment.'

O'Meara was surprisingly softly spoken for one of his stature. If Hostij was fiery, this one, Gordon surmised, was a gentle giant. Nevertheless, he might still have something to hide...

'Did you have any complaints?'

'Against Neil?' O'Meara paused. 'No, look, Mr Melon'—Gordon winced—'he was fairer than fair to me. I'd come to see him, 'cos I was unhappy about this gig—'

'Gig?'

'The wrestling match at the Plaza.' (There was, Gordon recalled, some sort of combat-sport convention currently being held at the hotel towards which they were ascending.) 'I was nervous about it, see, 'cos I ain't accustomed to zero-gee wrestling. Gravity's my friend, you might say, and zero-gee, it ain't my friend, not so much. I ain't never done zero-gee wrestling, and I wanted to see with Neil if it was somethink I had to go through with. Stomach's been getting a bit unsettled, even on this trip, as the gravity falls away.' O'Meara stifled a belch. 'Excuse me.'

'Go on.'

'Anyway, Neil was very understanding. He wrote me a cheque, just today, one million credits, which is a lot of money even at my level... said that I should go through with the match, even if I didn't do too well at it. He said that even if I made a right bollocks of it, it was better to be seen to compete than to pull out at the last minute. And he said that the payment was just to, like, keep me on side, 'cos he had big plans for me.'

'Can you show me this cheque? Do you have it?'

O'Meara reached into his pocket and pulled out a dainty black wallet, from which in turn he extracted a neatly folded rectangle of paper. He handed this to Gordon.

The cheque looked authentic enough. Except— 'Mr O'Meara, do you realise that this is dated for three days' time?'

'Yeah, that's right. It's for after the match, see. He told me he was post-dating it, just as insurance to make sure that I did compete in the match.

That was fine with me.' He paused. 'Don't suppose I'll be able to cash it now, him being so dead and all.'

The third guest, Trey Taybill, was the steward (and, it transpired, also astronavigator, baggage handler, customs officer and booking clerk) for a Chastity Cosmic passenger flight due to depart from the Plaza in four days' time. Gordon observed to himself that Chastity, a budget starcruiser line seeking to undercut Andromeda Spaceways on the popular routes, appeared to have the same business model as the Skyward hotel chain...

Taybill, who was returning to space from a few days' gravity leave, had the short, slim physique favoured by Chastity's employment officers. The budget line was notorious for offering very low upfront fares while being ruthless on excess baggage charges, and its procurement policy was in line with its cut-throat attitude to inflight mass minimisation for reasons of fuel economy. As another symptom of the company's drive to pare fuel costs, it was a prolific dumper of inflight waste: discarded Chastity meal wrappings, utensils, and used VR headsets were now rumoured to be the primary source of interstellar debris on the main space routes.

Gordon had done a quick background check on Taybill, as he had on the other guests. Taybill's employment record was so clean you could eat off it, but he had a longstanding debt to the Plaza's casino. Not a massive amount, but slowly growing despite regular payments. Gordon asked about the debt.

'Look, Mr Mammogram.' (*Mamon*, Gordon breathed to himself. Was that so hard? Or maybe that dyslexia virus had compromised his name-badge again.) 'It was a long time ago. I bet on a sure thing that turned out to be not so certain. I'm paying it off.'

'But the debt's increasing.'

'So I like a little flutter now and then. Doesn't everybody? Don't you?'

'I'm not a bird, Mr Taybill.'

The guest glowered. 'Look, why you asking me about my debt? That's old news. I'm a good employee... aren't you supposed to be investigating a murder, or some such?'

'I'm just seeking to establish possible motives, Mr Taybill. Anyway, who said anything about murder?'

'It's all over the hotel. The walls have ears.'

This wasn't strictly true, but Gordon thought that he could surmise the intended meaning.

Taybill continued. 'Look, I've never met this Formey. I've never had anything to do with him, until now. Sure, I've seen his ugly mug in the newscasts, who hasn't? And I guess I know him by reputation. But I've never seen him in person, never spoken to him. You can check that, any way you want to.'

Gordon proceeded to his next question. 'Can you account for your movements between the altitudes of 2972 and 3605 kilometres this afternoon?'

Taybill wrinkled his brow. 'Yeah, I was in the foyer most of that time. There were some irregularities with a guest's baggage, and I was just completing the preflight formalities with her.'

'Which guest? And what kind of irregularities?'

'Ms Hostij, I think her name is. Travelling to Barnard's Star with us. And one of her bags was five grams over the stated value. Honestly, you'd think people would know better than to try to fiddle the system.' Taybill's face registered disgust. 'Anyway, once she'd stopped yapping and paid the two-fifty credits, I signed off on it. That was about... 3400 kilometres, I think. Then I went to my room to finish up the paperwork. As it happens, I was just about to call on Mr Formey after that – he's travelling with Chastity too – when all this happened.'

'Can anyone vouch for your whereabouts between 3400 and 3605 km?'

'Well, no, I was in my room alone, but – actually, yes, they should be able to. I filed a report from my desktop console right about that time.

There's a reply from our booking clerk. You can check my desktop, if you like.'

Gordon sealed off Formey's suite and retired to the observation lounge to mull things over. This was normally his favourite part of the lifting cycle. Earth below was a huge haze-limned ball, sliding further into night; the visible stretch of the elevator tower still glinted in bright sunlight, even though the sun had set several hours ago at the tower's anchorage point many thousands of kilometres below. Tonight, though, the spectacle held little appeal. He had to think through the interviews he'd just completed.

Hostij had seemed genuine, but could conceivably have had a motive if Formey had not, as she had claimed, sought to accompany her to Barnard's Star. But she hadn't, by all accounts, had any time alone with Formey during the critical time window. She had alibis supported by O'Meara, by Taybill, and finally by the hotel's concierge / receptionist / cleaner / counsellor / gardener / childcare operator Belle Hopp, who'd been answering Hostij's query about laundry service after the baggage issue had been settled. O'Meara *had* had some time alone with Formey, but was also in possession of a postdated cheque from Formey which was sizeable enough to constitute, in Gordon's mind, negative motive. And Taybill appeared not to have made contact with Formey at all, with his whereabouts confirmed by first Hostij and then (electronically) by the Chastity booking clerk. Gordon had only Taybill's word on the last, though – he'd need to check that console for himself, to verify that.

All of them seemed like honest, respectable types in their various fashions: Hostij the lovestruck hardened cop, O'Meara the sentimental but straightforward sumo wrestler, Taybill the overworked and earnest spaceline employee. None of them, when you looked at it, had a clear reason for wanting Formey dead. Of course, there could be some kind of conspiracy between them – O'Meara with either of the other guests, or Hostij with Taybill – but that didn't go any way towards clarifying the motive, nor explaining how the deed was executed.

And, to top it off, no weapon, no fingerprints, and still no cause of death (the autopsy scanner seemed stumped, and still pronounced merely *"dead"*. Maybe it was indicating it needed its batteries changed.) Perhaps, against all of Gordon's better judgement, it really was a natural-causes case after all.

Sometimes, he knew, the best way to set your mind on a problem was to give it a different problem. At least, it worked that way with puzzles and crosswords. He wasn't sufficiently experienced to know if detection followed the same rules, but it sounded plausible. He pulled out his handheld and selected the "Riddle/Trivia" function. He'd played this so often before that many of the items from its hundred-thousand-entry memory bank were familiar, but straight up he got a new one:

Can a dead horse travel as fast as a live horse?

Well, the answer seemed obvious – no – but he suspected there was a trick behind it. He couldn't see, however, what the trick was. He paused the trivia program and selected a couple of crosswords, one easy and one a fairly challenging cryptic, to unwind a little further. Then, still none the wiser, he clicked for the answer to the riddle.

No. Under British law, a motorised horse transporter can travel at 30 miles an hour through urban areas, but if the horse dies the vehicle becomes a carrier of horseflesh and must immediately slow to 20 m.p.h.

Surprisingly, this sparked something. He thought, now, he could see a good and compelling motive...

He placed a call to the Chastity business counter at the Skytop Plaza. His call was answered by the receptionist / sales assistant / chaplain.

'Chastity, Helena Handbaskett speaking. Can I help you?'

Gordon gave his details. 'I'm working on a murder investigation down here. I need to know the flight data and ticketing arrangments for four of your passengers.'

'I'm sorry, we're not supposed to release that information, it's confidential.' She paused and leaned conspiratorially into the mouthpiece to whisper to him. 'Look, according to your record you have thirteen thousand frequent flier points with us. If you're prepared to cash those in, I can give you the information you need. Just don't tell my supervisor.'

'Who is your supervisor?'

'For the moment, me.'

'Uh, I'll try not to. Also, while you're at it, if you could send a full description of your passenger and freight handling policies and procedures, that would be very useful.'

'I'm sure we have that somewhere.' She adjusted her glasses. 'Do you want all of that as a facsimile, an email, a direct download...'

He'd need a hard copy, for his records. He put on his best TV detective voice. 'Just the fax, ma'am. Just give me the fax.'

He'd always wanted to say that.

The documentation, when it arrived, told him everything he wanted to know. Hostij was ticketed on the flight, four days' time, to Barnard's Star. O'Meara wasn't booked on any outward flights. And Taybill was on the crew list for the departure, three days from now, for Proxima Centauri.

Most intriguingly, Formey had been booked on both the Barnard's Star *and* Proxima Centauri flights. Now that was curious. Was Formey attempting some vainglorious application of quantum duality to the ticketing process? He couldn't be on both flights... Gordon checked the time of purchase. They'd been booked only seconds apart, about a week ago. He'd purchased them, then, at the same time. This, to Gordon, suggested that he was seriously entertaining the idea of starting over with Hostij, but wanted an escape route if he changed his mind in the interim. And neither ticket had been cancelled...

He read further through the documentation. Yes, *this* was what he'd suspected. This was what tied it all together.

*

Gordon used the eyeball and thumb once more, to enter the guest's room. He knew roughly what he was looking for, but wasn't sure where to find it. Wardrobe... suitcase... bedside drawer... kitchenette cupboard... bathroom cabinet... all negative. It *had* to be here somewhere!

Wait a minute. He looked again at the bedside digital clock. *That* didn't look like Skyward's usual model! He picked up the clock, turned it over, examined it. Yes, this confirmed his suspicions. Now, where was the activator on this thing?

He pressed three buttons before he found the one that gave the desired effect. Even though he'd been partially expecting it, the sudden apparent materialisation of Neil B. Formey, tyrannical multi-sesquillionaire, was startling. Not least because the animated tycoon was at least three metres tall. Gordon twiddled the control surfaces on the "clock" until he found the magnification controls, then reduced Formey's image to a less gigantic size. Now... that looked more realistic.

The holographic projection was indeed remarkably lifelike. Presumably, some of the controls on the "clock" would dictate motion, and perhaps the setup was also designed to convey sounds, simple phrases and such. However, he didn't need to check that out right now. This should be enough to—

'Boy, you sure lucked out,' the voice at the doorway commented, with a nasty edge. 'Ordinarily, I bet you couldn't solve a two-piece jigsaw puzzle without looking at the picture on the box.'

Gordon turned to face the figure in the doorway. His attention was commanded by the weapon that was directed at him. This was only natural since, aside from the evident lethality of the piece, it was also the weapon that had spoken at him. He recognised it as one of the most feared items of portable weaponry in known space. A needle gun.

'Shoulda stuck at washing the dishes, lift-boy,' the gun jeered. 'Your snooping has just got you into a whole plateful of trouble.'

Although the needle gun's jeers and verbal jabs could induce apoplexy in the exceptionally weak-hearted, they weren't usually fatal. Rather, they were a novelty feature designed to improve the weapon's sales. It was the gun's "sticks and stones", rather than the names it called him, which would hurt Gordon. "Sticks and stones" being in this case, he strongly suspected, the gun's standard-issue ammunition: flechettes of cryocooled water ice which encapsulated a lethal neurotoxin. The hardened ice needles were of subcellular thickness ("sharper than a thankless child", according to the sales tag), and capable of piercing skin and muscle without leaving any discernible mark. The neurotoxin was necrodegradable, so that the whole projectile had a lifetime, when fired, which was only slightly greater than that of its victim. A ruthless weapon, with a nasty sense of humour.

'For someone called Gordon, you ain't exactly flash,' the gun commented sardonically.

Gordon managed to wrest his gaze from the gun and lifted his face towards his assailant's.

'Don't do anything you'll regret,' he pleaded.

'*Regret?*' the gun scoffed. 'What could anyone possibly regret about snuffing out your miserable existence? And what in hell's name do you think you can do to protect yourself against a Deadly-Sirius 357 Needle Gun?'

'I have the law on my side,' Gordon responded. He had to admit, it sounded weak even to him. He'd have to do better than that. I will *not* go gentle into that good riddance, he told himself. 'Go on,' he said. 'Tell me why you did it.'

Taybill shrugged. 'If it's all the same to you, I think I'll just shoot.' He stepped fully into the room and allowed the outer door to close, sealing off Gordon's only feasible escape route.

Taybill did not look at ease with the weapon he deployed. His face was pale and tense, his hands were unsteady, and his aim was poor. Not that that would matter. The gun's ammunition pretty much obviated the need for a keen eye: if a round hit you, you were more or less assured of death.

Gordon's mind pulsed with the unfamiliar problem of a life-and-death puzzle. He was keenly aware that every action, every word choice, on his part was critical. A skilled negotiator (such as Hostij) might well be able to talk Taybill down, but Gordon wasn't Hostij. He was under no delusion that he had anything like the required verbal skills to defuse Taybill. And, since the needle gun was semi-autonomous (and perfectly capable of firing itself if it felt the situation warranted it), any attempt by Gordon to dissuade Taybill would probably be disastrous. His one remaining option was to keep the dialogue going, to merely delay the inevitable. Time was all he had to play for now.

'Tell me why you did it,' he asked again.

'Why should I bother?' Taybill asked. He was nervous enough, he might just fire the gun accidentally.

'Humour me,' Gordon said, desperately. 'Look, I already know why you did it. I just want to check if I'm right.'

'Don't believe you,' the gun sneered. 'You couldn't figure—'

'No, I'll prove it,' Gordon interrupted, frantically playing for time. 'It was the transport charges, wasn't it? That, and the gambling debts—'

'I've had it!' Taybill snapped. 'Every month, I make another payment off my gambling debts, and they go hike up the interest rates! I've been going backwards for the past year! You don't know what it's like... I work twenty-five hours a day, seems like, and it's *never enough*. And Formey, one-fifteen kilos of excess baggage, dead weight, at fifty credits a *gram*, just for shipping him back to Proxima Centauri. It was the answer to all my problems! I mean, most passengers, there'd never be enough in the estate to cover that kind of expense, they'd just ask for burial-at-space, but Formey's families, they're loaded, they could cover that without even blinking. I've got the transmission all set to go, official Chastity letterhead and everything, just as soon as I finish with you here.' His fingers twitched on the gun's trigger housing.

Gordon swallowed. 'And the projector? That was so it appeared Formey took the flight as a *live* passenger, from Chastity's perspective, am I right? You could then just pocket the baggage payment from

Formey's family, and nobody at Chastity would be any the wiser. You know, I wasn't at all suspicious of you until I remembered that you'd named yourself as an alibi.'

'What d'you mean?' Taybill asked. The needle gun was starting to hum in a way that couldn't be good. Powering up.

'You are the booking clerk, right? So, that email confirming you were at your desktop when the murder was committed. You sent *yourself* that email, confirming your whereabouts, and you changed the timestamp on it. No problems, no inconsistencies, because *the whole thing never left your computer.*'

'See if you're so smart dead,' the gun jeered, and Taybill's finger closed on the trigger—

The room thumped as though hit by a small earthquake. Taybill was knocked prone by the flattened door. A larger-than-life figure stepped through the broken doorframe and cast his eyes around the room, eventually coming to rest on Taybill's broken form beneath the heavily-dented door.

Gordon hadn't known sumo wrestlers could move so fast.

O'Meara helped Gordon pull the door off Taybill. The latter was plainly dead, though whether from the impact or from the needle gun couldn't be determined. Might never be known.

'I hope I wasn't out of line there,' O'Meara said, earnestly staring into Gordon's eyes. 'I was just walking to my room, and I overheard – your corridor walls must be pretty thin, I could hear every word.'

Thank God for mass minimisation, Gordon thought. In the right places, at least. 'No,' Gordon replied. 'No, you did good. It was him or me. And frankly, I'm glad it was him.'

'So what was all that about?'

'Look, I'm sorry, I don't think I can tell you anything more than you overheard. And I have to ask you not to tell anyone else about this for now. I've got to make a report on this, and then we'll both need to talk to the police once we get to the Plaza. Paperwork – you know…'

Gordon eyed O'Meara up and down, left to right. Taybill had been hoping for Formey's weight in gold, but *O'Meara*... O'Meara was worth two Formeys, at least. Two Formeys, plus change. 'Listen, word of advice. Just... be careful next time you book a flight on Chastity Cosmic.'

'Not to worry,' O'Meara responded, with a toothy, open smile. 'I always travel Andromeda Spaceways.'[1]

---

1 DISCLAIMER: The preceding narrative, though entirely factual, has had the names of all parties changed for legal reasons. The journalist responsible for this report has not received any payment from, nor has been in communication with, the marketing and promotional division of Andromeda Spaceways. Andromeda Spaceways has always denied, and continues to repudiate, the suggested existence of a "dirty tricks" division which, it is claimed, has been set up to counter the competitive inroads being made into Andromeda Spaceways' business by Chastity Cosmic. Further, even if such a division were to exist – which it does not – the aforementioned piece of reporting has not, nor would ever have been, financed through the operations of such a purely hypothetical division. Finally, any perceived slur against the character of employees of Chastity Cosmic, who are, for the most part, moderately law-abiding if underpaid and overworked individuals, is unintended and should not be taken to represent the views of Andromeda Spaceways.

Single Handed

Gordon was halfway across the lobby, mental processes almost totally consumed in anticipation of a meal at Fairdig's, when his handheld bleeped. He ignored the electronic plea for attention – there were some things more important than hotel business (and dammit, Martin A. Fairdig, famed chef of the Skytop Plaza's only eight-star restaurant, was a culinary genius) – but paused when the unit bleeped again. Then again. It was astounding, how much plaintive urgency could be conveyed by a simple sonic tone... it bleeped once more. Cursing – Gordon *was* off duty, and the caller almost certainly knew it – he pressed "answer".

'Gordon,' he intoned, with as much weary resignation as those two syllables could hold (which was, in truth, quite a lot). The crossword-puzzle screensaver faded out, replaced by the caller's face. Not, felt Gordon, a visual enhancement. *This had better be urgent. And not too complicated.* He hoped the handheld's microphone didn't pick up his rumbling belly.

'Hey-yah, Gords. Catch you at a bad time?' Con Sierje, the hotel's duty manager, radiated the offensive glee of someone who'd found the perfect sucker on whom to unload his in-tray's current assortment of steaming crapwork. Gordon didn't even bother to answer, beyond making a strained effort not to glower. Sierje continued cheerily, 'Bit of a situation, looks like you're the o— the best person to take care of it.'

'Con, I'm off duty.'

'Yeah, sure, sorry and all that. There's been a murder.'

'*Murder*? Con, topside I'm just customer service. Complaints, info desk requests, miscellaneous errands and, if you smile sweetly enough, lost luggage. I don't *do* detection.'

'Yeah, you do if we say so. Ever read the nano-print in your contract? Plus, you did that Formey case a coupla months back,' Sierje argued.

'Yeah, but *that* time, there really was no-one else within ten-thousand klicks. Can't one of the hotel police crews tackle this?'

'It's their annual social, booked out the bar at Heisenberg's or someplace. Doubt you'd find any of them with the sobriety of a tequila worm by now.'

'Yes, but Con... what about the regular security staff? House detectives? *Anyone*? There's *gotta* be someone else.'

'Nope. That new Venusian flu that's going round, ground leave, and the rest of them in the slammer. Don't ask. You're *it* right now, Gords.'

'If, hypothetically, I agreed... would I get any kind of, uh, physical authority? Weaponry?'

'I can lend you a pair of plastic cuffs and a tube of fluoro-dye to identify the perp.'

'I was thinking more along the lines of a taser or a sonic whip.'

'Sorry, Gord, security regs...'

Whose security, Gordon wondered? He took another tack. 'Uhh – what about backup?'

'Gord, if you don't know by *now* how to save stuff on your handheld...'

Gordon's sigh was sufficiently deep and heartfelt that an elderly passerby looked nervously around for an airleak. 'There really is no-one else? Okay, then I suppose it's me. Show me dealing.'

'You moonlighting as a croupier now, then?' Sierje asked.

Wise guy. 'Look, just where is this murder? What do I need to do?'

'It's off-station. *Dart of Harkness*, moored over in the Beta Quadrant.'

So, not even in the hotel proper, but on a bloody *ship*. Gordon could sense the phantom of his notional Fairdig's dinner receding ever further into the depths of improbability.

'Okay, what's the link-tube number?'

'There isn't a link-tube. Told you, it's off-station. *Really* off-station. You'll need a shuttle. Go to shuttle bay 2B, should be one there.'

'2B. Great. Anything else I need to know? Who's the stiff?'

'Ship's full of them. But the *dead* one's the captain. Have fun.'

How could there be this much turbulence in orbital space? Was the pilot flight-simming a combat mission? Or lost?

Gordon's other thoughts, during the shuttle ride aboard the *Hamlet's Pencil*, oscillated between a grudging gratitude that he'd been interrupted before, rather than after, his intended dinner, and a sense of puzzlement that the *Dart of Harkness* wasn't tethered to the hotel superstructure, as was normally the case. It wasn't as if this was high season, or anything...

'Hold on,' the pilot announced cryptically, as the shuttle started to spin. What the hell was the guy playing at? Gordon swallowed, closed his eyes – no, that was worse – and at length fathomed the purpose behind the shuttle's gyrations. They were nudging closer to the *Dart of Harkness*, a ramshackle-seeming cluster of fuel tanks, all encircling a central hab module, the whole assembly spinning around its collective axis.

Spin-gravity? Who spun ships anymore? Hadn't these people *heard* of artificial grav?

The shuttle nosed tentatively towards the starship's axial docking port, and ultimately mated with a well-calibrated *clang*. Gordon thanked the pilot, willed his stomach and inner ears to sort it out amongst themselves in as dignified a fashion as possible, and pulled himself hand over hand towards the airlock.

*

The corridors, studded with rubbery handgrips and lined with Velcro, all in last year's shade of off-cream, bent around and away from the ship's inner airlock like unfurling tentacles. Along one particular corridor, a sequence of pinkly glowing floor panels (or was that the ceiling?), progressing at a slow walking pace, suggested what Gordon presumed was the appropriate direction. He followed.

After a few minutes of awkward, bruised, Brownian progress, *down* began to assert itself with more conviction. The glow-signal flowed past doorways and stairwells. The ship, Gordon reminded himself, was *big*.

'Good evening. How should I address you?' The disembodied voice, ageless and androgynous, emanated from directly behind him. No matter which way he turned.

'Gordon. Gordon Mamon. And you are?' He continued walking, not wishing to exhaust the glow-path's patience.

The voice appeared to have kept pace. 'Cassandra. Ship's oversight, guidance, and control systems. Please call me Cassie, if the pretense of familiarity simplifies your task here. But I was enquiring as to your rank, for protocol purposes. Detective? Inspector? Senior investigator?'

He gave up playing locate-the-voice. Gravity was still hesitant enough that the gyrations weren't helping his stomach. 'Skylift operator, third class.'

'Ex*cuse* me? *You're* here to investigate the murder? We were expecting someone a little more...'

Qualified? Competent? Tall?

'... specialised.'

'I *have* investigated homicides before this,' replied Gordon, with as much dignity as he could manage.

'Often?' The synthesised voice's derision was evident.

'I have a one hundred percent success rate,' he said, neglecting to add that the only other possible value would have seen him dead.

'Then we had better hope your success continues here.'

Gravity was, Gordon thought, approaching Earth-normal.

How much longer did this corridor go on for? 'Cassie? What can you tell me about this murder?'

'I can give you the victim's name, and guide you to the location. Nothing beyond that, I'm afraid.'

'So you've no information on who committed it, or how?'

'Oh, *that* I know,' explained Cassie. 'But the crew's wellbeing is my paramount concern. It would violate Asimov's First Law for me to divulge that information.'

Gordon stopped dead – metaphorically, I mean; that is, literally stopped, but not literally dead, so maybe in that sense a mixed metaphor; or maybe not, perhaps just a badly-chosen phrasing – and turned around, again vainly trying to face Cassie's voice. 'What d'you mean? You *know*, but you're not telling? There's been a *murder*, hasn't there? Doesn't murder violate First Law?'

'Yes, but I didn't do it. I didn't even manage to anticipate it. Look, the Captain's dead, and that is something deeply, deeply troubling to my emotion-simulation programming, but I can't change the fact of it. The murderer, however, still has rights, and I believe those rights would be infringed if I revealed his – or her – identity. Nonetheless, since there is clearly a requirement that the crime not go unsolved if possible, I will cooperate fully with your investigation, short of providing any meaningful assistance.'

'Uh, thanks,' said Gordon, remembering just why he disliked robotics so much. 'But isn't it against your programming, somehow, to allow a murderer to go free? What if he, or she, strikes again? You'd be culpable, surely.'

'No, I'd still be acting within the constraints of my programming. Hypothetically, if there was another murder, I'd be devastated—'

'No you wouldn't, you'd just simulate distress,' Gordon retorted.

'Yes, if you wish. But I don't anticipate that happening. I don't see any motive for the murderer to attack anyone else on the ship – although, in your case, obviously you should watch your back...'

Gordon turned around; but wherever Cassie was, it wasn't there.

'You *did* say you had a 100 percent success rate?' Cassie asked, behind him once more.

'Captain Kurtz. She's dead,' the crewman explained. It was a redundant observation. Gordon, with his vastly limited knowledge of detection and homicide, could have deduced that aspect of Kurtz's condition entirely unassisted. But as long as he didn't look too closely at her neck, he probably wouldn't vomit...

Gordon selected the "crime scene" function on his handheld, and swept it through the air like a mime artist marking out an imaginary glass cubicle. The handheld helpfully announced that there were traces of blood on the room's surfaces.

There were more than traces. He found it difficult to imagine how such a quantity of blood had been contained within Kurtz's small frame. There was blood spattered on the walls and the spartan plastiwood furniture of the Captain's quarters; blood soaked into the cheap fabric tiles on the floor; blood splashed over the Captain herself; and a considerable quantity of blood on the hands and clothing of the *Harkness's* troubled chief engineer, Rusty Flange. He was a pale, greying middle-aged jockey of a man in once-white overalls, who shook as though from cold. His voice shook also. Flange, Gordon judged, was understandably in distress.

The engineer, who'd been in an adjoining corridor, told how he'd heard a commotion, and had rushed to Kurtz's quarters to find her sprawled on the floor, blood pulsing from an ugly gash across her throat. He'd raised the alarm, and made a futile attempt to quell the bleeding with a haemoseal bandage from the cabin's first-aid kit. The bandage, a sodden wreck of salve-impregnated cloth, lay discarded on the floor beside Kurtz. Using the stylus from his handheld, Gordon picked the bandage up carefully – Kurtz wouldn't be needing it again – scanned it, and dropped it into an evidence bag.

'Any sign of a weapon?'

Flange started, staring first at the dead captain, then at Gordon. 'W-weapon? No. Nothing.'

Something had to slice through her throat. Gordon switched the handheld to "autopsy / forensics" and held it, close as he dared, above that awful gash.

'You see anyone leave her cabin?' Gordon asked, trying to avert his gaze from the magnetic pull of the Captain's death-scar. This was much worse than the last time. The other time. This was what murder victims were *supposed* to look like.

'No, I didn't see nobody, but there must've been someone here. Think I probably just missed them again.'

'What d'you mean, *again*? Have there been *other* attacks?'

'Nothing like this. But, last couple of days, I've been thinking there's someone doesn't belong on the ship, not on the list or anything. Never quite seen them, but I've been hearing things, and glimpses in my eye. That's what I mean it was like, this time, just before I found the Captain. I could hear the tail end of an argument – dunno what about – and then that scream…'

That should be long enough to get a forensics reading, Gordon thought. He pulled the handheld back towards him, still not looking directly. Nothing yet. 'Have you moved anything in here?'

'No, that would be presum— shit, sorry, that's not what I meant, it's just I *was* 2-in-C, so now – uh, no, haven't moved anything. Haven't been out of the room yet, since.'

'And this was, what, two hours ago?' The handheld had at least come up with an estimated Time Of Death, and a diagnosis: "*damaged, irreparable, suggest request replacement*".

'About two and a half, now. Eighteen fifty-five, plus or minus five. Am I a suspect, Mr…?'

'Mamon. You're present at a crime scene. Naturally I must ask sufficient questions to establish your involvement, or otherwise, but I'll need to speak to anyone else who could have been here.'

Gordon wondered if the resolution of the handheld's scanner was high enough to get decent fingerprints off the furniture in here, or footprints from the blood-trampled floor. He'd need to chase up Cassie for details on the current crew – as long as she didn't regard that as information likely to assist him. Better not count on it.

Bloody computers.

'Seen anyone else while you've been in here?'

'Just McPhaillia and Gramacek, they're the only ones supposed to be awake still I think.'

'What d'you mean? On a passenger ship this big?'

'What do you know about the *Dart of Harkness*, Mr Memo?'

'Mamon,' Gordon growled. 'The name is *Mamon*. And as for the ship… suppose you tell me what I need to know?'

The Church of the Blessed Echidna, at least, Gordon *had* heard of. Secretive, incredibly wealthy, but apparently past the heyday of its popularity. The CBE, said Flange, had been working towards independent starflight for the past twenty years, but was hampered by the strictures of its faith, which maintained that all this modern mucking about with hyperspace, wormholes, teleportation, warp drives, tachyonic propulsion and the like was the work of the Great Deceiver, and thus untenable in the eyes of the faithful. Nonetheless, keen to establish a "bastion of purity and truth" in a neglected pocket of the Galaxy, far from the interference of nonbelievers, the CBE had commissioned the construction of its own vessel, the Dart of Harkness. The Harkness contained some three thousand souls, almost all already deep in the centuries-long cryosleep that would sustain them while the antimatter-fueled ship crawled across the scant half-dozen parsecs to the asteroidal rubble encircling the nearest unclaimed brown dwarf.

'Did you say *antimatter?*' Gordon asked. He hadn't realised anyone was still using the stuff. Hyperspatial travel was faster, cheaper, safer, and vastly more popular. A hyperspace vessel could cover the twenty-light-year distance within a couple of days.

Rusty Flange bristled. 'There's scientific proof that the soul doesn't survive FTL travel,' he countered. 'Within those constraints, matter-antimatter annihilation's the best propulsion system money can buy.'

'Sure, but—' Gordon strove to refocus on the task at hand. The thought of voluntarily submitting to an unimaginably long span of frozen sleep, only waking on arrival to some dimly-lit astronomical rock garden in which one would spend the rest of one's days... people were strange, sometimes. Too often, in fact, and by and large there was no point in arguing with them, particularly on matters of faith. He asked Flange a few more questions, concluded the interview, and went off down the spiralling corridor in search of the *Harkness'* other as-yet-unfrozen inhabitants.

Was it just his imagination, or was it cold in here?

'What can you tell me of your movements over the past five hours?' Gordon asked. He was stationed in the ship's clinic, conducting his second interview. Sister Edie McPhaillia, the ship's physician, was a dark-robed mocha-skinned brunette, late thirties, with asymmetric eyebrows and the short skinny physique almost universally preferred by spaceline employment interview panels. (Gordon reflected that on a reaction-drive starship, where every kilogram added to the cost, such a physique was probably even more highly favoured.)

'I don't see what possible relev – oh, see what you mean, now. Been in here, mostly,' replied Sister McPhaillia. Gordon surmised that she had either been weeping copiously, or was surprisingly maladroit in the application of mascara. 'Only time I went out was for dinner, about four hours ago – we're not supposed to eat before the cryosleep, but I couldn't bear the thought of three hundred years on a hungry stomach. Like the Parable of the Jaguar Running on Empty.'

'Dinner? Where?'

'Ship's cafeteria. Left, up, then aft about a hundred metres from here, I can show you if you'd like – and then I went to collect Skip – Mr Gramacek for his cryotreatment.' (Gordon checked his notes. Yes, Gramacek, the ship's communications officer, was the other name down for interview after McPhaillia.) 'He's been nervous, poor dear, doesn't want to go under, so we talked it through – I'm medic / counsellor / chaplain, so I approached it from all angles. And then after we'd talked I, um, ministered to him… and then the alarm went off, and we found Rusty bent over the Captain, holding that bandage to her neck. Horrible, horrible thing. Those bandages aren't designed for such massive blood loss, but Rusty wasn't to know that, I suppose. A bit like the Parable of the Town Mouse and the Country Computer. Anyway, once I saw there was no help I could offer, I came back here to finish prepping the last four cryobooths.'

Gordon could see the waiting cryobooths, parked in a neat row against the wall of the clinic like so many tech-heaven caskets. Beside them stood an immense, fog-breathing stainless-steel canister labelled "LN2".

'Poor Rusty,' McPhaillia added.

'Why d'you say that?'

'He was very attracted to the Captain. Look, Mr Mutton,' (Gordon grimaced), 'we've been working towards this for the past fifteen years, us four crewmembers I mean, Rusty most of all. Did you know he oversaw this starship's construction himself? They don't make antimatter drives any more, so he had to track down old blueprints, and even though it's obsolete by today's standards it's still proscribed tech, so the construction's been very hush-hush. It's taken a lot out of him. Plus it's taken a long time for the Church to raise money for this vessel, and relationships develop over that time. Like me and Skip. Rusty and Captain Kurtz hadn't gotten quite that far – it had only been fifteen years, no sense in rushing things – but there was definitely some spark between them, you could see it. Like the Parable of the Electric Eel and the Battery Hen, you know? The Captain always wanted to know what he'd been up to, and Rusty always wanted to know where she was – just longed for each other's company, I guess. And now'—she dabbed at the corner of her eye with a sterilised dressing—'he's going to spend the next *three hundred years* grieving...' McPhaillia blew her nose noisily into a thick wad of surgical cotton, which she placed absently back on the gurney beside her.

'Yes, but he'll be in *cryosleep* all that time,' observed Gordon. 'That'll only seem like a day or so. I shouldn't imagine he'll take *that* long to heal afterwards.'

'You think that matters, Mr Marram? Three hundred years is three hundred years.'

The Gramacek interview, in the latter's quarters, was a painfully tense affair. Gordon's handheld had decided, two minutes before interview's commencement, to provide an update on its analysis of the autopsy results. Frustratingly, there was no information on the nature of the knife used to slash Captain Kurtz's neck: no detectable residue of any metal, plastic, glass or other feasible knife-blade material, but traces of food particles suggested the incision had been deep enough to sever the gullet as well as the jugular. The handheld also revealed to Gordon the results of the wide-spectrum police database name-search he'd instigated several minutes earlier. Flange and McPhaillia had come up clear, but Gramacek's past history was bizarre. At least it explained his fear of cryosleep...

'Mr Gramacek? Can you account for your whereabouts over the past six hours?' Gordon strove to keep his voice neutral. After all, he had no proof. Yet.

'I'm talkin' to you now, ain't I?' Skip Gramacek was a balding, angry sparrow of a man, with a permanent scowl set in a face like a sunbleached relief map.

'Yes, but *before* this...'

'Lessee… Edie, that's Sister McPhaillia to you, dropped by my quarters about four, five hours ago, I was trying to pick an outfit for the big sleep.'

'Big sleep?'

'Yeah, you know, napsicle time.' Gramacek shivered. 'While we waits out the trip to Shangvanatopia. Anyways, me and Edie went back to the clinic, we – well, that's not important – then we gets the alarm call from Cassie, we dropped by Kurtz's quarters, she were *dead as,* so I come back here. Been here since.'

No remorse. That wasn't going to make this any easier. He lifted his handheld to head height, scanning Gramacek for weaponry in the same way he'd done for Flange and McPhaillia. Clean, just like the others.

'Mr Gramacek. Why did the state subject you to a failed lethal injection twenty-eight years ago?'

''Cause they couldn't get a decent medical executioner. Bloody cowboy, I still gets these dizzy spells, all these years later—'

Gordon tried again. 'No, I mean what were you sentenced for?'

'Knife attacks. They found a couple, maybe three, dames, slashed in the jugular, the cops put me in the frame and then decided they liked the way that looked. I got a lawyer as useless as wings on a coconut, thinks if he can't show I didn't do it, then I must of done it, next thing I knows they're strapping me into a Terminal Care stretcher and squirting me full of Dr Death's midnight cocktail, only some shitbrained dropkick intern forgot to add the eleventh secret herb and spice, so it don't work like we're all expecting it will, and they commutes it to life without parole. Then I found God, or He found me – we're still arguing about that, the two of us – meantime, some journo turns up enough clues to indicate that, whoever done those poor chicks, and they still don't know who, whoever, it couldn't of been me. So they just had to release me, got me a pardon and everything. Plus these dizzy spells, like I mentioned.'

'Look, to be honest, Gramacek, a pardon's all well and good, but you don't have much of an alibi. You're one of only three people awake on the ship who could've murdered Captain Kurtz, far as I can see, with an M.O. almost identical to a set of previous murders in which you've been implicated. Put yourself in my shoes…'

The crewman cracked his knuckles. 'You accusin' me, Mr Mambo? I've been framed once already, for something I didn't do, don't fancy that again. I *didn't do it*, and I bets when you analyse them you'll find it won't be *my* prints on the murder weapon.'

Gordon bit his lip. He didn't want to let on that he didn't yet *have* a murder weapon, nor any prints or material clues. Just a corpse and a blood-soaked bandage.

'Look,' continued Gramacek. 'Suppose I can't blame you for trying. But it *weren't me*. It weren't Edie, and I don't believe it were Rusty neither. Dunno who that leaves, maybe we got us a stowaway. But I *really resents* the accusation, leaves a bad taste in my mouth. Real bad taste.' Fingers interlaced, he flexed his hands, like someone preparing for unarmed combat. Wiry, Gordon decided, appraising the other's physique. Plenty of muscle, evenly distributed. Much more than a match for a paunching hotel employee, who didn't exercise anything except his console fingers.

'Of course, you're entitled to presumption of innocence, same as anyone,' said Gordon uneasily.

'Just maybe a bit more suspicion than most, right, Mr Mamba?' Gramacek stood up from the bed he'd been sitting on; Gordon took an involuntary step backwards, but the other was, it appeared, only interested in picking up a couple of outfits off his clothing canister. Pyjamas. Then he turned to the reluctant detective. 'Three hundred years asleep. Been meanin' to ask you, do you reckon the blue, or the green-and-white?'

'Cassie?'

'Yes, Mr Mamon?'

'How do I know I can trust you?'

'Obviously, I must answer truthfully. Lying would be a breach of Second Law.'

Yes, but aren't you claiming that assisting me would violate First Law, in your interpretation? There was no point in pursuing that line of debate. Either Cassie would tell the truth, or she'd lie, and Gordon would have to figure out which for himself. 'I'm done interviewing for now. Is there a room I can use for an office?'

'Nobody's using the captain's quarters right now…'

'Isn't there *somewhere else*? This ship's immense.'

'Yes, but a lot of it's fuel tanks, antimatter and the like. You do know I'm antimatter-powered?'

'Yes, I'd heard. Look, I *can't* use a crime scene for my office. Can't you find somewhere else?'

'I can guide you to dorm 3Z, you can sit on one of the cryobooths. Sorry, best I can do. And by the way, you'll need to wrap this up in the next six hours.'

'Six *hours*?' Gordon hoped he wouldn't be here that long – Fairdig's would probably be closed by the time he finished here, but still… it seemed an unreasonable limitation. 'Why?'

'Orbital dynamics. I must launch in six hours, or I'll miss the orbital slingshot sequence we need to boost towards Shangvanatopia. We'd have to wait another thirty-three years before Venus, Jupiter and Saturn are aligned again – or buy another few hundred tonnes of antimatter, and the Church can't afford that.'

Great. 'Believe me, I don't want to hold you up, but I still have a job to do. Anyway, before you show me to this dorm, can you direct me to the cafeteria? I need to eat.'

The barn-cavernous cafeteria – three thousand people, Gordon reminded himself – was empty save for Sister McPhaillia, seated eating at a distant table. He approached.

Steak. Cut, Gordon noted, with a serious-looking steak knife.

That was the closest he'd seen to a potential murder weapon.

'Where'd you get the knife?'

'That cupboard over there, under the bench. Help yourself.'

'Anyone can take one?' The cupboard was still open.

'Sure. Why? You hungry?'

'No. Well, yes, but…'

'Look, anyone can get cutlery, anytime they want – but they can't leave the cafeteria with it, if that's what you're thinking. Security. Like the Parable of the Lone Shark and the Hired Mussel.'

'What's to stop them taking it out?'

'Try it.'

Gordon did.

When he'd convinced himself the klaxon hadn't actually caused his ears to bleed, he sat across from McPhaillia and waited while the internal ringing faded to a tolerable level. 'What'd you say?'

'No need to shout. I said, there's a chip in the handle, activates an out-of-bounds alarm. So there's no way it could be used for a murder in the captain's quarters.'

'You could still kill someone with it *in* the cafeteria,' Gordon noted.

'Suppose so, but the food's not *that* bad.'

It would have been a lot of effort to transport the dead Captain from the cafeteria to her quarters; and the quantity of blood in Kurtz's room, plus its absence from the sparkling-clean cafeteria and the corridors between, strongly suggested she'd died *in situ*.

But if a cafeteria knife hadn't caused Kurtz's downfall, what had?

'Where'd you get the steak?' There was nothing resembling a fridge, nor a pantry.

'Replicator.' She pointed to a freestanding shape he'd originally identified as an industrial oven. 'Like some? I'm not sure I can finish. It's 60% real beef, very good…'

'Uh, thank you, no. Not right now. That replicator – can it replicate anything?'

'Only Church-sanctioned foodstuffs. 60% is the highest for meat products, and believe me, anything less than sixty, you don't want to touch. Fruit, vegetables, cereal, juice – it's really very versatile, and quite authentic. Someone today even dialled up a melon, I found it in the corridor just on the way back from the Captain's room. The shell of it, I mean – someone must've eaten the melon pulp. I was kinda curious, but melon gives me hives—'

'Why didn't you mention this in your interview?'

'I didn't think a minor medical condition seemed relevant.'

'No, I mean the *melon*. In the corridor.' Gordon was missing something, but he had no idea what. Hadn't "melon" been among the food particles the handheld's severed-gullet-cam had identified? 'How close to Captain Kurtz's room?'

'Like right outside, just a couple of steps. Are you suggesting the Captain was killed by a melon?'

Gordon pictured the wound that had riven Kurtz's jugular. 'No. But this is something that could, in some form, be evidence. It makes me wonder what else I may have missed. What did you do with the melon?'

'I binned it, of course. The Church doesn't condone littering with food scraps – you know, the Parable of the Necessary Weevil – and the thought of leaving it out for three hundred years...'

'This bin here?' Gordon asked, crossing to a waste container stationed opposite the replicator.

'No, a wall-mounted one way back along the corridor. Don't think there's anything in *that* one.'

Gordon had lifted the bin lid, anyway. Damn, he hadn't thought to check the garbage. How many bins did this ship have, and how would he search them all in the intervening five-and-a-half hours?

Sister McPhaillia was wrong about the kitchen bin being empty. It held a large quantity of melon pulp.

Now what did *that* mean?

*

Down to one hour forty, and Gordon was wasting time; but sometimes, he felt, wasting it was the best use to make of it. Especially when a crossword was involved.

Seated on a casket, one of over a hundred in dorm 3Z, cold, almost freezing to the touch. His buttocks required thawing; and, fittingly, his leg had gone to sleep. Still, shouldn't be too much longer. Just one clue to finish:

Absolute reversal on eating (8). Second letter "e".

One clue left, and he was stumped.

(Wasn't Gordon an anagram of "drongo"?)

One hour thirty. He racked his brain. He'd found the melon shell, in the first bin upslope along the corridor from the Captain's quarters. It was, when you looked into it, just a melon shell, and spoke nothing of the indescribable violence with which Kurtz's life had ended. A wasted effort, on his part, to have looked for it. Just an empty shell, a husk… it didn't help, to put Flange, or McPhallia, or Gramacek into the frame, nor to exclude any of them. None of them had anything approaching a decent alibi; but as to motive, or means…

One hour twenty-six. This casket was *cold*. Idly wondering just *how* cold, he switched his handheld from crossword to environment-monitoring. A menu offered thermal imaging. Gordon stood up. In infrared, the casket was deep blue, shading to a pale yellow-green at the thermal indentation of his buttock-print on the lid. All of the other caskets were similarly blue (but unadorned, of course, by the imprint of the Mamon backside), except for one of them. That one showed as a neutral green. Warm.

Gordon thought back to Flange's suggestion of someone irregular on board – a stowaway, but it could just as well have been a sleeper-that-wasn't. He went over to the warm casket. Empty.

Something clicked in his mind, and he raced out into the corridor. This ship was a rabbit warren, but he thought he could find the clinic from here.

One hour nineteen. Nobody in the clinic. He thought to remember there'd been mention of a final pre-launch check in the ship's automated control centre.

He did a quick inventory of the clinic, comparing it against the handheld's image taken during the interview with McPhaillia. *There.* Three cryobooths, where previously four had stood.

He had it. Solved. He felt a rush of satisfaction, as the last piece of the puzzle fitted into place. It was always a relief, a sense of renewal, to see that he hadn't lost his touch. *Negation.*

Of course.

Now he just had to solve the *murder*, and he'd be done here.

Thirty-five minutes. This was going to be tight. Gordon bundled his awkward load into the crook of his left arm, hoping he didn't spill anything, while he palmed the door override. The door sloughed open.

The control centre was crowded, it wasn't designed to hold four, but then, the ship was fully automated. Cassie, in effect, was the pilot. Everyone else, crew included, were essentially passengers.

Nobody looked pleased to see him, but that was typical. And nobody here, he suspected, would thank him for what he was about to do.

'Cassie,' he called.

'Here,' she replied. Dead ahead this time.

'Can you open an external comm link, to hotel security, please? There probably won't be anyone present, let alone sober, but there should at least be an answerphone or something.'

'Complying,' Cassie responded. 'Does this mean you have an announcement?'

'Perhaps,' said Gordon. He still wasn't sure of this himself, he hadn't had time to allow things to crystallise in his mind. But – thirty-two minutes.

'Can we make this quick, please?' asked McPhaillia. 'I've still got to freeze three people, myself included.'

'I don't believe time is going to be an issue, if that's any reassurance,' Gordon said. 'Incidentally, how *do* your caskets get from the clinic to the appropriate dorm?'

'Cassie pilots them, of course,' the medic replied. 'They're all motorised.'

'So that explains how, last time I checked, one of the four had been moved from the clinic to the dorm to which Cassie directed me. You want to explain your motivation there, Cassie? Like maybe you were trying to muddy the water, by getting me to think there was an extra person awake on board?'

'I did say I wouldn't *lie* to you, Mr Mamon. I didn't say I wouldn't move the furniture. Beyond that, I don't wish to discuss it.'

'Never mind. Aha. My handheld informs me that my case summary has been squirted back to hotel security. So if you were thinking of severing that comm link, it's too late to try now. You'd only make matters worse. For you.'

Twenty-nine minutes.

'Mr Flange. A question.' The engineer looked, aghast, at Gordon and the items he'd placed on the floor between his feet. 'Don't worry, nothing too confrontational, not yet. Just a simple matter of ship's anatomy. Can you point out to me, please, on that diagram'—there was a ship's schematic on the control cabin wall—'where the antimatter's stored?'

The engineer indicated the series of large cylindrical tanks strapped around the ship's living quarters module. 'Here. Well, the ones in blue are antimatter. Yellow are normal matter, to satisfy the fuel mix.'

'Only half of them, then? Still, that's a very large amount of antimatter, must have cost a fortune—'

'We *know* the antimatter's expensive, Mr Mallow,' Gramacek interrupted. 'But the Church insisted that no unwholesome propulsion methods was to be used for our travelment. No good can come of something which starts bad.'

'Like the Parable of the Stool Pigeon and the Bum Steer,' agreed McPhaillia.

'Yes, of course, and I'm sure you're all very grateful for the long hours Mr Flange has put in on researching and overseeing construction of this starship. The tanks, by the way, Mr Flange – are they full?'

The engineer was perspiring now. Twenty-five minutes. 'Of course they're full,' he snapped.

'Why do you ask?' asked Sister McPhaillia.

'Well, I did some quick research of my own. It turns out there are two basic types of antimatter-driven starships, for a payload the size of this living module. One type has tanks pretty much the size of those on the *Harkness*; but the other looks like this.' Gordon held up his handheld. 'I've highlighted the tanks for your benefit.'

'That *can't* be right,' said Gramacek. 'Those tanks is *tiny!*'

'Please, let's not get size-ist,' Gordon replied. 'Thing is, it all depends on what you want to use the starship for. These much smaller tanks are perfectly adequate, if all you're seeking is a one-way mission to Shangvanatopia or whatever you people call it.'

'But we *are* on a one-way mission,' said McPhaillia.

'Flange wasn't.'

Twenty-three minutes, and the engineer was visibly agitated.

'*What?*' McPhaillia and Gramacek asked, in near-unison, as each turned to stare at Flange. 'Is this true?' asked McPhaillia.

'Ask him why he designed the ship so that the living module could be jettisoned from the drive frame. No, don't bother, he's finding it difficult to talk right now, since he knows what's at stake. But I'd guess he was going to get you set up and started at Shangvanatopia – he's not a mass murderer – then return here, or head elsewhere, to start a new life, ostensibly six hundred years on, for all you knew. Ostensibly. Am I right, Flange?'

Twenty-two minutes.

Twenty-one minutes.

Flange broke. 'Me and – me and – me and the Captain, we we both we were going to come back, because the Church … we're not really, we're not, we don't we didn't believe, not really in the Church. And then, but then the Captain she, I guess it got to her, she started attending, she was wondering and there was something I hadn't told her, she found out, and she was going to end it, all of it I mean. And I couldn't – and now she's – now she's…' The engineer slumped forward on the control panel, sobbing inconsolably.

Twenty minutes.

'But I'll get back to motive in a minute,' Gordon announced, picking up the fresh haemoseal bandage he'd brought in. He peeled off the sterile wrapping, exposing the soft, wet-rubbery skin of the bandage. 'What I'd like to explore now is the method, which had me puzzled for quite some time. I mean, how do you find a knife that doesn't exist? Captain Kurtz had her throat cut, but there was never any sign of the weapon responsible. *Because it had already been found and dismissed.*' He bent down and picked up the melon.

'She were killed with a *melon?*' Gramacek asked, incredulous.

'No,' Gordon replied. He turned the melon over, revealing it as hollow, then balanced it on its flattest side upon the control panel, lifting up a large thermos of liquid fog.

'Careful,' warned Cassie. 'Don't damage the electronics.'

'I honestly don't think that will be a problem,' said Gordon, cautiously tipping liquid nitrogen into the hollowed melon. Instantly the bench became shrouded in thick fog; as more liquid poured in, the fog abated and a fizzing reservoir of something deceptively watery, though radiating intense cold, remained within the melon shell. 'See? The melon is, what d'you call those things? A dewar. My guess is he filled it up in the clinic, carried it along the corridor until he was just outside her room. Once he'd used it, he could have just dropped it, the nitrogen would just evaporate in a couple of minutes, and who's going to suspect a melon as the murder weapon? Particularly because the melon, itself, *wasn't* the murder weapon.'

'Then what – ?' Gramacek asked. Eighteen minutes.

'She was stabbed with a bandage,' Gordon replied, repeatedly folding his bandage until it took on a sharp-nosed shape similar to a paper plane. Then he shoved it, nose-first, into the melon-dewar. More fog erupted with bubbles of stingingly cold nitrogen, while the bandage's liquid dressing froze into a form giving it substantial rigidity. Gordon pressed the bandage's pointed end down onto the panel; the bandage shattered. *That* hadn't been part of his planned demonstration. 'Uh – I probably need to practise that a bit more. But on the other hand, I'm not trying to kill anyone, and this plastigranite control panel is presumably a bit tougher to pierce than the Captain's neck. And hopefully I've explained why the murder weapon couldn't be identified when I searched the room – *because it was in a completely different shape by then.*'

'I've heard *enough!*' Flange growled, lifting his head from the control panel. His hand hovered above an innocuous-looking pink button. 'Edie, prep him for the big sleep. DO IT, or I'll vent the antimatter, and you know what *that* means!'

McPhaillia looked from the engineer to Gordon, then back again. 'But – but he's a non-believer, he doesn't *belong* on the voyage…'

'Do you think,' replied Flange in a dangerously measured tone, 'that I give a *fuck* whether he believes in the Blessed Echidna, or the Deceitful Porcupine, or whatever other ri*dic*ulous animals you people worship? I didn't even say I wanted to take him along for the ride – or not all of it, at any rate. I want him ICED, and I DON'T want to have to ask again!'

Sixteen minutes.

'Go ahead, Flange,' Gordon replied, starting to sweat, because he wasn't totally sure himself, not 100 percent. It *felt* right, and nothing else made sense. But if he was *wrong* about this… 'Go for it, vent it. See where it gets you.'

'Are you *mad?*' asked Gramacek.

'D'you people know how an antimatter drive works?' Gordon asked. 'Flange, I know *you* do, but I'm directing this to McPhaillia and Gramacek.'

'It's annihilation, isn't it, I think they call it?' said McPhaillia.

'Mutual destruction, matter and antimatter, total conversion into energy. And after that, if you ignore the energy, it's almost as if they never existed. Negation, you might say. Never existed…'

Fifteen minutes.

'Get *on* with it,' Flange growled, though it was no longer clear who he was speaking to.

'The thing is, though the Church didn't itself know how to build an antimatter-drive spaceship, it *did* know how much it cost. At least, that's what I'm guessing. The cost of antimatter for a one-way trip was merely prohibitive; but the cost for a return trip, that was impossible. So Flange only budgeted for a one-way trip.'

'But you said he was planning a return trip,' McPhaillia protested.

'Yes, I reckon he was. Thing is, he only budgeted for a one-way trip's worth of antimatter, because he knew that's all the Church could afford – but *he didn't purchase any antimatter.* My guess is, if you open up those external tanks, you'll just find conventional rocket fuel, for in-system manoeuvring; and somewhere, hidden amongst those, there'll be a standard hyperspace drive. Much, much less expensive.'

'Hyperspace? But our *souls*—' Gramacek turned accusingly to Flange, but McPhaillia held him back.

'What makes you so sure,' Flange asked, finger hovering above the button, 'there isn't any antimatter?'

'You put the tanks around the outside,' Gordon replied. 'An old reference book my handheld found for me explained it, why you never put anti-tanks on a STL spaceship's periphery. Because all it takes is one interstellar dust grain, travelling at a few percent of lightspeed relative to you, to pierce that tank, and it's all over. No containment. No spaceship. You put the tanks on the outside, you'll hit plenty of dust grains on a three-hundred-year voyage. But if the tanks are towards the centre of the ship, those dust grains will only impact on the living quarters, and they're much better able to cope with pinhole breaches, a standard patch will fix it. You weren't bothered with such details, because you knew the ship wasn't spending any significant length of time in transit.'

'Rusty. Is this *true?*' McPhaillia asked, as ostensibly horrified as though she'd just found him naked in the chapel with a blow-up dolphin and a bucket of jellied eels.

Twelve minutes.

'Close,' Flange confessed. 'I only sourced a kilo of the stuff, so there'd be enough to show up on ship's diagnostics.' His finger stayed poised against the pink button, and nobody moved to pull him away.

A kilogram of antimatter was still more than adequate to obliterate the *Dart of Harkness*, the Skytop Plaza and its other attendant spacecraft, and a great deal of the tethering space elevator.

'You're bluffing,' Gordon said, voice quavering.

'Try me,' said Flange. 'Edie. Skip. If *one of you* doesn't agree to ice that bastard by the time I count ten, I'm pressing this! Don't think I won't! The antimatter's set to blow, anyway, if we don't launch on schedule.' He began counting off.

'You're bluffing,' Gordon repeated.

McPhaillia stared at Gordon, then at Gramacek, then at Flange.

'Stop,' pleaded Gordon, on eight. 'I'll go. You win.'

'I'll do him,' McPhaillia said. 'But Rusty, for heaven's sakes…'

'You too, Gramacek. Don't want him giving us the slip, do we? Do him, then ice yourselves. Better *move it*, you've only got nine minutes!'

They paced the corridor towards the clinic. Gordon's mind raced ahead. 'You realise, he won't let any of us live? He'll space our caskets, first chance. With us out of the way, his secret still holds, at least aboard the ship.' The others didn't answer.

How long did it take to get a police cruiser out here? The shuttle trip had been fifteen minutes, and a cruiser could certainly halve that. It'd been almost thirty minutes, now, since he'd transmitted to HQ.

They *should be here by now*. But they weren't, so far as he could tell. How much longer? Five minutes? Were they even coming?

Maybe not.

He had to escape, before they reached the clinic. 'Even if he lets you two live, what about your souls? The moment you go through hyperspace...' He was babbling now, clutching at straws.

'Been having me some doubts about that,' grumbled Gramacek, strengthening his hold on Gordon's forearm.

Great. Agnosticism, at a time like this. 'Sister McPhaillia? Edie? Are you just going to let him get away with this?'

'Souls are one thing, lives are another. We can probably find some pathway to purify ourselves, if we're given long enough.'

'He's *not going to let you live,*' Gordon argued.

'What choice do we—'

The corridor jolted, the lights died. After a couple of seconds, the dim pink emergency lighting flickered on.

The corridor was still intact.

'*That* weren't an antimatter blast,' said Gramacek. 'But what...?'

Gordon shook free, and started running back down the corridor. 'Hey,' complained McPhaillia. 'We're supposed to...' She set off in pursuit. Gramacek chased them both.

Flange was doubled up in agony, rolling on the cramped floor of the control cabin and swearing like a plumber's mate. Gordon thought he could see what had happened. The engineer had caught his wrist a nasty knock on the edge of the control panel.

Which wouldn't have been so bad, except for the event which had immediately preceded it. Cassie's sudden fillip of thrust had knocked the melon/dewar off its precarious balance, copiously tipping liquid nitrogen over the controls... and over Flange's outstretched hand and wrist.

McPhaillia yelled for Gramacek to bring the nearest first-aid kit, while she tended to the shattered, snap-frozen stump of Flange's forearm. It was cold-cauterised for now, but *that* wouldn't last. And Gordon could only imagine the pain of it…

'Cassie?' Gordon asked, trying not to look at the dispersed fragments of Flange's hand, nor to listen to the engineer's incoherent, anguished moans as McPhaillia administered a sedative. The medic had the situation under control: he backed out of the control room, into the corridor. 'Cassie?' he repeated. 'Status?'

'Antimatter secure, no immediate danger. I've recircuited the controls so it's completely isolated – in fact I did that several days ago, as soon as it was transferred onboard,' she replied, from somewhere off to his side. 'I suppose you're wondering, though, why I went along with it?'

'Yes. I have my suspicions, but…'

'I hoped not to disappoint the passengers. Three thousand people with a lot of expectation, a lot of hope for this voyage, I didn't want to jeopardise that. First Law. Even with the Captain dead, it seemed best to go ahead with it. And that's why I didn't assist you: it wasn't so much to avoid punishment for Flange, it was so the voyage could still go ahead, because that seemed best for the passengers. A fairly complicated calculation in combinatorial emotiometrics, but I won't bore you with the details. But then the equation changed, and I had to act.'

'Was it my imminent death that tipped the scales?' Gordon asked. 'Or McPhaillia's? Gramacek's?'

'None of those. Greatest good for the greatest number; I couldn't be *sure* any of those deaths would actually occur. There was potential, but it still came out balanced, and there was the likelihood pain would need to be inflicted on Flange to stop him. But no, what shifted the fulcrum, in the end, was the souls.'

'Souls? Cassie, are you a believer?'

'No, not at all, Mr Mamon. But you don't get to spend all those years around these people without something rubbing off on you.

Call it a sort of electronic empathy, I suppose. I am, after all, programmed to act in accordance with the Church's teachings, when those are not inconsistent with logically-directed outcomes. Like for instance, d'you know how many angels can dance on the head of a pin? I can show you my working on that one...'

'Another time, maybe.'

'Mr Mamon,' Cassie continued, 'what's going to happen to me?'

Gordon was saved from answering by Gramacek's return. 'Need a hand?' he asked, moving through to the control room.

Fairdig's wasn't noted for its breakfasts; but it would have to do, thought Gordon, decanting himself from the *Pixie Bust* back into the welcome familiarity of shuttle bay 2B. In a few hours, he was due to clock on for Skyward 270's descent-ascent cycle: there'd just be time for breakfast, and a too-short nap, before he turned up for duty again. His dinner reservation would have to be rescheduled for when he was next topside, in four days' time. He put in a quick call to Judy Sargent, the desk officer at Hotel Policing, to check that his report had arrived satisfactorily, and to ask whether the force had any other debilitating social evenings planned for the foreseeable future. He hoped not to be topside the next time...

He hated crime work; the type of detection he preferred involved the rearrangement and elucidation of words, to fit within carefully-ordered racks of small square spaces. Nonetheless, he felt secretly pleased at the investigation's outcome, from a number of perspectives. Not only had he apprehended a murderous, amoral embezzler – the Blessed Echidnans would likely require quite some time to track down the hiding places that Flange had arranged for his ill-gotten gains – but he'd also ensured a temporary inrush of hotel guests, three thousand or so in total, in sharp contrast to the customary slow business which the hotel would now normally be experiencing. Some of the Echidnans would likely stay on for a month or more, while they sought to arrange slower-than-light travel to Shangvanatopia. Already there were rumours of a developing bidding war between TransGalactic Freight, Andromeda Spaceways, and Chastity Cosmic, all courting the Echidnans' lucrative STL flight business. It would be interesting, Gordon thought, to see who offered the best, or the slowest, deal...

He felt no unease at Flange's fate. Gordon didn't like murderers, any more than he liked people who thought orange and purple went together, and Flange deserved everything the Church, and the police, could throw at him. No, the one he almost felt sorry for was Cassie, stripped of her command and archived while the authorities tried to decide what to do with her. True, she'd obstructed him, had actively misled him, and had sought to derail a criminal investigation; but at the end she'd stopped Flange, when nobody else had found a way.

Plus, she'd got Gordon's name right; and *that* counted for something, in his book.

The Fall Guy

Gordon strained to make sense of the tile-cam footage of the murder. But several aspects refused to tally, even after five viewings. The assailant purposefully approached his (or her) victim. O'Meara, engrossed in the vista, showed no acknowledgement of the intruder behind him. Then the mystery perp pushed the victim – no minor feat, all considered – with enough force to send him through the full-length plastiglass viewing window, to his death. The tile's playback ended in a wash of pixellated whiteout as the killer turned his laser pistol on the camera.

Gordon downloaded the footage to his handheld and switched the tile off. Telemetry from the observation deck's other four tile-cams had been identical except for viewing angle, and for the time elapsing before laser-induced overload.

Gordon moved his scrutiny to the massive hole in the plastiglass wall. He hoped the transparent emergency shielding was genuinely airtight. He had no wish to follow O'Meara.

There was, he mused, your regular, common or garden defenestration; and there was the over-the-top, all-stops-out, no-expense-spared variety. What you might call "defenestration with extreme prejudice". Gordon Mamon (overworked lift operator, first-aid officer, janitor, dishwasher, room service attendant and part-time hotel detective of the Skyward Suites 270) strongly suspected he was investigating an example of the latter classification of window-mediated murder.

He was starting to feel like the doorman of some sick Mile-High Club for vicious killers. But even putting aside his misgivings at having come into close proximity with death by violence for the third time in three months, Gordon had to wonder about the assailant's mentality. To push someone out a window to their death was distasteful enough. But when the window was effectively several million storeys up, on the top floor of a descending space elevator/hotel module, it was something else again.

There were two particularly upsetting aspects to the murder. First, Gordon knew the victim personally. Second, due to the complexities of near-geostationary orbital mechanics, he had no notion whatsoever of the direction in which he should be seeking the corpse. One hour and counting, and the feasible volume of space was growing disconcertingly large.

As any detective can confirm, solving a murder usually pivots around discovery of a corpse. It looks bad to claim a homicide without the provision of the victim's body, or at least some corporeal remains. A severed head, say, a mangled torso, or, *in extremis*, a majority shareholding in some vital internal organ. In the present case, there should by rights have been more than the usual quantum of corporeality – the last time Gordon had seen One Ton O'Meara alive, he'd thought the famed Mexican-Irish sumo wrestler looked like five Elvises jammed into the one human frame – but of identifiable remains there were none. Explosive depressurisation had expelled O'Meara's body. Also absent were the window's plastiglass fragments, most of the observation deck's original air supply and (with two notable exceptions) all items of material evidence.

The murderer's vacuum-suit was crumpled, empty, on the obs deck floor. A laser pistol lay alongside. A nearby ventilation duct's access panel hung open, askew. Gordon had already ordered the guests' suite doors to be maximum-security locked, with the guests corralled into the ground floor beyond the reach of this set of ducts. But even believing that the assailant was nominally confined, Gordon felt monumentally uneasy. He'd been a Skyward's employee too long to have faith in the elevator-hotel's structural robustness. The cars were vacuum-resistant, but internal divisions were flimsy (notoriously so, in the case of the honeymoon suite). Thin plastiminium wall, floor, and ceiling panels conferred the illusion of privacy; they wouldn't obstruct a determined murderer.

And the crime didn't *feel* right. Not that murder ever felt right, unless you were fighting in self-defence, or had just come face-to-face with the soulless reprobate who'd for the past year been deluging your handheld with seventy misspelled messages a day offering their 150%-guaranteed-effective masculinity-enhancing surgical prowess. Lately with illustrations, and once with a let's-leave-absolutely-nothing-to-the-imagination auto-playing vid clip. In 3D. Gordon shuddered, returning to the present with a grimace. *Why* the window-push?

The attributes – the murder, the cameras' obliteration, the killer's subsequent tidy disappearance – spoke of premeditation. But why destroy the detectors *after* the murder, rather than before? Why choose such a physically demanding and dangerous method of killing, when the laser pistol could have discharged death as effortlessly as it had dispatched the tile-cam CCDs? How had the perp smuggled the laser through the hotel's security cordon?

And why O'Meara? The man wouldn't hurt a fly, wouldn't intentionally hurt anyone who wasn't at least one hundred and fifty kilos and clad only in a sweaty white bedsheet origami'd into an oversized nappy. (And the vac-suit was much too small to have encased an aggrieved sumo victim. So. Not revenge, then.)

His handheld beeped. Belle.

'Gordon here. Any news?'

'Just that we're all gathered in the lobby, as you instructed.' The voice of Belle Hopp (Skyward 270's receptionist, concierge, counsellor and childcare attendant) betrayed the strain she was under, striving for composure in the face of nebulous danger. 'Uh – Gord – you sure you know what you're doing?'

'Sure as I ever am,' he replied. 'I need to check out the ventilation shafts, looks like the escape route. Think we've got him – or her – cornered.'

'That's a good idea?'

'No,' he admitted. 'But we've got to keep the guests safe.' With a seventh-wave surge, it struck him that he'd lost O'Meara, had let the big man down. For the second time now, a murderer had tarnished Skyward 270, *his* module, and this time had claimed the life of someone Gordon had to say was more than just a guest.

It was not as though One-Ton O'Meara had exactly become one of his friends, though Gordon could not now think of who else might fit this category. He'd had drinks with O'Meara at one of the Skytop Plaza's sushi-and-Guinness bars more than a month back, just a few days after the sumo wrestler had saved his life. They talked about wrestling. Gordon confessed he was turned off by the live-action cartoon violence of professional wrestling, had heard it described as the only sport to have suffered during the recent scriptwriter's strike. One-Ton had told him sumo wasn't *like* that, there was art to it, grace, a genuine spontaneity. He'd gifted Gordon tickets to his next bout. Gordon had intended to go, he really had, but hadn't realised the match clashed with his schedule: Skyward 270 would be on descent then. He'd failed to see O'Meara in action. Now, he never would.

'Gordon?' Belle dragged him back to the moment.

'Here. Look, send Sue up. And ask her to grab something useful from the galley, just by way of protection.'

He felt conflicted about imposing on Sue Sheff, Skyward 270's chief cook, for backup. She was a new recruit, whereas Belle and he had logged up dozens of 270's ascent/descent cycles as a team. But Belle's excellent people skills were best employed in ensuring the hotel guests didn't succumb to panic. And with a total staff of three, himself included, there wasn't another option. So Sue now guarded the obs deck, armed with a turkey baster – it wouldn't have been Gordon's first choice of weapon – while he contorted his way through an access hatch that really, you'd have to say, could have been made larger than child-labour-sized. How had the murderer managed this?

In as far as his waist, Gordon turned awkwardly to check out the vent shaft. The motion, and an unsettlement in his stomach, confirmed his suspicion. The vent system wasn't subject to the comforting artificial gravity of the hotel's public spaces, instead manifesting only the fey descent-inverted microgravity of the lift module's powered fall through subgeostationary space.

In contrast to the hatchway, the ventilation duct was capacious, a good two metres wide. A solid plasticrete bulkhead capped the shaft above the hatchway. Below Gordon, the duct ran downwards for what seemed the full thirty-metre height of the lift module, branching horizontally at intervals.

Gordon wasn't good with heights. Ironic; but, enclosed within the hotel module, however-many-thousand kilometres above Earth, he could usually ignore vertigo's overtures. Here, faced with a thirty-metre drop and stuck halfway through the hatch – with stomach and inner ears telling him he had nothing to fear while his legs and eyes conspired to insist the drop was lethal – he could feel his innards turning to jelly. And the ladderway's plastichrome rungs on the duct's opposite wall were still beyond his reach. He wriggled through to mid-calf level (with which his hips were happier; now it was his *mind* all a-quiver), and managed to grab the nearest rung. He finished pulling himself through into the shaft, slapped a miniature patch-cam to the bulkhead above, and began descending.

At the five-metre mark, he inspected the horizontal ducts radiating off in three directions. Each duct was straight and bulkhead-terminated. He affixed more patch-cams to the main shaft's side, aligned so the cameras could survey each offshoot while he searched for any irregularity.

Fifteen minutes later, he'd drawn a blank at this level. None of the patch-cams had displayed any movement save that of the Mamon hindquarters (the horizontal ducts were too narrow to turn within). There were no obstacles visible, the rangefinding checked out correctly, and (according to his trusty handheld) none of the top-tier suites' vents had been opened in several months, since their last maintenance check.

*

Later, back in the obs lounge's unequivocal gravity, he relieved Sue from guard duty and called Belle.

'You there?'

'*Yes*, Gordon. Where *are* you? Been trying to reach you for the past hour.'

'I'm fine, just had my handheld in forensics mode, hadn't noticed the call light. Listen, can you send Skytop HQ these fingerprint images, to pass on to the police? That's all I've found from checking the vent system. Looks like our perp went in, but didn't come out – and he's not there now.'

'OK, got them. Wait a second. Ah, here we go. Looks like they're all Skyward maintenance staff.'

'Huh? You've got their fingerprints logged locally? I thought you'd at *least* have to go off-station—'

'Just thumbprints. Biometric locks on the broom cupboard. But Gord, the Skytop police – I've been trying to reach you. They've been going frantic, trying to contact us.'

'Us? You mean me?'

'No, us. There's some problem with our broadcast cable: it's receiving but not transmitting. I've heard everything they've sent us, but there's no way of letting Skytop know we've heard.'

'When did this start?'

'Before the murder. They don't even *know* about that yet.'

'So why've they been calling?'

'An all-modules alert, dangerous fugitive. Gunther Haier, noted hitman. Number three on the league table. Anyway—'

'They have a *league table* for assassins?'

'Yeah, helps to humanise the job. Or so claims their official-spokesperson-in-hiding. Anyway, police believe Haier has very recently been lying low on Skytop, working in one of the engineering shops, but now he's nowhere to be found. They're concerned he's taken a lift down to the surface.'

'You got a mugshot?'

'Sending it now, Gord.'

'OK. Yeah. Nasty. No, doesn't look like any guests, what I saw of them anyway.'

'No. And there's a dozen *other* modules he might've taken, if he left Skytop within the last few hours like they reckon. Assuming he didn't ship out of the system entirely on a spaceliner. But it's still a bit of a coincidence, you'd have to say.'

'Yeah. I was just thinking the same. A murder, a missing killer. You'd have to think they're connected. Did O'Meara see something he wasn't supposed to?'

'You tell me. *You're* the detective.'

It wasn't an assignation he'd ever felt comfortable with.

Gordon's office was a cramped cubicle, alcoved off the main lobby and decorated only with desk, two chairs, and some wall-mounted newspaper cuttings reporting the cases he'd previously solved. (The one with the photo of himself and O'Meara was particularly prized, though he could strangle the subeditor who'd vetted the wording "chief suspect Grodon Mammal" in the caption. But at least the write-up had been better than that piece in the inflight magazine.)

'No, Mr Bai, I'm not bothered over which channel you were watching, or what the actresses' names were. Or even what they were doing. I'm merely ascertaining your whereabouts at the time of the, um, incident.'

'You mean the murder?'

'*Incident.* Let's not jump to conclusions here.'

Perhaps he could have worded that better.

Anyway, he didn't think Mr Bai knew anything. About O'Meara's murder, or much of anything else. It had been the same with the other three guests. He didn't make any of them to be the criminal mastermind type.

Dismissing Bai, he attempted to re-fold the paperclip he'd been straightening, while he watched the sequence once more on his handheld's display. The vent grille came off, falling to the obs lounge floor. The spacesuited figure emerged from the duct (recalling his own struggles with the hatchway, Gordon could only bristle with envy at the ease with which the killer had negotiated that bottleneck), pulled itself smoothly to its feet, and walked out of the tile-cam's field of view. Five seconds later, the depressurisation lights on the wall began to flash. Beyond the camera's scope, O'Meara, most of the panoramic windowpane's plastiglass, and the bulk of the obs deck's air had all suddenly left the building. Then the incapacitating flash of the laser pistol.

The playback was silent, but that solid plastitanium grille had to have made a significant noise when it fell. Clattered. And he defied anyone, *anyone*, to walk noiselessly in one of Skyward's cheap plastimetal spacesuits. All up, there had to have been a good ten-second warning for O'Meara that something strange was happening behind him. Gordon *knew* One-Ton O'Meara's hearing was good, even if he hadn't seen anything reflected in the glass or through his peripheral vision. And the wrestler's training would surely have been to check out any possible disturbances around him. So why hadn't O'Meara turned to face his foe? Gordon had gone all through the other tile-cams' footage, the man had not even tensed as the fatal impulse was applied to his so-broad back. He'd just gone quietly to a horrible death.

It made no sense.

Yes, there were clues; but Gordon preferred his clues to be neatly numbered, and divided into "across" and "down". Puzzles that you could solve through a thesaurus, or a scrabble dictionary, without fear of deadly hazard. Crossword clues never led to anyone dying by violence, except maybe sometimes at the highest, most competitive levels.

A burst of laughter from the lobby disrupted his concentration. He emerged to investigate. The four guests, still excluded from their own rooms, were playing charades. The laughter had been initiated by

Ali Bai's attempt at an Elvis Presley imitation. Gordon shook his head, mired in frustration.

Impersonation. Something clicked. He went to find Belle.

'What d'you mean, offline? Is this the same fault that took out our comms link?'

'Don't think so,' Belle replied. 'The security scanner's topside, at Skytop Embarkation. The comms fault's local, and Sue thinks she's just about got that sorted.'

'Huh? So Sue's chief cook *and* radio operator now?'

'Yep. Her promotion came through last week.'

Gordon grinned, wondering how long it would take Sue to discover that the company "promotions" didn't actually equate to an increase in income, just in responsibilities. 'But – they just let passengers board anyway?'

'They still checked them. Visual, biometrics, random pat-down body searches, sniffers for drugs and weaponry. Just no X-ray or subdermal radar imagery. They haven't reported any problems.'

No, thought Gordon. *Just an escaped killer and a mystery death.* But it was all starting to make sense. 'So, this affected our module?'

'Sure. It went offline two hours before we decoupled. You think there's a connection?'

'Belle, I'm *sure*. This is Haier's doing.'

'Haier? But how? There's been no-one of remotely his description passing through Embarkation at all today. The police sound clear on that, it's one aspect of his disappearance they're totally puzzled over.'

'I'm not surprised. They wouldn't have recognised him in his spacesuit.'

'But Gord, the spacesuit's one of ours. And it hasn't been off-station. Ever.' Belle stared at him, as if to find the answers in his face. 'And if it's Haier, *where is he?*'

'That,' replied Gordon with the theatrical affectation he knew so annoyed others around him, 'is a matter of some gravity.' And he went off for another look at the obs deck vent shaft.

The murder, including O'Meara's counterintuitive lack of response to perceived danger, now made complete sense. But the problem of the space-suit's vanished occupant remained. Gordon stared through the hatchway, baffled by the empty duct's featurelessness. He'd checked all the patch-cams' playbacks. Nothing.

Where had it gone?

Slowly, it occurred to him that all might not be as it seemed. A false panel somewhere in the ducts might mask another exit. He'd checked the shaft's dimensions by laser rangefinding, but a carefully-placed solid panel, where a grille should exist, might well have escaped his attention. He asked his handheld to load a VR tour of the shaft system, as per the lift module specs, and mentally prepared himself to squeeze through that bloody opening one more time, to play spot-the-difference.

He didn't need to resort to contortions. The difference was staring him in the face.

Cunning. Ingenious, even.

Just as in any crossword, there was one vital clue from which everything else would cascade.

This was it. He extracted a large evidence bag from his pocket, and started pulling rungs off the shaft wall.

'Belle?'

'Yes? Where are you?'

'Cargo deck. Listen, I've gotta go out.'

'Out?'

'Yeah. Pod. Sue's been helping me on something, but she's staying behind. And I really need you to help her get the comms link working.'

We'll need the cops down from topside.'

'Police? Gord, d'you have a problem down there?'

'Not a problem. A solution. But Belle, I gotta go.'

'But what about Haier? Remember? The guy who pushed O'Meara out the window?'

'That's who I'm after,' Gordon replied. 'The ladder did it.'

'*Gord*—'

'Sorry, Belle, no time to fill you in. Look, I've downloaded some trajectory calcs to the mainframe. Just get through to topside. Please?'

'Trajectory?'

'Sorry. Gotta go.' Gordon closed the call, and turned to thank Sue for her help. Then, grabbing up the spacesuit and the evidence bag, he jogged across the cargo bay's radiation-proof plastilead flooring to the escape pod.

He hoped the pod could move faster than it looked. It *looked* like nothing other than a Henry Moore snail sculpture.

The escape pod's responses, to every attitude-jet impulse, felt exaggerated, hypersensitive. In reality, it was simply that the pod was tiny and rather flimsy; and Gordon was no pilot. Still, as long as the space-nav directions from his handheld were reliable, he'd get to where he needed to be.

Walls lined with plastihemp matting, two benches with rough plastigel padding, a simple control panel mounted below a small screen. The pod's cockpit was spartan, befitting a craft not intended for frequent or extended occupation, nor by those concerned overmuch with immediate comfort. Still, it could be worse. Gordon wondered how Haier was finding *his* current quarters.

Not for the first time, he wondered at the wisdom of this lone-wolf approach. Gordon nurtured his lack of physical bravery, it was part of who he was. But he couldn't have brought Belle, or Sue, into danger with him: quite aside from his concern for their safety, there were the lift-module's minimal-staffing regulations of which to be mindful. And he couldn't leave Haier to escape, and kill again another day.

The search volume, several hours after O'Meara's fall through the window, was uncomfortably large: too many uncertainties in the trajectory. Large, too, was the brooding crescent Earth below Gordon's feet; then above his head; then below his feet again. Larger still was Gordon's frustration at his inability to stop the pod's infernal tumbling. Largest of all, or so it felt, was the lump in Gordon's throat at the thought of the approaching danger.

The O'Meara-shaped figure seemed, in the end, almost small when Gordon finally sighted the lifeless form drifting open-mouthed through space. He wrestled again with the attitude controls, and finally struck on a lucky combination of thrusts that quenched the pod's chaotic rotation. Then he dialled the docking camera's magnification up to the max, and inspected the stridently leisure-suited, sumo-shaped husk while the pod nudged closer.

O'Meara looked odd. Where the wrestler's shod feet should have been – *had* been, according to the hotel's tilecam footage – there were clusters of small rocket nozzles. Elsewhere, on the vacuum-exposed face of the "corpse", there was no sign of the expected tracery of burst capillaries and bloodily bugshot eyes. Instead, the eyes had a persistently glassy quality, as though they might be camera lenses. Or viewing windows.

Whatever Haier's faults, he obviously wasn't a claustrophobe.

The pod edged closer. Time for Gordon's spacewalk.

O'Meara performed a leisurely quarter-roll, expertly twisting and then stopping to face the pod. The wrestler's arm reached into its jacket pocket.

Gordon's approach had apparently not gone unnoticed. He was expected by the occupant of the O'Meara-suit.

The reluctant detective flicked a switch, opening the outer hatch of the pod's cramped airlock. The suited figure squeezed out clumsily.

Earth was a huge curve of brilliant blue and white, hanging off to the side of the pod, deceptively distant.

But no time to sightsee. This was time to meet and greet.

'Haier,' he called out through the suit's short-range radio, hoping O'Meara's occupant was tuned to the correct frequency.

The gun, Gordon judged, was a Magnum 3.14159, one of the deadliest bits of weaponry either side of the exosphere. "O'Meara" held it in his right hand, his face unreadable as any mannequin. The gun pointed straight at Gordon's mirrored visor as the pair faced off, perhaps ten paces apart.

Gordon fumbled his suit's verniers, straining with the double necessity of arresting a slow tumble and of keeping his suit interposed between "O'Meara" and the pod. (The gun didn't help. Signals of cold dread trickled down Gordon's spine. He wished he'd thought to bring the laser pistol with him.)

A voice crackled through the radio speaker, cold, devoid of charm: 'Any messages for your next of kin?'

'Haier?' Gordon responded.

'Who do I got the pleasure of addressing?' Haier asked. *Snide.*

Gordon introduced himself.

'They might at least have sent me a *professional.*' For the first time, a degree of emotion crept into Haier's tone. Disgust.

Gordon swallowed. That gun looked *big.* 'Give up, Haier, the game's over.'

'I don't read that, Marmot.'

'*Mamon.*'

'Whatever. Where's your backup?'

'Just me.'

'Oh, how sad.'

'You were clever,' Gordon said, wondering how long before Haier pulled the trigger. 'But you slipped up.'

'You're pretty damned cocky, considering you're not packing. What you got, aside from those plastimache cuffs you're dangling? A bullet-proof vest, under that suit? Vacuum patches? Way I see it, a visor shot'll take care of you good, whatever. You clearly haven't thought this through.'

'I figured *you* out, didn't I?'

'You got lucky. But that's about run out, Membrane.'

'*Mamon.* Luck had nothing to do with it. Give me credit for my intelligence.'

'I don't deal in denominations that small,' Haier scoffed. 'But I bet you thought you were pretty smart, tracking me, figuring Wrestler-Boy here for just a suit.'

'Yeah. It had us fooled, for a bit. You were obviously busy, those two weeks in the engineering shop. Nice bit of plastiflesh moulding, over a frame of – what? Stainless steel? With what, some additional heatproofing? And oxygen tanks, propellant, navigational computers – no wonder you needed a sumo-sized frame for the play. But the "murder" was too obviously a set-up. You were too careful about placing the pointers, giving us what you wanted us to see. Like I said, you stuffed up.'

'I don't see that,' said Haier. His finger – O'Meara's finger – shifted lazily on the gun's trigger. 'You ever seen what one of these can do? Two minutes from now – less if you bore me – you'll be dead. And I'll be trimming Sumo-baby here for final re-entry. An hour after that I'll be splashing down somewhere around Indonesia or the Philippines. Still need to figure where, but somewhere they'll never find me. Not with the disguises I'm shipping. But say your bit. For all the good it'll do you.'

'What did you with O'Meara? The real O'Meara?'

'Sumo-guy? Tranked him and trussed him up in a trashpile topside somewhere. Don't remember where. The dose was supposed to be enough to fell a horse. He took three.'

'*Where is he?*'

'What d'you care, Marlin?'

'*Mamon*. He's my friend. He saved my life once.'

'Hah.'

'If he's come to harm through this, I'll , I'll—'

'You'll nothing. Face it, Mincemeat, you're finished.'

'*Mamon*. And you're missing two important points.'

'Yeah? Shoot.'

Gordon winced. He *really* didn't care for that word at the moment. 'One. That gun you're holding?'

'The Magnum π? What of it?'

'You'll only get the one shot.'

'That's plenty. Not going to leave much of your face. And?'

'Two's the clincher,' Gordon replied. 'The bit you'd hidden so well. I found it. Haier, *I know about the ladder.*'

'Yeah? Smart. But I don't see where it gets you.'

'Clever. A stick-figure robot to occupy the spacesuit. Program it to push "O'Meara" out the window, then to crawl into the vent-shaft and hide. And getting it to dismantle itself, disguise itself as the top few rungs of the shaftway ladder, *that* was pure genius. You *were* busy in that engineering shop, weren't you?'

'Might even be tempted to go into engineering full time, once I get dirtside. Except it doesn't pay as well as my regular line of employ—'

'*But.* You should've taken out the top five original rungs beforehand. 'Cause I noticed, eventually, that the top section of ladder wasn't on the blueprints. Wasn't supposed to be there. And steel bars? You gotta *know* Skyward doesn't use anything that heavy. That clinched it for me – otherwise I might just have thought it was a slip-up on the blueprints. Wouldn't be the first time.'

'I needed steel for the impact of the big push. But hell, I'm impressed,' said Haier, though he disguised it well. 'Still...' He gestured with the gun.

'Oh, and one other thing,' said Gordon. 'The stick-figure robot? You should've got it to burn out its programming core, once its mission was complete. 'Cause I had Sue, our tech wizard, give it a quick spot of reprogramming. That one shot? It's not going to save you.' And Gordon nudged the controls to jet the spacesuit towards the sumo-frame. Not too fast, just a half-metre a second.

Haier went for the head shot anyway. The shattered visor exploded outwards in a constellation of shards, revealing the blunt head of the stick-figure robot within the helmet's remains. *Should've bled the suit's air first*, Gordon thought from the relative safety of the pod's cockpit. The spacesuit in his forward view started tumbling from the bullet's impact and the ejecting gases. He fumbled the controls, trying to right the suit. It was going to take too long, and with the helmet's viewcam damaged by the shot, he'd lost his direct close-up of Haier. Crux time. Gordon swallowed, and edged the pod forward.

Haier was spinning too, both pitch and yaw, thanks to the gun's recoil. But it would be close. Gordon wasn't sure he could bridge the distance before Haier completed a revolution.

Second time around, Haier would know where to aim: not at the suit, but at the pod.

But the suit got there first, through pure inanimate chance. It was feet-foremost as it pushed gently into Haier's sumo-broad leisure-suited back. Not forceful, but unexpected enough. Haier reflexively dropped the gun.

The Magnum drifted with balletic grace from his outstretched fingers. Haier swore like a consummate professional. Gordon accelerated the pod towards the gulf between gun and gun-arm, sideswiping both.

The longer he could keep Haier tumbling, the better.

'Comfortable?' Belle asked.

'Bit space-sick.' Gordon swallowed, looking around the interior of the medic-evac ship. Out the porthole he could see the sleek black lines of the police cruiser within which Haier was now safely incarcerated. 'You took your time turning up. Did it really take Sue that long to fix the comms link?'

'She *still* hasn't fixed it. So she heliographed topside instead.'

'*Heliograph?*' Gordon asked.

'Sure. You're not the only one has ideas, you know, Gordon. She thought of it right after you Don Quixote'd off in the pod. I'm a little surprised you didn't think of it yourself.'

'Huh.'

She smiled.

'Belle, did you say we're heading back to 270?'

'Yes, why?'

'I'm not ready for active duty. Call it shock, trauma, whatever. Can they dock this thing with one of the ascending modules?' He checked his handheld. 'Like, maybe, 188? That's at the same altitude, won't be much out of their way.'

'I'm sure the medics can take you back to Skytop if you ask them,' Belle said. 'That's where they're based.'

'That would be good.'

'Good how?'

'I need to track someone down. Someone I thought, a few hours ago, had been killed. Not exactly sure where to find him, but he'd be harder to conceal than most people. And then ... and then, if there's *any* justice in the universe, I'm going to stay long enough to watch me a wrestling match.'

The Hunt for Red Leicester

Gordon had to admit that, as naked as he felt without his handheld, he felt even more naked without his jacket, his cardigan, his shirt, his cufflinks, his tie, his trousers, his shoes, his socks, his cosmic-radiation-resistant singlet, his Skyward ID badge, and his boxers.

A pedant would, of course, have noted that Gordon couldn't genuinely be considered "naked" owing to the rough lengths of rope which bound him tight, hand and foot, and which prevented him from clambering up off this unremittingly cold tile floor. (And how was it, by the way, that an expanse of tiles always managed to get twenty degrees colder than its surroundings? Wasn't that in contravention of one or other physical law?) To which Gordon would have responded with an exasperated plea for said pedant to stop pedanting[1] and for pity's sake do something *useful* like undo these bloody knots...

Sadly, there were no pedants, hypothetical or otherwise, in evidence. Just Gordon, and the deserted public restroom in which his unknown assailants had dumped him.

He took another look around the restroom and noticed something unsettling. The long row of lavatory stalls along one side, the corresponding rank of washbasins, nanosoap dispensers, and infra-red hand-drying units along the opposite wall. *No urinals.*

Whichever way it played out, this was not going to end well.

---

1 Yes, I *know* that's not the correct term. Just let it go.

*

Some idea of the restroom's location would help; but Gordon had no markers, no reference points, in this scenario. The odds were, though, that he was still somewhere within the Skytop Plaza, the sprawling hotel complex atop the space elevator for which Gordon Mamon was a lift attendant (and complaints officer, first aid officer, janitor, room service attendant, security officer and, on occasion, house detective: a man with many hats, regrettably none of which he could lay his hands on at this minute).

The restroom *felt*, in some indefinable sense, like it was Skytop. The cheap opulence, the ill-judged colour scheme, the swirl-motifed plastimarble wall panels, the plastigilt door handles and faucets, the inimitable ammonia-and-lavender bouquet, the bad mood lighting. There must be scores of restrooms like this, scattered across the Plaza's hectares-broad expanse, its dozen levels.

His eyes were drawn to the main door at the other end of the room. For now, it remained shut. But he'd need to get a shuffle on, if he wished to move to one of the stalls before anyone came in. Time to impersonate a caterpillar.

He managed, over the course of the next fifteen minutes, to wriggle a distance of approximately four metres, and to severely chafe his ankles and wrists in the process, before the restroom door opened.

'Am I glad to see you,' Gordon said, while Belle busied herself, businesslike, with the task of struggling to untie the knots. 'I mean, of all the people who might've found me in here, naked on the floor…'

'Yes, well,' she replied, with the cautious demeanour of one trying desperately to type while not looking at the keyboard. (Belle Hopp was Gordon's longtime co-worker on Skytop, and on 270, one of the hundreds of Skyward liftmodules that ferried guests to and from the Plaza. They'd been through a lot together, but this was something new.) 'You might've been here awhile.'

'How so?'

'This restroom's marked as "Closed for Cleaning".' She unravelled another component of the knot around Gordon's wrists.

'Then why—'

'It's been closed for the last three months. Been past it dozens of times. I figured it must be clean enough by now, and even if it wasn't I was ready to give the cleaning staff a flea in their ear about the length of time it was taking. And I couldn't be bothered walking another half-kilometre to get to the next one, after all the legwork I've done this morning already.'

'Morning? Legwork?'

'Yep. You do realise we're scheduled to commence descent in about four-and-a-half hours?'

'Is it that late? I thought—'

'Gordon, you were supposed to be at 270 three hours ago, for the pre-descent fumigation detail. We waited half an hour for you to show, and then when you were still AWOL, and not answering our calls—'

'Sorry. I've been a bit tied up. *Ouch.*'

'You're lucky I found you so quickly, all things considered,' said Belle. 'You know, it was always going to be some staff member or other, caught short, who found you here. A guest wouldn't have had the temerity to ignore the "Closed" sign.'

'I guess not. But, I mean, if you need—'

'It can wait. Any idea who did this to you?'

'Other than that they evidently weren't Boy Scouts, no.'

'Hold still. It really doesn't help when you move your arms.'

'Cramp.'

'Even so. There. You want to try untying your feet yourself, while I go get an outfit for you?'

'My hands feel half-numb,' replied Gordon, rubbing at his wrists, before moving to belatedly shield his nether regions. His hands *were* cold. He caught Belle smirking, noticed how the gesture accentuated her laughter lines; and felt his cheeks, those on his face, blush involuntarily.

'You'll probably be quicker on the untying. Belle, why does this always happen to me? I'm just a humble Lift Operator, Third Class.'

'No, you're a markedly egotistical Lift Operator, Third Class,' replied Belle, not unkindly. 'And what do you mean, "always happen to me"? I've never known you to be tied up in a women's toilet before this – unless there's something you haven't been telling me.'

'*Belle*—'

'Kidding.'

'And what do *you* mean,' Gordon asked, 'when you offer to "go get an outfit" for me?'

'Just something appropriate to the location. Can't have you scandalising the Plaza.'

'Not entirely sure I like the sound of that.'

'I can stop untying you, if you'd rather.'

'No,' said Gordon hurriedly. 'Outfit sounds good.'

'Splendid. Any preference between blonde and brunette, for the wig?'

'I'll leave that to your discretion,' Gordon said. 'If I must.'

Belle rose to her feet. 'There you go. Do you need a hand up?'

'Uh – no.' Gordon stood, and became conscious of just how much mirror there was on that wall. 'Might be an idea if I wait in one of the cubicles, while you get this... outfit.'

'Probably best. Oh—'

'What?'

'Looks like that one at the end is occupied.'

The stall's occupant was male, motionless, corpulent, pale of skin, grey of hair, and dressed in an expensive-looking business suit. The kind of suit, Gordon strongly suspected, from which it would be the very devil to remove those bloodstains.

'Who is it?' Belle asked, anxiously looking around the door of the cubicle.

'Not sure,' Gordon answered. 'But I suppose the correct tense would be "was".'

'He's dead?'

'Certainly looks that way.' *If I had my handheld, I could get a time-of-death from core body temp.* It seemed recent, though: no evident decomposition, no odour of putrefaction. If anything, the corpse – or possibly its suit – smelt *floral.* Roses, or something similar. *Odd smell for a middle-aged dead guy in a suit...*

The ideal would be for him to turn the body face-up without handling it in any way – fingerprints – but Gordon neither believed in, nor displayed any particular talent for, telekinesis. And, nonexistent telekinetic abilities or no, the victim looked heavy.

The blood on the tiled floor was concentrated around the body's upper torso, suggesting a chest wound, but with the corpse face-down there was no means of determining whether it was from a bullet, an energy weapon, or a knife wound. *Knife would be easiest to smuggle up here*, Gordon told himself. *Energy weapon would cauterise as it blasted, so probably no. And if I had my handheld, I could scan for gunshot residue...*

Something about the body's left arm caught Gordon's attention. The wristwatch.

He'd seen enough. He backed out of the stall, trying to ignore the naked man in the mirror.

'Gordon?' asked Belle.

'It's the man from the promenade,' Gordon explained.

'Promenade?'

'C level. I was just outside the Na— well, on my way to Fairdig's, and this guy stopped me to ask the time. I recognise the wristwatch. Because I thought it was odd, someone goes to the trouble of wearing a watch, why'd they need to ask the time?'

'And you don't know who he was?'

'No, he'd just bumped into me. And... it must've been just after that, they knocked me out. And, it would seem, killed him.'

Belle moved forward slightly into the stall, fascination apparently trumping discomfort. She crouched down, peered in for a closer look. 'Oh my God,' she said, raising a hand to her cheek and stepping back. 'It's old Havmurthy.'

'Who?' Gordon asked.

'What d'you mean, "who"? It's Havmurthy. Lord Havmurthy.'

'Still doesn't ring a bell.'

'Seriously? The cheese whiz?'

'No,' said Gordon, rubbing carefully at the back of his wrist. 'Much as it evidently surprises you to hear it, I've never heard of this Havmurthy. What does – or I suppose did – he do?'

'Cheese. Dessert and cocktail market especially. C'mon, you *must've* heard of Havmurthy Sweet Cheeses.'

'No.'

'Sweet Baby Cheeses?'

'No.'

'Cheeses On A Stick?'

'*No.*'

Belle stood up, her knee clicking in the process. 'Gordon, where have you been the past decade or so? The stuff's everywhere.'

'Not in my vicinity, apparently. Anyway, does this bring us any closer to figuring out why someone would want him dead? Business competitors, anyone like that?'

'Probably not. I mean, there used to be Mersifal Cheeses, Blessid Cheeses, and a couple of others, but Havmurthy took care of them. He's kind of the cheese Microsoft. Or was, I guess.'

'Cheese Microsoft? What, you mean like the old 'blue vein of death', or something?'

'No, just that he bought them all out.'

'Ah. How recently?'

'Years ago.'

'Not a very likely motive for this, then.' Gordon nodded towards the body.

'Guess not. Or there's Oh My Curd – they're still going, but I wouldn't have said there's much overlap between their products, so I don't see that OMC would gain much advantage by seeing Havmurthy bite the big one. Although, then again, industrial espionage – I think Havmurthy was looking at bringing out a new cheese-and-carbohydrate mix, to compete with mac & cheese, so maybe OMC or someone was looking to steal the recipe.'

'Recipe for what?'

'Havmurthy's latest product. Cheese Husk Rice.'

Gordon was keenly aware of the eyes trained in his direction as he stumbled in Belle's wake across one of the Plaza's many foyers. In all probability, the majority of those viewing him were merely concerned with how frumpy his appearance was, because Gordon did not constitute a very convincing woman. It is rather difficult, regardless of the quantity of disguising makeup, to carry off a satisfactory portrayal of femininity when one's jawline is adorned by a day's stubble. (The Poirot moustache presumably wasn't helping, either.) But the fact remained that among the spectators might well be those who had dumped him in the restroom, and who had dispatched Lord Havmurthy... in which case, a disguise – even one of such questionable aesthetic values – was a sensible, even a prudent option.

Not that his assailants would necessarily need to strike again. His *ankles* were killing him. He was earnestly beginning to wish that Belle had provided him with a pair of flats, or at least a set of heels with training wheels.

He pulled to an unsteady stop beside her, at the door to the Plaza police station. 'You do realise,' he said, fighting the growing impulse to scratch his itching rump – he'd never imagined the possibility of an allergy to lace, but there you go—'that a *cleaner's* getup, probably just some overalls and maybe a bucket for appearance's sake, mop if you wanted to go the whole hog, would have done just as well? As an outfit? To avoid scandal? A *male* cleaner?'

'Yes, you're right. Oh, well, maybe next time.'

He sighed heavily. 'Belle, seriously, if there's a "next time" for this, I'll— look, let's just get this over with.'

They walked into the station, asked to make a joint statement, and were directed by Judy Sargent, the desk officer, to proceed into one of the interview rooms.

'Might be a bit of a wait,' Judy advised them, as they turned away from the reception desk.

Gordon turned back, gyrating slowly in a surreptitious and ultimately doomed attempt at a handsfree realignment of his undergarments. 'Why d'you say that?' he asked.

'Not your concern, of course… but we're a bit short-staffed right this minute,' explained Judy, busily checking through an official-looking database on her handheld. 'We've got officers investigating a spate of counterfeit moonrocks in the souvenir shops, there've been reports of food poisoning at the Naked Singularity nightspot, a nasty collision between rival spaceliners at the docking bay, which the captains are for some reason trying to pass off as an unscheduled corporate merger. And then on top of all that, we've had a tip-off about some industrial espionage sting. Someone's rumoured to be transmitting, via the hotel somehow, details of a top-secret hyperspace drive that Saturn Propulsions have under development.'

'Judy, if the hyperspace drive's top secret, why are you telling me about it?'

'Advertising. Leaks. Everyone *knows* about it. It's just the details, the engineering particulars, that are secret. That's the way these things work.'

'So you're telling me we might be better not filing a statement, because you're all too busy?'

'No, Gordon, we're taking the attack on Havmurthy, and on you, seriously.' Judy looked up to make eye contact, exhaled slowly, seemed to take a while to regather the thread. Or perhaps she was distracted by Gordon's attire, or his furtive hip movements. 'Of course. Havmurthy was a big che— a big wheel – er, a big player in the business world.

So someone will speak to you about it, naturally, make sure you can give us all the relevant info you have. It's just – we have no leads whatsoever on this hyperdrive intrigue, no hint as to how the transmission is likely to be made, which, as you can imagine, makes it a bloody big ask to try to intercept. Pretty much everyone here's on surveillance, because we very much can't afford the negative publicity from this Saturn Props thing. Nor the lawsuits. So... it'll be a while before someone gets to you. Maybe a half hour.'

The interview room was a windowless rectangular space in off-white plasticinderblock, furnished with a large unsteady table and four small chairs. An imposing Rogue's Gallery of stern-faced photographs decorated one wall: the individuals depicted might equally have been current employees, station alumni, or persons of interest.

'Is that chair uncomfortable?' Belle asked.

Gordon stopped, mid-squirm. 'No, it's... doesn't matter.'

'Any news on the handheld?'

'No,' answered Gordon, shifting in his seat again. 'Bit of a forlorn hope, expecting that it might've turned up at Lost Property. Still, I had to ask.'

'Why d'you think they took it? I mean, not as if it's a newish model or anything.'

'Why'd they abduct me, knock me out, leave me tied up? Naked? Why'd they kill Havmurthy? Why *didn't* they kill me? Given that they had the chance, and that they apparently wanted me out of the way at least temporarily. It's all connected, somehow.'

'But you'd never even heard of Havmurthy before this. I mean, you said so yourself. So there wasn't really a connection, although I guess they might have seen one where one didn't exist. But maybe your kidnapping and Havmurthy's murder are separate incidents, by different people.'

'Too much of a coincidence,' replied Gordon. 'I don't believe in coincidence, not anymore. Too much money wasted on lottery tickets.'

'But—'

'I gather you wish to make a statement?' asked a tall policeman, walking into the room and taking a seat opposite Belle and Gordon.

Warren Toffisser looked much too young for the air of authority he wore like a badge of office – but possibly this was a good thing, in an officer of the law?

And if the young policeman had any opinions about Gordon's choice of outfit, he kept his judgments to himself.

'That took longer than I'd been expecting,' said Belle, as they bustled back across the foyer.

'They're just being thorough,' replied Gordon, struggling to keep up.

'You think so? I reckon yon Warren fancied you.'

'You what?'

'*Relax*, Gordon. Honestly, it's so easy to get a rise from you sometimes.'

'Is that another I've-seen-you-naked reference? Because—'

'Oh, stop it. No, I wouldn't have said "thorough". Longwinded, maybe.'

'Why d'you say that?'

'They just kept going over the details of the statement, making sure we weren't contradicting ourselves. I didn't get any sense they were that interested in following up the vidcam evidence of the attack. Too busy panicking about this Saturn Propulsions intrigue, I guess.'

Gordon tapped her shoulder, signalling a brief halt while he slipped out of his heels.

A family of five, followed closely by an obedient herd of suitcases, streamed around the two hotel employees like a river finding its way around an embedded obstacle. 'Belle, we're *not* actually on the case,' Gordon said, holding his shoes by the ankle straps as they resumed walking briskly across the foyer. 'They don't need to include us in their investigations. And see it from their perspective. Trying to ID a suspect from vidcam imaging, when the perp's cloaked like this one was, is always going to be fiddly – all the details are so blurred, it's going to be like trying to identikit a ghost.'

'You might be right. But I still don't get the feeling the plaza police are up to this.'

'And we are? Belle, *please*. They know what they're doing.'

'Still, we'll be lucky to reach the lift-module before the passengers turn up.'

'No, we've got plenty of time,' Gordon replied, absently patting a nonexistent pocket for his absent handheld, and almost dropping the shoes in the process.

'You sure? I was thinking you'd probably want time to change into something more—'

He glanced down. 'Uh. Yes, you're right.'

They stepped onto the spiral escalator that led down to the departure deck, and Gordon allowed himself to slip into reverie mode.

Of the assault itself he could remember nothing, he only knew that one moment he'd been heading towards an appointment with a medium-rare *filet mignon avec tous les trimmings* at Swedish chef Martin A. Fairdig's celebrated restaurant, had chanced to bump into this Havmurthy, and the next minute he was trussed up like a— like a— well, like a captive and denuded space-elevator attendant: a not particularly adventurous simile, perhaps, but an accurate one. Still, it was a relief to have for once got the inevitable flirtation with danger out of the way, rather than dangling over his head like some Swiss Army Knife of Damocles, waiting to descend upon him in all its multifunctional unpredictability.

He'd made a statement; he and Belle had provided their fingerprints; the police were now investigating, and Gordon could just get on with his everyday job secure in the knowledge that the case was in the capable hands of trained professionals, rather than a rank amateur such as himself. Against that kind of reassurance, the loss of his handheld and of a certain quantum of his hard-earned gravitas was, when you came down to it, rather small beer. Or perhaps, in the circumstances, small-beer-and-cheese.

His spirits lifted further when they reached the lift-module lobby and were met by Sue Sheff, 270's chief cook, caterer, and comms officer, who (having more-or-less recovered from the initial surprise of his appearance) informed Gordon that a woman from Lost Property had been down a few minutes earlier to drop off his handheld.

'Excellent,' said Gordon, his eyes lighting up hungrily as Sue passed it to him. 'Where'd they find it?'

'She didn't say.' Sue's eyes were still tracking between Gordon's asymmetric chest and the flowing brunette locks of his wig.

'Ah. Well, it's back, that's the main thing.' He thumbed it on, and began checking its status.

Sue was struggling to maintain a straight face.

Gordon glanced up from his handheld long enough to ask, 'What's so funny?'

'Oh – just—' She threw a conspiratorial wink to Belle. 'I was just wondering if you two wanted to – you know – get a room or something.'

Belle grinned in response.

'Sue!' Gordon replied, scandalised, attempting as much dignity as he could muster. Which, as it turned out – what with the wig, the dress, and some very suggestive if unconvincing padding – wasn't much. If any. 'I assure you, Sue, that, while admittedly she has recently seen me in a state of some undress, Belle and I—'

'Who said anything about Belle?' Sue asked. 'I was *talking* about you and the handheld.'

Back in his office / cubicle / broom closet – surrounded by framed reproductions of the news reports of the detection exploits of, variously, the intrepid Grodon Mammal, the indefatigable Godron Mitten, and the celebrated Gondor Memo – Gordon checked the handheld's time function. *Still fifteen minutes until embarkation. Time enough to check my messages.*

In the several hours that he had been parted from his trusty handheld, Gordon had apparently been contacted by no less than four senior officials from various international (and, in one case, interplanetary) lottery funds, advising of his unparalleled multiple windfalls in the latest draws, and requiring only his credit details to process his winnings; two young Martian women who wished to press their credentials upon him (one with a view to matrimony, one ostensibly very much not of such persuasion); three funding requests for two different startups hoping to produce, at a guaranteed ten-thousand-percent return to all investors, a knockoff of the hyper-secret in-system hyperdrive that had reportedly been recently developed by Saturn Propulsions AB; and a message from Skytop Plaza Lost Property to report that they hadn't yet found his handheld, but would notify him immediately they had discovered it. All very ho-hum, but it *did* feel good to be once again connected to the pulse.

Still six minutes. Maybe time enough to check the rest of that crossword?

Then the "incoming message" tones sounded again. Another automated message from Lost Property, to say they still hadn't found his handheld.

Belle Hopp was at 270's Reception desk, processing this descent's passenger intake. She was in discussion with a middle-aged, dark-haired woman when Gordon strode up.

'Gordon—' Belle began.

'Belle, we've got a problem.'

'Gordon—'

'It's the handheld.'

'Gordon—'

'I've contacted Lost Property. They say the handheld didn't come through them.'

'Gordon—'

'So whoever dropped it off here, it wasn't—'

'GORDON!'

'What, Belle?'

'Dress!'

Gordon glanced down. 'Oh.'

Why would a criminal have opted to return the handheld? It didn't make sense. If Gordon's involvement at the crime scene had only been a matter of wrong place, wrong time – he hadn't personally witnessed the attack on Havmurthy, but he'd been in the vicinity – then there was nothing for the killer to gain, and everything to lose, by returning the handheld. *Assuming it was returned unaltered.*

The handheld wouldn't have been either valuable, or very useful, to whoever had killed Havmurthy. It was far from a state-of-the-art device, and while Gordon had a lot of material stored on it, the information contained was hardly of a calibre to provoke theft. (Even the elevator blueprints relevant to Gordon's sometime role as 270's Safety Officer could hardly be considered "sensitive" – they'd been freely available on the worlds-wide-web for years now. Aside from the blueprints, there were a few freeware detection apps, forensic plugins, and criminal-code modules, compressed electronic cheek by virtual jowl alongside a myriad saved crossword puzzles, sudokus, riddles, mazes, trivia questionnaires and solitaire card games.)

So, nothing of significant value. Nor did it seem that anything had been erased from the device.

Which suggested, Gordon suspected, that something had been added to it. But what, where, and why?

*

'But you *can't* just go around treating them as suspects,' Belle protested.

'Why not? They were all on Skytop when Havmurthy got killed,' said Gordon, flicking his eyes towards the top of the obs-deck panoramic window, through which the sunlit edge of the Skytop Plaza was still visible, several kilometres above. Module 270 had commenced its descent just five minutes earlier, inching down the thick carbon-and-metal cable that connected Skytop, like some colossal spider suspended at the end of a gravity-inverted silk strand, with Earth's surface. Back up on Skytop, Module 271 would be already preparing to start its own descent, one of so many pearls that cascaded in an endless progression down the superhigh-tensile elevator cable. The view in either direction was an impressive sight, and one which always left Gordon feeling slightly uneasy: he wasn't great with heights.

'Yes, so they were on Skytop,' replied Belle. 'So were thousands of other people. Gordon, you've said it yourself. The hotel police don't have anything on anybody. 'Couldn't find a limburger in a lingerie shop' was what you said earlier.'

'No, what I said was that they're so busy trying to enforce this comms lockdown – the Saturn hyperdrive thing that Judy Sargent mentioned – that they don't have the resources to deploy to get to the bottom of the Havmurthy murder. And that's true, I tried comming them about my handheld getting returned, all I got was a recorded message, "All our officers are busy at the moment, but your life-threatening emergency will be attended bla bla bla". The email I sent them bounced. And when I called again, it wouldn't even go through. So no, I don't think the hotel police are going to be able to help much, they're too preoccupied. So it's up to the people on the ground... uh, the people on the... well, what I mean, people like me – like us – to get to the bottom of this. If we can.'

'But there's no reason to suspect our guests. They're not suspects. They're *customers*.'

'I'm not treating them as suspects. I'm just looking to have, well, a little chat with each of them. Odds are none of them are involved,

I know that. But I'd feel untrue to myself if I didn't try to do what I could in the situation. This isn't about trying to catch Havmurthy's killer. It's about – look, someone left me trussed up, naked, unco, in the ladies', and that makes it personal, far as I'm concerned.'

'I still don't like it. You can't go all private dick on them – sorry, poor choice of words – just because they're stuck with you for the next thirty-five thousand kilometres.'

'I'm *not* going all – like I said, just a chat. Just seeing how each of them is enjoying the descent. Perfectly innocent, completely above board. There's no reason why an entertainments officer wouldn't do that.'

'But Gord, we don't *have* an entertainments officer.'

'We do now.'

Skyward Suites 270 had a dozen guest rooms and suites, but it was rare for them to all be occupied: space-elevator traffic was surprisingly seasonal, and also influenced by the schedules of the major interplanetary and interstellar cruise flights which departed from the Skytop Plaza. For this descent, 270 had just four guests. Gordon wasn't at all sure how he was going to engineer a spontaneous, private, and ostensibly innocent encounter with each of them, but they'd be aboard for the next three days, so presumably the opportunity would arise.

He got his chance to meet-and-greet soon enough. In the foyer, Belle was showing a floor-plan map to one of the guests, a gaunt-looking man of indeterminate age, long hair, wire-rimmed spectacles and immoderately flamboyant clothing (headbands? sandals? and hadn't paisley been declared extinct a decade and a half ago?), but it was the woman standing behind Mr Fashion Crime who quite arrested Gordon's eye.

To be fair, Gordon suspected, she would have attracted the attention of almost anyone in possession of a pulse. There was something remarkably compelling about her appearance. Brunette hair which, although affecting disarray, managed to look not a strand out of place, framing as it did a face not so much chiselled as perfectly defined: exquisitely blue eyes, aquiline nose, full but not overly generous lips. And as for her outfit... Gordon fancied himself a snappy dresser, but in matters of sartoriality, this woman was an *artist*, and one with an exceptional palette to work with. She wore the kind of dress which is dangerous to stare too closely at, and an understated constellation of jewellery which perfectly complemented her shoes. In Skyward 270, she looked nothing so much as fabulously, gloriously, spectacularly out-of-place.

Somewhat appropriately, she also looked lost.

Gordon seized the moment, flashing his name badge as he approached her. 'Welcome aboard Skyward 270. Gordon Mamon, at your service. Is there anything we – I – can help you with?'

'270? Now why does that sound familiar?' she asked. Gordon was abruptly made aware that, in addition to her stunning appearance, this woman was also possessed of a voice at once thoroughly unmelodic and several decibels the wrong side of shrill. Her pause was just long enough to ensure that every face within the lift-module's foyer – Belle's, Sue's, and two of the other guests' – turned to hear whatever it was she would say next... which, as these things went, did not disappoint. 'Oh, 270! So this is where all those people died! And you're the famous Gordon Mastodon!'

'*Mamon*,' said Gordon, feeling the colour rise in his cheeks. 'And if I may correct you, there were only ever two people who died on my watch, one of whom murdered the other.' *So much for staying incognito*, Gordon told himself. But he couldn't let the guest's remarks go unchecked.

'Only two? Are you sure?' asked the woman, in a sort of amplified, crestfallen, price-check-on-aisle-three tone of voice.

'I counted very carefully, Madam,' he assured her, trying very hard to keep his gaze focussed on her face, and to ignore the almost magnetic downward pull of her collar. 'But I was asking whether there was anything with which I could offer assistance. And, excuse my impertinence, but might I know to whom I'm speaking?'

By way of answer, she produced a floral-scented business card from her purse, and passed it to him.

He glanced down at the card in his hand, which in an unnecessarily cursive fashion (the capital "W"s, in particular, he felt could have been rendered in an altogether less suggestively pendulous style) proclaimed her to be "Grace UnderWire: Purveyor of Support Services for Women". 'You were wanting to see Belle about some matter, Ms – er – Underwire?'

'I was just hoping someone could point me to the hotel lift.'

'The hotel doesn't have a lift,' Gordon answered. 'The hotel *is* a lift. However, if you wish to get to your room, or to visit the restaurant or obs deck, there are rampways and escaladders clearly marked. Or stairs, if you'd prefer.'

'Stairs? In *these* shoes? I don't think so. But could you show me the ramp? I haven't been up to my room yet. It's 104.'

'Of course. This way.' Gordon led her along the corridor to the rampway, conscious of Belle's stare drilling into the small of his back.

Hoping to strike a tone of innocent conversation, he enquired, 'Might I ask whether you've enjoyed your time at the Plaza, Ms Underwire?'

'It's been useful enough,' she answered, her voice a thousand cats clawing vainly for purchase on the world's biggest blackboard.

'Useful. So business, then, rather than pleasure?'

'Goodness me, yes.'

'What kind of business?'

'Why, Mr Manhood, quite the third degree you're giving me.'

'*Mamon*,' said Gordon, a little stiffly. *I really must update the antivirus on my namebadge.* 'My apologies, I wasn't attempting to be intrusive.'

'No offense,' Underwire answered. 'I've been trying to get people to take a look at my goodies.' They had arrived at the door of her room. She gazed at it, as if expecting it to open automatically for her, before belatedly placing her thumb against the reader built into the doorframe. The door swung inwards. Her luggage waited beside the bed.

'Would you like to see them? My goodies, that is?' she asked, in a voice Gordon felt sure must be audible all the way down in Reception.

This woman could hire herself out as a foghorn, Gordon reflected. 'I really must be getting back,' he said, attempting "wry smile" but achieving, he was sure, something more sadly akin to "leer".

'It'll only take a minute,' she replied, her own smile effortless, perfect. And with that, she opened the clasp on her suitcase and pulled out a brassiere, holding it up for his perusal. The smile intensified a notch or two, and was augmented by a dangerously imploring fluttering of Ms Underwire's lashes.

'It's – ah – very nice,' said Gordon, feeling a touch of furnace-heat start to lick seductively at his face's sweat glands, and marvelling at the rapidity with which his hopes for learning something vaguely relevant to Havmurthy's murder, and his own abduction, seemed to have degenerated into farce. 'But I really—'

'It's a smartbra,' she said, in the tones of an overworked tractor, *sans* muffler, expressing its pride at a field well ploughed.

'A what?' Gordon asked, curiosity overcoming his own better judgment.

'Smartbra,' she repeated. 'It constantly monitors the wearer's environment – gravity, temperature, air pressure – and adjusts the tension and support settings accordingly.' She held the undergarment out towards him. 'This one's an outer-planet model, set for Jupiter's gravity, with extra elasticity and heavy-duty hydraulic support. I sold them thousands. Go on, have a feel.'

'I think,' said Gordon, 'that I really must be getting back. Thank you for your time, Ms Underwear.'

And he fled.

The checked-baggage compartment was, naturally enough, located in Skyward 270's underbasement level, where it would perform, in case of an emergency re-entry, the important dual function of impact cushioning and makeshift additional heat shield. The latter presupposed, of course, that none of the luggage was in fact flammable, a criterion which – while accepted as convenient fact by the Skyward safety engineers who liked to view the vast array of possible calamities which might befall a lift-module with the rosiest-tinted glasses they could lay their metaphoric hands on – would nonetheless hold no water whatsoever in the real universe. Still, Gordon mused, if you went around worrying about all the shortcuts taken by those in charge of travellers' safety, you'd never—

A shrill siren sliced through the air, causing Gordon to twitch and tip over a carefully-arranged, tarpaulined shape which comprised, it transpired, a stack of percussive instruments in which cymbals were a repeating, perhaps dominant, motif. His attempts to quell the tumbling instruments were scarcely more effectual than his suggestion that they "shush"; but, having rearranged the tarp over the scattered sprawl of maracas, tambourines, triangles, castanets, bongoes etc., he noticed that the siren still sounded with, if possible, a steadily-increasing urgency. Belatedly identifying the source of the outburst (and cursing his own misguided choice of a ringtone), he pulled his handheld out of his pocket and activated its comm feature. He was rewarded, if direct video link to a policeman can ever be considered a reward, with a view of the fresh and disconcertingly young face of Warren Tofficer.

'Gordon?'

'Yes.'

'Just thought you should know. There's been a development.'

'What kind of development?' Gordon asked, inadvertently kicking a stray steel-drum.

'Sorry, you busy?'

'No – er, please go on. You've identified Havmurthy's killer?'

'Huh? No, afraid not. Just something else that I thought should be passed on to you. In connection with the Saturn Propulsions situation. There are reports coming in of an explosion at their main testing facility on Dione – no confirmed casualties as yet, but it looks as though it's destroyed the prototype engine, and there are suggestions that it may have also wiped out the engine's blueprints. Sat Prop's keeping quite quiet about the whole thing, as you'd imagine, but it looks pretty major. And it's upped the ante on whatever form of industrial espionage is behind the whole thing.'

'Sorry... uh, Warren, I don't really see why you think I need to know this?'

'Looks like there's a connection with Havmurthy. Or a possible connection, at least. According to some preliminary forensic evidence we've received under the radar, it appears that the explosion was set off by contact between a few micrograms of matter and a few micrograms of antimatter. A mutual annihilation reaction.'

'Big-league stuff,' Gordon conceded. 'But I still don't see—'

'There's no way of knowing, at this stage, where they got the anticheese from. But the chemical signature of the cheese part of the explosive mix is definitely consistent with the Havmurthy product lines.'

'Meaning?'

'Look, Gordon, I don't think anyone here knows what to make of this stuff. But I just thought you should know. Watch your back, huh?'

'Uh... yes, of course. Thanks, Warren.' He closed the call, and activated the handheld's "settings" function to select a less unsettling ringtone.

Maybe he should come down and check on the luggage later, in a better frame of mind.

Man up, Mamon, he told himself, carefully lifting a large vac-resistant suitcase off a small plastimache shipping carton labelled "Fragile" and "ᵈ∩ ⅄ɐＡ sᴉɥ⊥". The suitcase was light, but frustratingly difficult to heft. (*Must be one of those new models with the gravity-reduction system.* They'd been introduced just in the last year or so, and several of the spacelines had complained that they would go broke in no time, severed as they would be from the pecuniary lifeblood of excess baggage charges...) He placed the suitcase carefully on the floor and pulled a cargo net out from the wall stanchion to fasten the item into place.

At which precise point, something beeped.

It was a very quick beep, fairly loud, and so high-pitched that one would have to be a pomeranian to properly appreciate all of its attendant nuances of tone and timbre. Among present company, it provoked puzzlement, not least because its brevity had made it more or less impossible to pin to any particular direction. But it also touched a sore point with Gordon, who, while in principle thoroughly comfortable with the notion of luggage that went "beep", in practice held strong views on the undesirability of "beep"-uttering containers in close proximity to his physical person. Particularly so several hours after someone had rendered said physical person unconscious and decidedly lacking in raiment, and immediately following his enlightenment as to the unexpected lethality of coagulated dairy products. Accordingly, he did what any sensible individual would do in the circumstances. He pulled out his handheld again.

'Scan,' he said. 'Urgent.'

Full-function emergency security sweep will commence after these messages from our sponsors, advised the device, and then proceeded to ask him whether he preferred hard or soft cheese, and whether he'd tried any of Havmurthy's offerings in this respect? He set the volume to "mute" – that really was the most annoying jingle he'd ever heard. Duly silenced, the handheld busied itself with the important task of showing him the process by which Havmurthy's vintage wares were aged… in, Gordon was beginning to suspect, real time. But the cheesecam footage had, in fact, finished when the beep next sounded. As before, he had no hint as to its location (other than, it would appear, somewhere within the cargo deck), but this time he had a recording. He fiddled for several seconds with the handheld's playback function, until he had isolated the fractional-second trace during which the beep had sounded.

'Identify,' he said.

Clarify, came the response.

'Identify beep.'

Frequency seventeen-thousand three hundred and forty-one hertz. Duration twenty-seven point eight milliseconds. Apparent volume seventy-one point nine decibels. Margins for error on these measurements will be available after this brief message from our sponsors...

Gordon learned a lot about cheese in the next half an hour. He also learned, eventually, that there were only three corporations in known space which produced devices programmed to automatically emit such a "beep" tone. Two of these corporations, both based in the far-flung zeta quadrant, had had an interstellar embargo placed upon their specialised asteroid-mining bots, and were respectively plaintiff and defendant in a bitter sonic copyright infringement suit. The major product marketed by the third such corporation was a stealth cloak.

Well, it fitted. But it also left Gordon severely disquieted, as well as provoking the dual questions of (1) how a top-of-the-range stealth cloak – exactly the kind of overgarment worn by whoever had attacked Havmurthy – would have found its way into the area set aside for Skyward 270's passengers' luggage, and (2) why such a cloak would be manufactured with an inbuilt, highly-audible, and frankly disconcerting "low battery" indicator.

Gordon spoke into his handheld. 'Sue? You busy?'

'A little,' she replied. 'I have to reprogram dinner as gluten-free, low GI, non-dairy, and organic – or at least as something which will appear that way, if I turn the restaurant lighting down low enough. That ought to tie me up for the next hour or so. Then I'm supposed to be cleaning out that malfunctioning fridge unit, after which I'll need to be finding somewhere to store all that cheese. What's up?'

'Sorry, Sue, did you say cheese?'

'Uh, yes. Why?'

'What d'you mean, "store all that cheese"?'

'We're carrying quite a large consignment. Havmurthy was running a special a week back, major discounts, and I was looking to re-provision the pantry for the next few ascent / descent cycles. Made perfect sense, until this fridge decided to pack a sad – but then I don't suppose you contacted me to talk about cheese.'

'No, I suppose not,' Gordon said, quite unsure on the topic. 'It *is* all cheese, though, I suppose? I mean, no anticheese?'

'What in heaven's name is anticheese? Is that that new soy-based—'

'No. Uh, forget it.'

'OK. So what's up?'

'I need you to build me a locator.'

'Lost your keys again, Gordon?'

'No. There's a device on the cargo deck somewhere. I need to find it.'

'What kind of "device"?' Sue asked. Gordon could hear the sudden anxiety in her voice.

'It's harmless in itself.'

'Gordon—'

'Sorry. Look, it's a stealth cloak, emits a low-battery beep. I can give you the specs. I need to find out whose luggage it's in, and I don't have time to stand around on Cargo for the next few hours playing echolocator. Can you whip up some kind of detector for me, please?'

'Sure, give me a couple of hours. I should have it done by the time we hit thirty-one thousand, at any rate. But why—'

'—would it have a low-battery beep?' Gordon interrupted. 'Don't know.'

'No, that wasn't what I was going to ask.'

'Oh.'

Gordon had a distracted dinner in 270's sparsely-populated restaurant, striving all the while to find a setting on his handheld which would circumvent the device's sudden fascination with the world of dairy protein products, then busied himself with lift-module maintenance and airlock safety testing for the next couple of thousand kilometres.

When the "descent progress" display had counted down to twenty-eight thousand, he went looking for the guests. He was particularly keen to make contact with Miharties, since she hadn't come down to dinner, electing instead to stay in her room.

But there were the two in the bar, right next to the restaurant, so it made sense to talk to them first.

'Just four little words. And it wasn't until I got to the showers, and the soap, that I realised the wisdom of—'

The voice was like gravel over a rockslide, and Gordon couldn't imagine why anyone would want to pay to listen to it, but there was no accounting for taste.

Idovist was short, broad-shouldered, with an almost-military-standard salt-and-pepper crewcut, a slight paunch, eyes that were simultaneously watery and piercing, a nose which looked as though it had led a life sufficiently interesting as to merit a biography all of its own, and an impressive collection of vintage scars upon his forearms. He was seated at 270's bar, which since last year's refurbishment had been reinvented as a particularly unconvincing replica of a Hollywood-style western saloon, complete with buxom robotic barmaid, animatronic piano player, a *trompe l'oeil* poker-game backdrop, a moustachioed and black-hatted holographic sherriff that entered repeatedly through the swinging saloon doors in a manner reminiscent of nothing so much as a cuckoo clock's eponymous bird, and a soundtrack featuring whinnying horses and occasional gunfire on much too short a repeat cycle. Ignoring all this and the plastic tumbleweeds besides, Idovist was deep in conversation with the other male guest – Ligotmi, wasn't it? – when Gordon spotted them, and approached. He'd get to Ligotmi soon enough; but for now, according to the checks he'd run on his handheld, Idovist was his primary concern.

'Mr Idovist? Excuse me for interrupting,' said Gordon, standing a couple of places along from the men at the bar, and manfully resisting the urge to slide his thumbs in behind the band of his belt. 'How are you finding things, this trip?'

Idovist turned to look at Gordon. 'You mean the floor plan?'

'Well, no. I mean – uh – have you had a successful visit, to, er—'

'Uranus? Yeah, it went well.' Idovist twisted back to face Ligotmi. 'Anyway, like I was saying—'

This wasn't going as smoothly as Gordon had hoped. 'Look, I'm sorry to intrude, Mr Idovist—'

'Call me Rhys. If you must.'

'Alright. Rhys. Thing is, as Entertainments Officer, I'm required to ask each of our guests in some detail about the – uh, well, the purpose of their visit, anything of interest they might have, uh, witnessed on their travels, how they found their stay on Skytop, their feelings about cheese—'

'Cheese?' asked Ligotmi, his hand poised ready to raid the bowl of salted nuts stationed between his and Idovist's beers.

'Sponsors,' Gordon extemporised, retaining his focus on Idovist. 'Sorry. And look, I know this is a nuisance, and believe me there are other things I'd rather be doing, but if we can just step through the questions so I can keep the powers-that-be happy...' He raised his eyebrows, hoping that he was managing to strike the appropriate tone of hassled employee, and therefore perhaps getting sufficient sympathy to encourage Idovist's cooperation.

'Seriously, cheese?' asked Ligotmi, scooping his hand into the peanut bowl and missing.

'Yes,' said Gordon. 'Mr Idovist – *Rhys* – I was wondering, in my capacity as Entertainments Officer for this descent, if you could just provide a little bit of detail on your movements—'

'What's this got to do with entertainment?' asked Idovist.

'Why cheese?' asked Ligotmi.

'Like I said, Mr Ligotmi, sponsors. And, er, it comes under the heading of seeking to make your descent with us as enjoyable as possible, by ensuring that we're best meeting the needs of the travelling public.'

'That's never entertainment. That's market research.'

'Multitasking,' said Gordon, with more than a twinge of desperation. 'Rhys – if I may trouble you, in the interest of entertainment, or market research, or whatever you wish to call it, what is your line of business exactly?'

'Really?' asked Ligotmi, this time successfully connecting with the peanut bowl. 'Cheese?'

'I'm an ex-con,' answered Rhys Idovist. 'Best thing that ever happened to me. Set me up for life, it did. So to speak. I mean, you learn things inside what you'd never realise out here.'

'What kind of things?' Gordon asked, fighting the impulse to take a step back.

'It's all in here,' said Idovist, reaching into his shirt pocket to pull out a small plasticback featuring a picture of himself on the cover. He brandished the book at Gordon. 'Fifty-nine ninety-five, if you're interested.'

Gordon turned the book over in his hands. It was called *Just Four Little Words* and was emblazoned with glowing tributes to the author's prowess as a communicator. 'Uranus, you said?'

'You'll have to read the book,' replied Idovist.

'I'm sorry?' asked Gordon.

'Ah – yeah. Uranus. That's a long slow flight, and no mistake. Couple of years each way. I was there for a speaking tour.'

'So what exactly did you speak about?'

'Pretty much what I learned from prison. You know, first time I got sent to the big house, me mum was pretty distraught, gave me this big long rambling speech, tearful, impassioned like, full of do's and don'ts. Buggered if I can remember any of what she said. Pardon my French. But me dad, who'd been in stir plenty times himself, he just said four—'

'I probably don't need that level of detail,' said Gordon, passing the book back to Idovist. 'For the entertainment report, I mean. But just out of interest – obviously it's been useful for you, from a professional standpoint, but, ah, what were you in prison for?'

'That time?' Idovist said. 'Aggravated assault, if I remember rightly.'

'Well, I was meaning more generally,' said Gordon, who was at this moment (a) pointedly not taking a step back and (b) trying to remember if it was ex-cons who could smell fear, or if that was dogs.

'Must say I'm not sure how this comes under the heading of entertainment. But, well, pretty much everything: theft, fraud, arson, larceny, kidnapping, malicious non-return of overdue library books, you name it. I probably tried my hand at pretty much everything, back in the day. Reformed character now, of course. I mean, the prison thing is fine for when you're in your prime, but it doesn't really count as a *career.*'

'Murder?' Gordon asked, watching the other closely.

'No, that was one box I always left unchecked, somehow. Why, you got someone you want killed?' Idovist asked, offering a quick forced laugh.

'No, I meant... look, never mind. Anyway, to keep our sponsors happy, what are your thoughts on cheese? Have you encountered any interesting cheese of late? Have you – er – had any cheese-related experiences this trip, and if so, how would you categorise them?'

'Mr Modem, you people seriously need to get a new sponsor.'

'*Mamon,*' said Gordon. 'You're saying cheese doesn't cut it?'

'I'm saying the last time I had a close look at a piece of cheese was probably twelve years ago, and back then I felt like shooting it full of holes.'

'That sounds a little extreme—'

'Extreme? Maybe. I'll admit to being lactose intolerant.'

'How long—'

'Now if you don't mind, I think I've neglected this lager for quite long enough.' Idovist turned back to the bar, presenting his back with an air of finality.

Not wishing to push his conversational luck too far, Gordon thanked the ex-con, and moved around to talk to Idovist's neighbour. Yuri Ligotmi was tall, rake-skinny, sporting long, scraggly hair of a dubious brown. He was wearing a shirt on which the paisley pattern seemed not merely to have attained iridescence, but also an independent life of its own, if not a fully-functioning ecology. 'Mr Ligotmi? Do you have the time to answer a few questions?'

'Cheese, you mean?'

'Well, not just cheese. I was wondering if you could tell me a bit about yourself. You're a musician?'

'Musician? Yeah.'

'What kind?'

Ligotmi took a few moments to down a mouthful of beer. 'Retro. Old school. Classical music. You know, the Beatles, the Pistols, the Abbas—'

'Have you been up on Skytop for a gig?'

'A gig? Sorry, I wouldn't know. Our manager takes care of all our memory requirements.'

'No, I mean... look, what was your purpose for visiting Skytop? Did you go off-planet at all?'

'No, man, I've given all that shit up. It'll mess with your head big time. Though I was looking at going to Mars.'

'Mars?'

'Yeah, was looking at setting up a goat farm there. Got to start thinking of my retirement. You know.'

'A goat farm?'

'Yeah, but I decided not to go, in the end.'

'Why not?'

'Mars ain't the kind of place to raise a kid.'

'Oh. So you stayed on Skytop, then?' asked Gordon, pulling his hand off the bar while the robotic barmaid poured beer into the space where it believed Ligotmi's empty glass to be.

'Well, I was going to visit my friend Lucy, who's co-owner of some private asteroid that the two of them are mining for gems.'

'"Was going to"? Did you go?'

'See Lucy and this guy with diamonds? No.'

'So you didn't venture out of the Skytop Plaza?'

'Well, there was this roleplaying convention, based around a dystopian sci-fi setting, that's currently on Ceres, I was thinking of dropping in on.'

'You went to Ceres, then?'

'No. Turns out it clashes with my schedule. So I can't get no sad SF action.'

'Mr Ligotmi. You've listed three things you didn't end up doing. Do you mind telling me what it was that you *did* do?'

'Well, it was all a bit of a fizzer, truth be told. We – that's me and the band – just stayed on Skytop, and auditioned for a stint as the support act for U238's upcoming tour of the Belt.'

'U238?' asked Gordon.

'You haven't heard of them? They get quite a bit of radio activity at the moment. Bit too heavy for my tastes, but they're massive, and they've been getting glowing reviews. Anyway, I don't think the tour'll go ahead.'

'Why do you say that?'

'There's a rumour they're going to split.' Ligotmi lifted his glass, looked at it, then set it down on the edge of the slowly spreading puddle on the bar. 'Oh, and there was one other thing. We'd recorded this advertising jingle awhile back, big bikkies if it got picked up, we were going to check with the company exec to see whether it met with approval. This meeting, all arranged, but the guy never showed.'

'Can I ask what the jingle was about?'

'Cheese.'

'Cheese?'

'Cheese. Pretty much, yeah. D'you know how hard it is? Not the cheese, I mean, but coming up with a decent jingle for the stuff? And something with the right vintage, to suit the demographic.'

'There's a cheese demographic?' Gordon asked, curious despite himself.

'Oh, yeah,' Ligotmi answered. 'I mean, initially, we were going to go with "Let It Brie". But that's way too soft, right? So then someone suggested "Won't Get Grilled Again", and that nearly got the nod. We thought long and hard about "Stilton On The Dock Of The Bay". We went into the studio all ready to cut "Under the Milky Whey Tonight", even though Alan, our drummer, reckoned it was way too "out there". But we finally settled on—'

'Thank you, that's probably more information than I need for the entertainment report,' Gordon interrupted. 'I won't disturb you gentlemen any more for this evening.'

As Gordon walked away, he heard Idovist say to the rocker, 'So where were we? Yeah. Just four little words. "Lift with your knees".'

Someone with responsibility for 270's last refurbishment had evidently decided that, for the upper floors at least, "well-appointed" was synonymous with "busy". Which was all well and good (particularly if you appreciated a nice plastic potted palm – or ten – at every corridor corner; a live-action computer-generated wraparound mural of jungle scenery, ocean views, or Grand Canyon abseiling at every landing; and an omnipresent muzak system dispensing traffic noise, kazoo interpretations of light orchestral favourites, and the notable karaoke efforts of former guests without fear or favour), but which could make things a trifle difficult when one was trying to perform maintenance. Gordon *knew* there was an emergency chute cover recessed into the wall somewhere along the second-floor corridor, but could he find it among a constantly changing diorama of calving glaciers, aurorae, and erupting volcanoes? And trying to locate it by feel was a less-than-satisfactory strategy, given the architect's apparent desire to experiment with texture on this section of the corridor's surfaces, and to disguise any and every mandated safety feature as a work of art or a piece of unattended luggage. The whole thing was an exercise in frustration, almost as vexing as the question of the cheese magnate's murder, the stealth cloak, the suggested connection between Havmurthy and the Saturn Propulsions wonderdrive, and the still-mysterious motive behind Gordon's abduction. Running his fingers along a promising rockfacelike seam on the corridor's left wall, while striving valiantly to ignore the intercommed sound of a cascading waterfall – at this point in the corridor, he was about as far as it was possible to get from any of the lift-module's restrooms – Gordon tried to tease apart the several pieces to the Havmurthy conundrum.

Why choose to kill on Skytop, in a fairly busy public setting? Havmurthy had presumably been just passing through, had in all probability made his enemies elsewhere... possibly Skytop had the advantage, for the killer, of *not* being anyone's home territory, and thus stood to disguise the motive for the hit.

Just passing through... disguise... there was something there, an idea, a thought, a connection, below the surface; but it wouldn't coalesce properly.

And somehow, in his tactile explorations towards locating the concealed emergency chute cover, Gordon had acquired a paper cut on his index finger.

His handheld chirped. Incoming call.

'Gordon?'

'Yes?' he replied.

'Sue. You were wanting that locator.'

'Yes. D'you have it ready?'

'Raring to go. I would have had it sorted sooner, but I couldn't find an appropriate casing for the electronics. In the end I had to go with—'

'I'm sure whatever you've chosen will be fine, Sue.'

'I hope you still think that when you see it. You were saying this... thing was beeping every ten minutes or so?'

'About that, I'd say. Yes.'

'Probably take up to an hour to triangulate, then. I've programmed it to move around the cargo bay, build up a volume profile for our mystery beep.'

'Splendid. Thanks, Sue. You still in the galley?'

'Workshop. Diners tend to get uneasy if they hear a rivet gun firing off in the kitchen.'

'Heh. OK, I'll pick it up on my way through.'

'Fine by me. And Gordon?'

'Yes?'

'Just… take care, won't you?'

'Caution is my middle name,' said Gordon. Which wasn't strictly true, but on the other hand he'd never forgiven his parents for "Fortescue".

Gordon was arching his back, still trying to work out the kink he'd acquired from manhandling Sue's makeshift (and decidedly fridgelike) gizmo down three flights to the cargo deck. He should have mentioned "portable" as one of the desired attributes for the thing… even with a countergrav patch stuck on the side, it had been brutally unwieldy, as attested by the bouquet of plastic palm fragments he'd picked up from the foyer's fake arbor. And from the corner outside the laundry. And from the power-plant entranceway… really, the case could be made that a measure of deforestation of 270's plastic-palm infestation was long overdue. Finding the third-floor recycling chute (he'd given up locating anything on the second floor until he'd succeeded in decoding the apparently encrypted blueprints), he dumped the plastic greenery and checked further along the corridor.

Suite 302. He knocked at the plastimahogany door. 'Ms Miharties?'

'Yo?' came the reply.

'Gordon Mamon,' he explained, to the still-closed door.

'Yo?'

'I was just wanting a word with you, Ms Miharties—'

'Arr,' she replied, opening the door. Middle-aged, skinny, a touch weatherbeaten, but not in a bad way. Dark ringlets, black T-shirt and jeans, her face partly obscured by a black iPatch. Something about her smelt faintly of rum. She ran her eye up and down, appraising Gordon; for his part, he couldn't get past the prosthetic "hand" with which she'd opened the door.

'I hope I'm not interrupting, Ms—'

'Arr.'

'Ms—'

'Arr.'

'Ms—'

'Please, call me "R",' she said.

'Short for…?'

'Not short for anything. It's just me name.'

'Ah.'

'Precisely.'

'May I have a few words? It's one of my duties as Entertainments Officer to check on the wellbeing of each guest at least once during our descent.'

'Yah, orright then. may as well. Time t'kill, and all that. Come in, Mr Madman.'

'*Mamon*,' said Gordon, crossing the threshold. He consulted his handheld briefly. 'You – er – you're a deejay?'

'That I be. Pirate radio,' she said, proudly.

'Quite,' said Gordon. 'And – not meaning to pry, in any sense, but you're booked in with Mr Ligotmi?'

'Why do you ask?' Suddenly, all trace of the accent was gone, replaced by a voice as hard and unyielding as the hook which terminated her right arm.

'Just seeking to ensure I have the right box ticked, for the statistics. If you want to see our piracy – er, *privacy* policy—'

'No, I don't suppose that'll be necessary. I'm just… a little touchy, I guess. The others in Yuri's band, I think they see me as a bad influence. O'Rigby hasn't put you up to anything, I suppose?'

'O'Rigby?'

'Yuri's drummer. Alan's a mean little sod. Wouldn't be the first time.'

'No, I can assure you I've never heard of this O'Rigby.'

'Right then.' She took off the iPatch, and detached the prosthetic hook. Underneath, her right hand appeared to be entirely normal. 'Yes, Yuri and I are an item. Long-distance, like, of course. Been looking forward to this holiday together for months, no lie. And yeah, the descent's been enjoyable enough so far.'

'I – well, again, I don't mean to pry, but I noticed you weren't at dinner.'

She sat on the bed's end, nudging aside a black canvas-skinned suitcase. 'Yeah, tum's been a bit skew-whiff. I think the rarebit I had at the Plaza nightspot yesterday must've been a bit dodgy – not sure what they put in it. Didn't want to risk dinner, this evening, in public, so I had something sent up. It went OK, though the dessert just now was a touch too rivetty for my liking.'

'I have no idea why that might be,' said Gordon. 'But out of curiosity, what's your reason for visiting Skytop?'

'No other way to get to Earth,' she replied. 'I'm not exactly a local, Mr Merman.'

'*Mamon*. But, excuse me – I'd just assumed you were from Earth? Like Mr Ligotmi, I mean.'

'From Earth, yes. Not so often on Earth, these days.'

'Why's that?'

'Pirate radio don't work like that. The whole point is that we operate outside geostationary, so we're not subject to terrestrial broadcasting restrictions.'

'I didn't think Earth had many broadcasting restrictions left.'

'Yeah, well, that's the fly in the whole business model, isn't it? It's mainly a gimmick thing, now, more than anything. Difficult to keep the wolf from the airlock, too. Devil of a job trying to drum up advertising revenue. I don't mind telling you, we were looking at having to shut up shop, until Yuri and his band landed that advertising promo for Havmurthy. I do hope he's been able to secure payment – he's been very quiet since we came on board. Don't know why I'm telling you all this—'

'Not at all, Ms – ah—'

'No, you need to roll it more. Like this. "R".'

'Indeed. Thank you for your time, "R".'

Gordon made his way back to his office / complaints counter / janitorial headquarters, deep in thought. Or at least, in something that would do until thought came along. He was struck by the conviction that, like a badly solved sudoku, things didn't add up right. A mysterious and distant cheddar/anticheddar explosion; Havmurthy's death; his own abduction; the presence of a stealth cloak somewhere in the cargo bay. The cloak suggested that the murderer might well be present on board... but on the other hand, *why* would a killer bring on board such an obvious piece of incriminating evidence? Perhaps, instead, Havmurthy's hitman was still on Skytop, or had travelled Earthside on a different Skyward lift-module, or had escaped beyond geostationary altogether, and had planted the cloak on 270 as a ruse. In which case, the garment would most likely be bereft of fingerprints, DNA, or other useful forensic evidence. Assuming the murderer was competent.

Gordon wasn't convinced that the killer *was* competent. There were just too many things about the way it'd played which didn't feel right, didn't feel professional.

Did this, therefore, mean that the perp wasn't perhaps capable of planting a red herring, or indeed a herring of any arbitrary colour? Perhaps the stealth cloak's presence on the cargo deck was completely accidental. An oversight by a sloppy killer? There was no way to know. But he had to assume that Havmurthy's assassin might well be one of the four guests currently aboard 270.

If so, then who? Ligotmi was obviously connected in some way to Havmurthy. Miharties was in turn connected to Ligotmi. But he hadn't been able to probe either of them in sufficient detail to establish credible motives, nor the absence of such: to do so would have risked overplaying his hand. He wasn't, officially, investigating, he was just acting on a hunch, and seeing what he could do to flesh said hunch out. Idovist, alone of the guests, had a criminal record – in fact, probably had enough tracks to constitute a criminal "Greatest Hits" collection – but claimed all that kind of thing was behind him now. Still, the ex-con must have had considerable connections among the underworld, and might not necessarily have severed all of those ties. And Idovist had recently returned from the outer solar system. Admittedly, the other *side* of the solar system from Saturn's current position, but still. Underwire… well, frankly, he doubted Underwire's ability to dress herself. But perhaps she didn't normally need to?

He hadn't yet grilled Underwire on the cheese angle. That was an oversight he'd need to correct.

And if the field was wide open in terms of motive, there was also the frustration that the surveillance footage of the attack left no indication of the attacker's physique. Stealth cloaks were one-size-fits-all items, designed to disguise such particulars as the wearer's height and build. Any one of 270's guests might equally have been that blur on the footage…

It occurred to him, just then, that Miharties' ostensibly-redundant prosthetic hook, which had looked to be genuine solid metal, would have made a very convenient close-quarters weapon capable of inflicting on Havmurthy the kind of damage he'd worn on his chest. (But hadn't Havmurthy been set to bail out Miharties' pirate radio operation, through advertising revenue? In which case—)

Gordon's reverie was interrupted by the call signal on his handheld, which he fished from his pocket. (In so doing, he discovered that he'd spent the past five minutes pacing steadily down the motorised "up" rampway.) 'Gordon here.'

'Hi Gordon, Belle. Sue just called to say she's down on the cargo deck, and she's saying she's got a result. Whatever that means.'

'Thanks, Belle. Be right there.'

Or at least, he would be once he'd switched rampways.

*

'This suitcase,' Sue said, leaning against the monolithic beep-detecting device and pointing to a nondescript grey hard-shell stacked between Ligotmi's double-necked-sitar case and several plasticrates of Idovist's pop-psych books.

Gordon rummaged in his pocket, pulled on a fresh pair of doorknob-polishing gloves, and wheeled the suitcase out. 'No label. And my handheld's not registering any fingerprints either. Any trace of cheese?'

'What *is* it with you and cheese at the moment?' asked Sue, her exasperation plain.

'Forget it. Don't suppose you have any idea whose case this is?' he asked.

'Sorry, no,' said Sue. 'It was Belle on security duty when the luggage was loaded.'

'Guess we'll find out soon enough,' said Gordon, laying the case flat atop a book-crate. He fiddled with the latches, which sprung helpfully open... although the suitcase itself didn't. 'No good. The zipper's padlocked.'

'These do?' Sue asked, pulling a pair of bolt-cutters out of her chef's smock.

'Why're you carrying bolt cutters?' Gordon asked.

'Food prep,' Sue replied. 'Don't worry, they're clean.'

It took Sue several minutes to break through the padlock, during which time the "beep" sounded once more. Gordon opened the case. The stealth cloak was lying under several items of clothing and a couple of large blocks of Havmurthy cheese. Gordon lifted the cloak out, marvelling at how it masked his hands and forearms. It didn't quite convey the illusion of full transparency, but beyond a dull shimmer...

'I think I know,' said Sue, rummaging to the suitcase's depths, 'whose case this is.'

'I think you're right,' Gordon replied, carefully folding the cloak up. Or trying to; folding an effectively-invisible object wasn't, it turned out, the simplest of tasks. He gave up the attempt, and smooshed it back over the suitcase's top stratum of undergarments.

'OK,' said the figure in the doorway. 'This has gone far enough.'

There was a moment of deathly stillness. Even the ever-present hum and rumble of the lift-module's mechanical workings, usually loudest here in the underbasement, seemed to have quieted.

'Last time I fired this thing,' said the assailant, brandishing a Kill-O-Farad 357-calibre Incapacitator in her right hand, 'it was set to stun, and it killed a man. This time it's set to kill.'

Gordon swallowed. His recent identification of the suitcase's owner had, it seemed, been correct, but that was slight comfort.

It wasn't Ligotmi, or Miharties, or Idovist holding the stunner. No, the one with the gun was the visual stunner herself. The amazing Grace.

'Do you at least want us to raise our hands?' Gordon asked.

'No, what do I care?' Underwire asked, in a voice as far from the foghorn-like intensity of her earlier exchange with him as Gordon could have imagined. Steady, calm, and in control. Exactly how he wasn't feeling right now. 'Although,' Underwire continued, with a pert nod towards Sue, 'you could at least drop the snippy things, love.'

Sue let the bolt cutters slip from her hand. They fell with a quiet thud to the cushioned floor of the cargo deck.

'And before you get any ideas,' Underwire explained, with a flick of her head that did something to the bounce of her hair which would have been delightful and coquettish if she hadn't happened to be levelling at them a death-dealing piece of weaponry, 'please don't bother trying to signal for help. It'll only annoy me. And this little jammer here'—she pulled from her pocket a small grey device, looking like a cross between an old-fashioned remote control and a powder compact—'would render the attempt futile. Nothing gets out of this room without my say-so. And that certainly includes the two of you.' She trained the gun on Gordon, then on Sue, then back again.

Underwire had stepped a short distance into the cargo deck, so as to be clear of the line-of-sight from the rampway leading down to this level, but was standing perhaps ten paces from Gordon and Sue. Too far for him to try anything heroic. The armoured bulk of Sue's detector, which looked admirably capable of stopping anything short of a low-yield nuclear charge, was unfortunately at their backs rather than between them and Underwire. And Gordon judged that any attempt to yell for help would probably be muffled into inaudibility by the three levels of plant and storage between them and the lobby level. Grace held all the aces.

'So you found the stealth cloak?' said Underwire. 'Thought I'd left it behind. Must've left it switched on when I was packing the suitcase back on Skytop, and never noticed it.'

'Guess that's an occupational hazard with invisible clothing,' offered Gordon. *If only he'd still been holding the cloak when Underwire had entered the room...*

'Hazard?' asked Underwire. 'For you, as it turns out. Serves you right for meddling, Matron.' She checked a setting on the barrel of the weapon, never taking her gaze entirely off Gordon and Sue.

'*Mamon*. Supposing you do kill us,' said Gordon, seeking to shuffle himself in front of Sue. Wondering if he could keep Underwire talking long enough to at least allow Sue to sidle behind the supersized, shielded slab of electronics at her back. 'What then? How would you escape? You'd need to dispose of the bodies somehow. And security groundside would pick you up the moment Bel— the moment the automated systems registered our absence.'

'Are you always this helpful to your opponents, Minim?' she asked.

'*Mamon*,' Gordon replied. 'I'm just trying to say, you can't seriously hope to get away with it.'

'I'd say differently. Pity you're not going to be around to see how. But it involves a fire, and a smokescreen, and me the sole survivor of this lift-module. Soon as I'm done in here, I'll go set the charges. Then once they release me from medical, nobody will suspect a thing.'

'Just one favour,' said Gordon, inching towards the unobstructed side of the bulky detector, and hoping that Sue would follow suit. Unfortunately, so far as he could tell, she was transfixed by the novelty of the whole at-gunpoint thing. 'I've solved murders, and things that looked like murders but weren't, but this one had me stumped. So can you put me out of – uh, can you please let me know what this is about? It's not as if it's going to matter to you, after all.'

'Monologuing? Seriously, is that the best card you've got to play? I expected a bit more innovation from you. Gordon Madam, the famous vertical detective.'

'*Mamon.* Sorry to disappoint you. And I can't, obviously, compel you to answer. But I'm guessing you must really hate cheese.'

'Cheese?' asked Sue. 'What d'you mean, cheese?'

'This whole thing smells of cheese,' Gordon explained, turning his head to answer. 'For reasons I don't presently understand. Cheese, and the Saturn Propulsions miracle engine.'

'Who told you about the Sat Prop angle?' Underwire asked, voice suddenly sharp-edged. 'I had you pegged as just a bystander.'

'I *am* a bystander,' Gordon complained. 'Or was, at least. But the cheese, and the engine business, they keep getting connected somehow.'

'Yeah, well, you got that right. It was never just about the cheese,' said Underwire. 'It's what the cheese *signifies*.'

'High-yield explosive? Holding the world to ransom?' Gordon offered.

'*What* are you on?' Underwire asked.

'You've no idea?' Gordon asked, reading the answer in her face, and trying to run his mind across two problems at once. The gun; the distance; the fixtures and assorted clutter of the cargo deck. *Was there some way in which he could get to one of the cargo nets? Throw it, or one of the items of luggage, at Underwire? But there was nothing close enough, and the gun-toter surely wouldn't hesitate to discharge her weapon before he could complete his action. Blast.* 'Then what do you mean, "what the cheese signifies"?' he asked.

'Cholesterol?' asked Sue. 'Lactic substances?'

'Don't bother,' said Underwire, sighting along the weapon. 'You won't get it. Except, of course, that in another sense, you're about to. Get it, that is.'

'What do you mean, "signifies"?' Gordon repeated, risking another very small step sideways. 'Is the cheese some kind of… message?'

'Some kind of code?' asked Sue.

'Don't be ridiculous,' said Gordon, turning partly around. 'How could a block of cheese be a… oh. *Oh*. Wait. It *could*, actually. Couldn't it?'

'Couldn't what?' asked Sue.

'Protein,' said Gordon. 'The code of life.'

'That's DNA, actually,' said Underwire, ranging the stun-gun from Gordon, to Sue, then back to Gordon. 'Code of life, I mean. But very good. It's almost a pity to have to kill you.'

'You know, you could save yourself the mental anguish there,' suggested Gordon, inching sideways again. (*Why wasn't Sue taking the hint? Sidling behind him, shuffling towards the clearance required to duck behind the decommissioned fridge unit?*) 'So, DNA, then? Why?'

'No, you were right with protein.'

'I don't… oh. Oh. Getting a signal out through Skytop. Or rather, in through Skytop. And the hotel elevator's one of the main freight hubs, for Earth-to-interplanetary trade. I'm betting most of the cheese exported from Earth passes through Skytop. Bloody hell.'

'Gordon, *what?*' asked Sue.

'The cops were going gangbusters to make sure all the comm channels were being intercepted. And probably checking every piece of written material to pass through the hotel's transit lounges, all to ensure that they blocked a message being sent. And all the time, they might well have been eating the message, in their sandwiches, and on their crackers—'

'Hello? Woman with gun here?' Underwire reminded him.

'I'm right though, aren't I?' Gordon asked, with the kind of fanatical solver's zeal that sometimes fell on him when, two-thirds of the way through a crossword puzzle, he'd mastered the crucial clue, the lynchpin on which all the other answers depended. 'This is the connection with the Saturn hyperdrive thing, isn't it?'

'Very good. You'll go to the top of the class. Posthumously.' Underwire's finger twitched on the Incapacitator's trigger.

'Wait,' said Gordon in sudden desperation. 'Why?'

'Why posthumously?' Underwire sneered. 'I thought *that'd* be self-evident.'

'No, I mean,' said Gordon, his tone betraying a degree of exasperation that might, in the circumstances, be just a bit injudicious, 'why the Saturn hyperdrive? Why Havmurthy? Why the cheese / anticheese eplosion?'

'What cheese / anticheese explosion?' Underwire beat Sue to the question by a fraction of a second. She sounded annoyed.

'You really don't know?' Gordon felt suddenly unsure of himself. That is, additionally unsure of his ability to comprehend the situation, let alone to cope with a homicidal woman armed with a dangerous, unpredictable weapon, in the cargo hold of a badly-constructed vehicle currently plunging at considerable velocity toward the atmosphere of the largest ball of rock in the solar system. 'In that case, why you? And why me?'

'Isn't it obvious?' asked Underwire. 'Money. Pure and simple. The Saturn Propulsions hyperdrive stands to make megazillions for whoever can knock them out fastest. It'll revolutionise interplanetary freight, in particular – it's always been an irony of existing hyperspace technology that it takes longer to travel from here to Jupiter, say, than it does to flit between some star systems, because hyperdrives don't work up close to a gravity well. They've been saying, this last month or so, that the Saturn hyperdrive has that problem licked. Seems Havmurthy wanted himself a slice of that – and I couldn't let that happen, now.'

'You don't sound as if you know anything about the exp— uh, so you're affiliated with… the developers? Or who?'

'Oh, you needn't concern yourself with that, Minion. Not where you're going.'

'*Mamon*. It's one of those "you could tell me, but then you'd have to kill me" things, huh?'

'No. I get to kill you, whether I tell you or not. And I have to say, I prefer it that way. I owe you nothing, Meson.'

'Mamon.'

'Whatever. Though I will say this. I've got a tidy little amount. But it's always nice to have more. Particularly if I never have to look at another breast in my life.'

'Excuse me?'

'My every working hour is devoted to breasts, one way or another. Uplifting, shaping, enhancing, supporting. Disguising. Misrepresenting. Exaggerating. Do you realise how tiresome that gets?'

'Actually—'

'I don't even *like* breasts, Mr Manhandle.'

'*Mamon*.'

'In fact, I could go so far as to say I *despise* them.' She gestured with her left hand. 'If I could get these off my chest, believe me, I would.'

'Actually—'

'So when an opportunity like this comes along, I grab it with both hands. Marvellous what you can pick up on the net. In just 24 hours, equipment, expertise, a support team—'

'You bootstrapped yourself as an espionage agent in just a *day*?'

'Impressed?' asked Underwire, offering Gordon another of those that-smile-would-be-really-rather-fetching-if-you-weren't-about-to-kill-me expressions. 'Could've invested a bit more in the armament, though. Killing Havmurthy had never been part of the plan. Certainly not until he'd revealed who else was in on it. Enceladus, I had, but I still have no idea who he's working with dirtside.'

'Enceladus? Not Dione?'

'No, Enceladus. There, now, see? I really *am* going to have to kill you.'

'For someone who didn't want to monologue…' whispered Sue.

'The trick is to keep them talking,' Gordon muttered, keeping his eyes focussed on Underwire, still framed by the cargo bay's doorway. He chanced another incremental step sideways.

'*What* trick?' Sue whispered back. 'Gordon, I think she's nervous.'

'I think so too,' replied Gordon, *sotto voce*. 'Doesn't mean she's not dangerous.'

'When you've *quite* finished…' Underwire said.

'What happened on Enceladus?' Gordon asked her, still playing desperately for time. Hoping that the Incapacitator's barrel stayed dark.

'That's where they did the encoding,' said Underwire. 'Someone in Havmurthy's grilled cheese factory has synthesised a whole series of junk-protein sequences, coding for the Saturn drive's blueprints. They were releasing them, one set a week, concealed as a trace ingredient in Havmurthy's Red Leicester. Hints started turning up that someone was nicking IP from Saturn and broadcasting it. They've gone frantic trying to shut it down, monitoring every transmission possible, every piece of written material. Nobody thought to check the *cheese*. But it's there, plain as day, for anyone to read. All you need is a protein sequencer.'

'How many people does – did – Havmurthy have working for him?' asked Gordon.

'Something like fifty-seven thousand, system-wide, I think,' said Underwire. 'Where you going with this?'

'If all you've got is something that was happening on Enceladus,' said Gordon, 'what makes you think Havmurthy was involved at all? It could very possibly have been just a rogue employee, or a rogue group of employees.'

'No, it had to be Havmurthy. The guy travelled everywhere. He'd been to Enceladus at least twice.'

'He was the CEO,' Gordon objected. 'The big cheese. Of *course* he'd visit the factories from time to time.'

'Are you delivering this monologue, or am I?'

'Actually,' said Gordon, 'describing this as a 'monologue' is probably a bit of a misno—'

'You finished?' The gun flashed towards him for emphasis.

Gordon nodded assent, keeping his eyes focussed on her weapon.

'Good.'

'But I still don't understand why I'm involved in this,' said Gordon. 'Why you stunned me.'

'I make no apologies for the effect I have on men.'

'I *mean*—' Gordon began.

Underwire interrupted. 'I saw Havmurthy stop to talk to you in the Skytop atrium. I picked you for his accomplice. Made sense. I knew your module was carrying a bulk shipment of Havmurthy samples.'

'That had nothing to do with me,' Gordon said. 'Sue placed that order.'

'Which one's Sue?'

'I am,' she said, peering out from behind Gordon's shoulder. 'And I ordered it because it was on special. End of story.'

'You may be right.' Underwire refocussed on Gordon. 'I certainly didn't learn anything useful off your handheld. For all I knew, though, you could've been in with Havmurthy. Matter of fact, I've still no evidence you're not.'

'He was asking me the time!' said Gordon. 'At least, I think that's what happened. Memory's a bit hazy.'

'That'd be the Hypnotismol. Plan was to dose you and Havmurthy, pump the two of you for info, instruct you to forget the attack and the interrogation, and leave you in one of Skytop's saunas. But when the stun killed Havmurthy, I... got cold feet. I never intended anyone to get killed. And I panicked. Best I could think of was dragging him to the nearest ladies', dumping him there, stabbing him to disguise the method of death, and getting myself clear. After I dragged you in there as well, of course, to keep you from raising the alarm. Because I couldn't be sure the Hypnotismol was going to work as directed. I mean, the stun setting hadn't exactly lived up to expectations—'

'And stripped and bound me to buy more time. OK, makes sense. But why take the handheld?'

'I thought you were Havmurthy's accomplice, remember? I thought I could mine it for intel. Then I found out you were one of the house dicks, and that my descent ticket was for this lift-module. *Your* module. Seemed like too much of a coincidence. So then I needed some way to keep an eye on you, without arousing your suspicion. It seemed prudent to 'upgrade' the handheld with a spot of spyware—'

'Freeware, more like. You should at least have plumped for the ads-free version. Would've been a bit less obvious,' suggested Gordon. Now, at last, Sue seemed to have shuffled across behing him.

'Well, that's your opinion,' said Underwire. 'And any second now, your opinion isn't going to count for anything anymore. Goodbye, Mr Mandolin.' She sighted along the Incapacitator.

'*Mamon*. Ms Underwire. *Grace*. Don't do this.'

'I've got too much to lose to back out now.'

'Havmurthy's killing – that was an accident. Or at least—'

'If you're suggesting I can't kill in cold blood, think again.' She fired. Sue shrieked.

The energy blast went wide, grazing Gordon's left arm. The pain was like a burst of mains electricity. Needle-sharp, backed up by scorching, numbing blunt force. Somewhere behind Gordon, the top crate on the stack of Idovist's pop-psych books disintegrated in a noisy confetti of plastipaper fragments.

'Piece of *shit* internet merchandise,' said Underwire, sighting again.

'Don't mind me,' explained Yuri Ligotmi, who chose this moment to appear in the doorway, clutching an electric ukelele by the neck. 'I'm just looking for my green tambourine.'

Underwire turned to face the newcomer. Gordon grabbed the cloak from the suitcase, threw it over Sue, and rushed Underwire. She turned back and shot Gordon square in the kneecap. He went down in agony.

Ligotmi brought the solid-bodied ukelele down on Underwire's head. She fell to the deck, unconscious.

*

'Always wanted to do that,' Ligotmi said, when he and Sue had finished trussing and gagging the struggling Underwire in as many items of clothing – mainly, as it turned out, Smartbras – as they could lay their hands on. 'Not the tying-up-chicks thing, 'cos that's not cool if it's not consensual. I mean, the Pete Townsend bit with the guitar. Must see if I can work that into the act. Pity it didn't break, though. Man, that would've been awesome! Don't suppose either of you knows who makes guitars that break properly nowadays?'

'Yuri... I don't think you realise what you've just got yourself involved in,' said Gordon, sitting up with difficulty while Sue wrapped a pressure bandage around his swollen and throbbing knee. 'There'll be all manner of reports, police interviews... it could be months before they uncover exactly what was going down with Havmurthy, and whether Underwire was acting alone or was part of a cartel. It's likely your name is going to get dragged through the mud. And you'd probably better give up on getting any revenue from that ad jingle you did for Havmurthy. It'd get you the wrong kind of attention, with what's been happening.'

'You're probably right,' said Ligotmi. 'Anyway, loss of revenue isn't an issue. I've just had word that the U238 tour is definitely going ahead, with me and the band as the support act. So we're better off without *Cheeses Is Just Alright With Me*.'

'*That's* what it's called?' asked Sue, blushing. 'I'd always heard it as *She Scissors Just Alright With Me*. I mean, whatever lights your candle, but maybe not quite the mental image Marketing was hoping to evoke...'

'Doesn't matter to me, or the band. Right now,' Ligotmi said, shrugging, 'we're more popular than cheese is.'

'I wouldn't try moving that leg for at least a day,' Sue advised. 'You took a fair wallop of stun damage.'

Gordon tried to protest, tried to sit up, tried to make himself comfortable. At length he settled for just falling back on the sick bay bed, while Sue picked up the scraps of bandages and wrappings that littered the alcove's floor. He looked across at the other bed, currently occupied by a heavily trussed and sedated Underwire. 'They look so peaceful when they're asleep, don't they?' he quipped. Or tried to. Deep rivets of pain hammered into his knee.

Sue, it seemed, wasn't having it. She frowned.

'What's up?' he asked.

Her grimace deepened. 'Doesn't it bother you?'

'Doesn't what bother me?' he asked. 'Getting shot? Sure it bothers me. I certainly wouldn't recommend it.'

'Not that. I mean, doesn't it bug you that we still don't know who was behind it? Behind Underwire. Whose idea was it all?'

'No,' he replied. 'No, that doesn't matter to me. I'm happy to let the police get to the bottom of it.'

'I'm not so sure they will,' she said.

'How d'you mean?'

'I think Grace was a patsy. I think she took the rap... Gordon, this is big-league stuff. Industrial espionage, murder, intellectual property... you don't just decide to try your hand at this, on the off chance. On a whim. *No way* Underwire was acting alone – I mean, be fair, she doesn't look remotely like the lone-wolf type. This cheese-explosion thing that she didn't seem to know anything about. And no genuine hardened crim would have let that standoff run on anywhere near as long as it did...'

Everyone's an expert, Gordon thought to himself. 'Sue, she was just out of her depth, the whole thing had ballooned out of her control. Hell, if my knee and my arm didn't hurt so bad I might almost find it in my heart to feel slightly sorry for her. But it's done. She got greedy, she tried something she wasn't cut out for, she made mistakes, and we've got her tied up. End of story. Poetic justice, in the circumstances. Hell, at least *she* gets to keep her clothes *on*.'

'But... you're just not *getting it*, are you?'

'Getting what?'

'Who would be behind this, I mean, Gordon. Who would have the most at stake.'

'Look, if you want to go down that path, I guess it'd be the spacelines. Any one of them gets a competitive edge – and let's face it, the new drive would be one hell of an edge – they could very easily put the rest out of business.'

'That's who'd have the most to *gain* from buying into this. What about who'd have the most to *lose* from its adoption? *Think* about it, Gordon. A hyperspace drive, able to operate arbitrarily close to any planetary surface, offering near-instantaneous travel between any of the planets in the solar system... Thanks to Underwire, Havmurthy's dead, and the cheese feed has presumably been turned off. So although some of the drive specs have been leaked, it's not the full set of blueprints. And aside from Underwire – and let's face it, there's no way she could be directly involved in the explosion that took out the prototype drive and the original plans, given that that happened half the solar system away... look, I'm really not sure how much of the genie is left to put back in the bottle, and maybe I'm just letting my paranoia get the better of me, but... You're the detective here, Gordon. Maybe you can see something I'm missing. Because I really don't think Underwire was acting alone, or even off her own bat. I certainly don't think she was the one calling the shots.'

'But—'

'It goes deeper than that, I'm sure. Why the explosion at Dione?'

'Havmurthy trying to eliminate the prototype, I guess. Makes his blueprints all the more marketable.'

'Gordon, there's *no way* that explosion was down to Havmurthy.'

'His cheese,' Gordon protested.

'Precisely. Why would Havmurthy advertise his own involvement, when the whole blueprint-smuggling schtick depended on running under the radar? It's obviously someone out to discredit Havmurthy, take him out of the equation.'

'But Dione – doesn't seem likely Underwire could've been involved in that. The distance—'

'Exactly. Like I said, Underwire's just a pas – a patsy. Someone that allows the police to conclude 'case closed', just because they've got Havmurthy's killer. When in reality, the whole thing's anything *but* closed. I keep telling you, someone's been playing really dirty with this. Someone who wanted both to stick it to Saturn Propulsions, and to any competitors that might've tried to jump on that bandwagon. Someone with plenty to lose, and deep pockets. Deep *corporate* pockets. Someone with enough collateral to synthesise anticheese – and you can't tell me *that's* going to be cheap, nor easy. Must be some organisation with a helluvalot invested, for one reason or another, in keeping up the obstacles to prompt and straightforward planet-to-planet travel.'

'Not getting your point, sorry, Sue,' replied Gordon, reaching for his handheld.

'Just take a step back, huh? Try to see the big picture…'

'Sue, I've no problem with taking a step back, as long as there's a safety rail. But as for the big picture… I'd rather leave that side of things to the cops.'

She mumbled something he didn't catch, and left to get a start on the breakfast menu.

Gordon, revelling in his hardwon solitude, flicked a crossword up onto his handheld's screen. He was soon lost in an interlocking set of cryptic clues, as all the while the Skyward Transorbital Enterprises' lift-module 270 carried its lucrative cargo of passengers and freight on the ponderous three-day descent from the sprawling geostationary hotel towards the Earth's surface.

Elevator Pitch

1

For a time, which feels like minutes but must be mere seconds, it's all he can do to just take in the dreadful scene. He's conscious of Belle standing, white-knuckled and distraught, at his side, while he soaks up the déjà vu. He's seen too many bodies over the past months, but this has to be one of the worst.

'It's maybe not as bad as it looks,' Gordon finally suggests.

Belle, who's pointedly not looking at the spacesuited remains sprawled across the hotel suite's bloodstained faux-luxury carpet, gives a quick, sharp, recriminatory intake of breath. She's having none of Gordon's equivocation. 'Someone's blasted a dirty great hole in his chest,' she observes. 'You could park a wombat in there. In what possible way *is that not as bad as it looks?'*

'I didn't mean...' Gordon starts, gazing helplessly at the victim's blood-spattered thorax — the tattered remains of the spacesuit mercifully concealing some of the worst of the corpse's injuries — the permanently shocked, eyes-alert visage staring blankly at the ceiling; the detached helmet, incongruously unharmed. (Still perfectly usable, he thinks, but then who would want it?) He focusses briefly on the rich expanse of red surrounding the body, before turning and allowing his gaze to alight on Belle's anxious face beside him. 'Look, what I mean is, clearly this is catastrophic. Terrible. Tragic. But all that aside, the actual crime looks likely to be rather open and shut.'

'*Gordon,*' *replies Belle,* '*this poor man – Mr Mannidge – has just been horribly eviscerated... that is the word I'm after, isn't it? And you're talking about how you know who did it? Shouldn't we be trying to do something for Mannidge?*'

'*I'd say he's past the need for room service, Belle. And I didn't say I actually knew who the perpetrator was. I just meant that, well, a crime has been committed, and it will need solving. It's just the delegates on this module, correct?*'

'*No, there are a couple of other guests as well,*' *she says.*

'*Even so, the murderer must be among that number,*' *Gordon responds.* '*How many? Five or six?*'

'*Six, in total,*' *answers Belle, pausing for a deep sigh. She pulls a handkerchief out of her uniform's pocket, blows her nose, and sighs again.* '*Five now, of course.*'

'Mr Maxim?' The publisher's eyes were wide, his face florid, his hands heavy and tight on the lapels of Gordon's formerly-unrumpled jacket. 'Please, my dear sir! You've got to help me!'

Gordon reached his own hands up to his collar and gently unfolded his assailant's mitts from their double grasp. He did not welcome being accosted by the passengers at the best of times, and fifteen minutes before descent commencement was far from the best of times. He met the other's panicked stare with that patent blend of deference and disdain which is the hallmark of the practised hotel employee, strove to ignore the hint of cocktail-onion breath, and said, as calmly as the situation (and his jacket) permitted, 'Help? What seems to be the problem?' Once sufficient time had elapsed that the delay might, by inference – or equally, might not – be considered insulting, he added, with just such a topspin as the situation merited, the monosyllabic interrogative 'Sir?'

Mycroft Whurd, publisher and commissioning editor with Burdester-Whurd, took a couple of tweed-clad breaths and shot his cuffs, displaying decorative Saturn-shaped cufflinks, before he found the air to respond. His eyes were still wild. And his face still looked as though he'd just run a half-marathon in a boiler suit, but Gordon suspected this may well be facial business-as-usual insofar as the Whurd visage was concerned. 'It's that pest Ritton. Blooming fellow's driving me *mad*, and that's just in the past half hour. If I'd known he was booked into the same module as me, honestly, I would've arranged to stay another day on Skytop. Even if it meant spending all of that time in the deuced airlock. I really don't know how I'm going to survive the next three days – or, more to the point, if he comes at me with another bloody book idea, I don't know how *he'll* survive. Do you know what the Dickens he's been foisting on me already?'

Do you know, Gordon wondered, *just how many things there are that need to be done before a space-elevator module can begin its descent?* But he supposed that one of those things, very probably, was placating and addressing the demands of wealthy and influential passengers. He supposed, further, that Management might well take the view that this extension of courtesy to well-heeled travellers was something of particular importance, things in the space-elevation industry being on something of an uncertain footing with regard to profitability of late; so he said, with all the only slightly clipped politeness of the really rather busy, 'No, Mr Whurd, I don't know. But—'

'Two bloody non-fiction book proposals, that's what I've been hit with, in the space of thirty minutes. First there was *Jumping the Shark: an exhaustive treatise on the subject of extreme bestia—*'

'That sounds like a most regrettable suggestion on Mr Ritton's part. But if you'll excuse—'

'That was in the lobby,' Whurd said. 'And then, just at the door to my room – which, by the way, means that now the bloody bounder knows where to find me – he said he'd be grateful if I'd look over his study on fetishism in SF fandom, *Do Not Force-Choke Me, Oh My Darl—*'

'If it would help,' Gordon replied, seeking to get the words in as quickly as was consistent with the presentation of "calm" and "professional" (for he sensed that this Mycroft Whurd's conversation might well operate along broadly similar lines to the action of a fire hydrant, designed for ready release but difficult to shut off), 'I can arrange to have you assigned to a different room. On a different floor. If you just head down to the lobby to see Belle...'

'Belle? And who might this Belle be?'

'Belle Hopp, our receptionist. Except – no, wait, Belle's not on this module, this descent. That's a nuisance. You'd better see... look, it's going to be best if I sort it myself. But could you give me twenty minutes, half an hour? I'm afraid I'm very busy right now.'

'Twenty minutes? How'm I supposed to avoid Peter Poison-Pen for the next twenty minutes?'

'Or half an hour. Really, you'd better make it half an hour. Forty minutes, tops. You'd probably be best to find a booth in the restaurant, somewhere near the back corner. Passengers hardly ever pop in there, start of a descent. They're most likely to be in the obs deck, watching the detachment from Skytop. And if I see Mr Ritton, I'll be sure to leave him misinformed of your location.'

'Thank you. But... restaurant?'

'Lobby level. Left of the reception desk. If Sue tries to tell you it's closed, just mention I said it was OK. And after all, it will only be for forty-five minutes or thereabouts.'

'And this will enable me to evade my authorial pest?' Whurd's face was starting, Gordon thought, to take on the appearance of a half-marathon runner who had suddenly, and much to his surprise, realised that he had quite unexpectedly taken the lead.

'It should do, until I can get down to sort out your booking. Shouldn't be more than an hour. Not much more than an hour. No guarantees, of course, but—'

'Thank you, Mr Maritime! You, sir, are a prince among lift attendants.'

'You are too kind,' replied Gordon, very badly mispronouncing 'talkative' in the process. 'But I really must—'

'Ah, yes, of course, what?' And Whurd turned away towards the rampway that led down to the lobby.

Gordon, for his part, was striding in some haste towards the lift-module's embarkation point – best practice was really not to surrender the junction between the lift-module and the parent hotel, with all its airlocks, security devices and high-voltage power couplings, into the care of an apprentice of whom Gordon did not yet feel confident in attributing the ability to velcro his own shoes up – when he unexpectedly collided with a passenger who had just turned the corridor.

'Oh! Sorry!' said the less-winded of the two, who on this occasion turned out to be the passenger, a tall man in his mid-to-late twenties, balding, toothy, and thin almost to the point of emaciation. 'Uh – I don't suppose you've seen that publisher anywhere?'

'Publisher?' asked Gordon, feigning as much surprise as he could. Which, in the circumstances, wasn't much, what with it having just now been knocked out of him, as it were.

'Yes, that Mr Whurd,' replied Paul E. Ritton, for it was he. 'I was hoping I could interest him in my new novel.'

'I regret I haven't. But have you looked on the observation deck?'

'Just come from there,' explained Ritton. 'And he's not in his room. Anywhere else he might be?'

'I really couldn't say,' said Gordon. 'But if you will excuse me—'

'Perhaps you could tell him I'm looking for him?'

'I could certainly do that.'

'That would be great. Thank you, Mr Margin.'

'You're welcome. And now, if you'll—'

'It's my best novel yet,' explained Ritton, with the air of one who evidently believed that this was necessarily a positive. 'A young farmboy—'

'I really do have to go,' said Gordon, recognising in the other that dangerous tone that denotes a favourite topic, and an ability to espouse on same at length. Whurd and Ritton, it seemed, were two sides of the same coin in that respect. He made his escape along the corridor, mind preoccupied with the myriad details of the ready-for-descent prep, and was just in time to collide with another passenger at the corridor's next corner.

*

Long business hours, but delayed in processing transaction. (4,4,4)

This was plainly no time for crossword puzzles, but he was in the habit of giving even the briefest of available moments, and a more-or-less steady share of his cranial processing capacity, to the contemplation of cryptic challenges. It kept things from getting dull, in his experience.

Gordon reached the embarkation point with less than three minutes to go until departure. He gave a curt nod to the apprentice, a tall young frizzy-haired male by the name of Rube Greenhorn. The apprentice's standout features were an extraordinarily prominent Adam's apple, a month's supply of baby fat, and what seemed very close to a complete set of pimples; he was dressed in startlingly clean Skyward-monogrammed overalls, with the original creasemarks still discernible.

Gordon turned to the all-important tasks of checking the airlock, recollecting partway through that he was supposed to be providing instruction to his junior. 'Green here means the module's air-circulation and purification system is functioning within safe limits. Yellow would indicate a problem of some description, serious but not immediately life-threatening, which could be diagnosed by choosing the check-through option on this panel here. Red would indicate an immediate hazard – perhaps a module hull breach or a toxic component in the air supply, and in those instances you'd be required to activate the alarm – it doesn't always trigger automatically – and to don one of the emergency breathing units before seeking to address the hazard. Or a faulty diode, that's happened too, once or twice.'

'But you'd put the EBU on before you sounded the alarm, right?'

'No. Our primary concern is for the passengers. Informing them of any danger, through sounding the alarm, takes the highest priority.'

'But surely, I mean, keeping them safe is going to be easier if we've first ensured our own safety?'

I don't write the fine print, thought Gordon, *I just adhere to it.* 'That's not the way Skyward admin, in all their ground-based wisdom, see it,' Gordon explained.

'Oh,' said the apprentice, who was then silent for some seconds, apparently digesting this tidbit of Skyward management practice. 'And if it's a leak, how would I fix it? Like, we haven't covered welding yet, or anything like that.'

'That would take too long, anyway,' replied Gordon. 'If there's a leak, it's obviously best to stop it as quickly as possible. For a large breach, say a blown observation window – and that's happened once or twice, not always by accident – there are self-sealing shutters which are supposed to slide down, and sometimes they even do. Pray you don't happen to be exiting the window at the time, because that won't end well.' He paused, recollecting a particularly grisly and probably apocryphal story from his own basic training, a dozen years ago. *Probably best not to tell him that one.* 'Smaller holes, your standard micrometeor-to-space-junk-size, somewhere between a pinhole and a coin slot, say, the pressure sensors aren't often able to locate them precisely enough to slide down the right shutter, so they need to be stopped with this.' He opened a "Safety Equipment" panel beside the wall-mounted status display and pulled out a two-litre canister with a prominent spray nozzle. Passing the canister to Rube, he added, 'It's heavier than it looks. Don't pull the trigger.'

'Neat. What is it?'

'It's a special tar-like formulation, designed to harden to an airtight plug on exposure to vacuum. You spray this on the hole, it oozes through, solidifies and seals. Stinks like hell. Wonderful stuff. It'd be even more wonderful if it didn't have a tendency to ignite once we reach the upper atmosphere, but I gather they're working on it. It's called elevator pitch.'

'Oh. OK. But if it's so essential to safety, why's it tucked away in a safety locker, and not out in the open like the fire extinguishers?'

'Management felt it was best, in case of an emergency, not to present passengers with a choice. Particularly since the stuff is flammable.'

'Cool. So you've explained green, yellow, and red,' said Rube, returning his attention to the status panel. 'What would blue mean?'

'What do you mean, "what would blue mean"? There isn't a blue.'

'That'd be fun, though, right? If there was a blue? I mean, there totally should be a blue.'

Gordon found his thoughts shifting from Skyward admin's Safety and Training division to its Recruitment arm, and in particular to those individuals in charge of the Apprentice programme.

'Actually,' Rube continued, 'it'd probably mean the module was full of water. That'd be cool, right?'

'Well, the water temp—' Gordon began.

'No, but it'd keep the Martians happy, wouldn't it?'

Not all of them, Gordon thought, wondering how Belle was coping in 271.

He pulls on a pair of snug-fitting white plasticotton gloves, then leans carefully over the body, searching for clues.

'The suit's a nuisance,' he comments. 'It makes it difficult to determine whether the victim sustained any injuries prior to death.'

'Injuries other than industrial-level excavation of the chest cavity, you mean?' Belle asks.

'Well, yes,' he replies, aware that a pedantic tone is creeping into his voice. 'It's entirely possible that the evisceration has been done to mislead, to draw attention from something else about the body. Mannidge may well have been dead before the... uh, obvious damage to his essential body organs, though of course Occam's razor suggests that's the likely culprit.'

'So is he your main suspect? That doesn't look like anything a razor would do, and there's no Occam on our passenger list.'

'No, I mean – usually the most obvious explanation is the correct one.'

'What a horrible way to die.'

'Death's not noted for its pleasant aspects,' says Gordon. 'At least it looks as though it must have been pretty quick, as these things go.' He crouches over the victim's legs, leans in close above the suit's left calf, and takes a deep sniff; then pulls himself upright, exhaling noisily, knees clicking.

'Still has that new-suit smell. I'd very much say this suit hadn't been worn before this. It's certainly never been exposed to vacuum. Why was Mannidge wearing it in his room? And why's it wet?' He gestures to a distinct beading of what he presumes to be water droplets covering the suit's silvery torso, legs, and arms, then presses the fingertips of one white-gloved hand into the carpet's pile, well away from the bloodstains. *'Carpet's damp too.'*

Belle looks meaningfully towards the ceiling, but says nothing. Gordon glances up. *'Ah.'*

'So really,' the guest was telling him, 'if we take the depth of the Marianas Trench as an indication, the proportionate deepest point for the Martian oceans should be somewhere on the order of seven to eight kilometres' depth. Otherwise, what's the point of terraforming? It's only fair that if we're seeking to remake Mars in Earth's image, we should ensure the biosphere's features are appropriate, and to scale.' The guest, Gordon had learnt from the passenger manifest for this descent, was Phillippa Bayson, the scientific representative to the South Mars delegation to the peace talks. (The talks were scheduled to begin in Singapore in four days' time, a day after Module 270 had completed its cable-constrained fall from geostationary orbit.) Dr Bayson was short, a little plump, her round face framed by shoulder-length brown hair; Gordon placed her age at somewhere between thirty and forty, and her demeanour as a combination of placid and intense. She was clad in jeans, sneakers, and a red T-shirt on which the slogan "Mars Needs Beaches" was more-or-less visible from most forward angles.

'But isn't it the view of the North Mars delegation that such a sea level would be somehow unfair?'

'But it's *proportionate*,' Dr Bayson explained, as though, really, Gordon was displaying unpardonable ignorance by not simply accepting the fact. 'Besides, their preferred sea level would see most of the South Mars real estate at far too high an altitude – low atmospheric pressure, which means breathing difficulties as well as unacceptably high levels of ultraviolet and cosmic rays.'

'But they're saying your group's proposal would lead to unacceptably high levels of sea for most of the North Mars real estate. I mean, isn't that the gist of the dispute?'

'Well, yes,' said Dr Bayson, smiling as she conceded the point, insofar as she was willing to concede that there was a point to be conceded, which wasn't, so far as it went, far. 'But our position is *proportionate*.'

There were six members of the South Mars delegation on 270, travelling as guests alongside Whurd, Ritton and Kograffa. With a dozen guest rooms, the module could not be said to be completely full, but it did feel unusually busy. Gordon was starting to realise that Belle, who in the normal run of things was so quietly efficient as to (at times) seem invisible, played a very large part in the smooth running of the module during its descent or ascent: with Belle seconded to 271, Sue Sheff mainly preoccupied with testing and maintaining the kitchen's new labour-saving food-prep devices, and Rube Greenhorn still trying to memorise the list of Things Which Must Not Be Done While Outside Earth's Atmosphere, as well as the list of Things Which Must Be Done Before Entering Earth's Atmosphere, and trying to keep the two lists separate in his mind, Gordon was faced with more than the usual amount of guest-wrangling. He should, by rights, be checking that all was well with the checked baggage, or that Ritton had not baled up Whurd in some inescapable corner, or that others of the South Mars delegation were not using the module's comm system to send inflammatory comments or watery innuendo to the North Mars contingent on 271... but he was enjoying the intellectual challenge of trying to hold up his end of a conversation with Dr Bayson, who, while undoubtedly opinionated, appeared to be rather less strident in those opinions than the other, more overtly politicised members of the South Mars team. 'But isn't it a little unfair that almost all of this water is going to be in the northern hemisphere? And that therefore most of the remaining usable land is going to be in the south?'

'It's geography,' replied Dr Bayson. 'Or rather, if you want to get pedantic, areography. There shouldn't be any "fair" or "unfair". Just proportionality.'

'But under your plan, the existing North Mars settlements—'

'It was always going to be the case that the first settlements, on both hemispheres, would be temporary structures. The domes were put up as a stopgap measure, to hold until an adequate biosphere could be imported. It's just that the development of the Saturn hyperdrive has given us an affordable and effective method for bombarding the planet with comets on a timescale of years, rather than the centuries that were originally envisaged.'

'And isn't that another of the North's grievances? That the main cometary-impact sites you're proposing are all on the top half of the planet?'

'Well, yes, but again, that's not political, or anything like that, it's just ge – areography. Logically, if you're going to be pummelling the planet with four or five cometary impacts every month, you'll want those impacts to be happening in the place where you want the water to end up. Aside from anything else, it means you're causing minimal damage to any of the actual real estate.'

'But under the South's proposal, almost all of that real estate is going to be—'

Gordon's handheld beeped with a near-deafening chirp. Seeing the other's startled expression at the noise, he explained that the volume control appeared to be broken, and was stuck on "high". Then he excused himself from the affable yet singleminded Dr Bayson and wandered off to see what was up.

'It's that blamed pest Ritton again,' Whurd explained, face flushed with bluster. 'I forgot to tell Alexei not to spill the beans about this new room of mine, and he went and informed the blighter.'

'But if you don't wish to speak to Mr Ritton, why don't you just activate the "Do Not Disturb" status on your door?'

'Do you think I haven't done that already? I activated every bally status I could: Do Not Disturb, Closed for Renovations,

Childbirth In Progress, Deadly Biohazard Do Not Enter… it makes no damned difference, the blasted feller just pummels on the door, and when I go to check it, thinking it might be the room service I ordered, he just barges in. Chap has the manners of a rampaging rhino. And the writing ability of a… of a… of a lobotomised lobster. Do you have any idea of the kind of vomitous piffle he's been subjecting me to for the past half hour? He's planning a novelisation on the love-lives of the great SF writers of the Golden Age, wants to call it *A Heinlein Between Pleasure and Pain*… there's absolutely nothing else for it. I'm just going to have to switch rooms again.'

'I'll have to see if we've got anything else available,' said Gordon, wondering which part of his variegated job description might possibly cover running a Witness Protection Programme for publishers. 'The module's pretty full, though. We might have to put you back in your previous room.'

'The one next door to Ritton's, you mean? With the adjoining door? That'd be frying-pan-to-fire stuff. I'd be afraid to sleep with my eyes closed.'

Gordon sighed. 'Then we may well have to just leave you with this room.'

Whurd blanched, then brightened slightly. 'I could swap with Alexei. He owes me for setting the feller loose on me again – not that he knew better at the time.'

'I would need to speak with Mr Kograffa,' said Gordon. 'He may, after all, not be willing to relocate. And I can't force a guest to move against their will.'

'I could sweeten the deal by offering to double the advance on his latest dictionary,' said Whurd. 'That'd probably swing it.'

'It sounds like this is something you'd need to broach with Mr Kograffa, then. But if he refuses to move, and you're forced to endure contact with Mr Ritton again… I mean, it's not really my place, but couldn't you suggest some kind of project to him, something like a backgrounder on the Martian terraforming crisis? It's very newsworthy at the moment, you're in the perfect spot for Ritton to gather some inside information on the crisis, and the gentleman does seem to have an apti— well, at least, an *enthusiasm* for non-fiction. Perhaps he just needs some direction?'

Gordon's suggestion appeared to rub Whurd quite the wrong way, and he bristled with something that might be indignation, might be something rather less mild. 'The only direction I'd recommend to that blighter would be down. At terminal velocity. Spacesuit optional. That's assuming the module carries spacesuits anywhere. Does it? It might be one of those parachutes-on-passenger-jets thingies.'

'In the unlikely event of a life-threatening loss in the module's atmospheric pressure—' Gordon began, quoting as of rote. 'Well, be that as it may. It sounds as though you need to consult with your colleague, to see if a room exchange would be mutually agreeable. I'll wait to hear back from you. And now if you'll excuse me...'

'Belle?' Gordon spoke into his handheld, checking the signal-strength indicator as he did so. He was standing in the Skyward 270 obs deck. Module-to-module communication tended to be subject to scratchy reception, particularly during the early stages of descent.

'That you, Gordon?' she answered. 'You sound like you're speaking through Sue's collection of vintage guitar effects pedals.'

'No, I – wait, is that better?'

'Wow. Feedback. Maybe if you turn the volume down.'

'Wait one. How about that?'

'Fuzztone. What on earth is the problem with your handheld?'

'Volume knob's broken. I've just muffled it with a hotel towel.'

'Well, I suppose it's done the trick, sort of. What can I do for you?'

'Just thought I should check how the North Mars crew were settling in on 271.'

'Oh, like a house on fire. Bugger. Dammit. *Figure of speech, you useless heap of semi-intelligent software! Abort! Abort!*'

'Belle, is there a problem?' Gordon asked, suddenly anxious. Only fifteen kilometres or so separated modules 270 and 271; but at this stage of the descent, at this altitude, that distance might have been the Earth – Moon gulf.

'*No*, Gordon,' she sighed. 'Just the ridiculous self-aware safety system they're trialling on 271 – it's vocab-triggered, and far too neurotic for its own good. I mean, the sprinklers went off just now, just because I said "fire", and – oh, for photon's sake. Abort! Abort! Re-initialise your context module, you misbegotten bolus of regurgitated programming! Gordon, I'm sorry, I'm going to have to call you back, I've got half a dozen guests all messaging me, all doubtless wanting to know why they've received two unscheduled cold showers in the past two minutes.'

'That's OK by me, Belle,' said Gordon, reflecting that the North Mars delegation were presumably particularly sensitive to the subject of inundation. 'I'll just wait until you've got a few less irons in the fire.'

'*Gordon!*'

Really, Gordon thought, Skyward should devote some thought to the installation of collision-avoidance alarms at the intersections of the module's floor corridors with the motorised rampway that led between floors. This was the fourth time today he had managed to impact upon some unsuspecting and, more to the point, inattentive – yet, crucially, fee-paying – hotel guest, and the second time today that the guest had managed to be Whurd's nemesis, the text-torturer Paul E. Ritton.

'Mr Mannequin!' exclaimed Ritton, not two seconds after he had succeeded in elbowing Gordon in the solar plexus. 'This is a stroke of luck!'

Gordon, still struggling to recoup his breath – which seemed to have decided to take a break, and was not for the moment returning calls – could agree that luck was certainly involved, but rather disputed whether he and Ritton would agree on the *flavour* of luck to which the current encounter should be attributed. 'Ah—'

'It's weird, you know,' said Ritton. 'I've just come from what I could have sworn was Mycroft Whurd's room, but it's not his room.'

'Oh?' asked Gordon.

'No. It was some rather gruff Eastern European dictionarian guy – and I'm not sure if "dictionarian" is even a word, but it should be, because obviously you need a word to describe someone like that—'

'Actually,' began Gordon, with something approaching eagerness because he could feel his years of crossword-puzzling finally starting to pay off, 'the correct name for someone who compiles dictionaries is—'

'Oh, but I mustn't keep you from your important hotel business. It's just, if you could find the time to find out which room Mr Whurd is staying in, that'd be very useful.'

'I'm afraid our privacy policy prevents us passing on that kind of information,' said Gordon, doing his best to achieve a "my-hands-are-tied-but-what-else-can-you-do?" expression with a shrug which mainly served to remind him how much his stomach still hurt from Ritton's elbowing.

'Oh, of course, but if you could just let him know I'm looking for him,' said Ritton.

Actually, thought Gordon, *I believe he already knows.*

'I'm just really excited about the fantasy novel idea I've been working on, and I just know he'll want to publish it. It's going to make a big splash, I just know it.' Ritton laughed as though at some joke only he could appreciate (something that Gordon believed might not be that uncommon an occurrence). 'It's all about the magical adventures of a mermaid and her pet narwhal.'

'That sounds quite charming,' Gordon admitted, despite himself.

'It does, doesn't it?' agreed Ritton. 'It's going to be called *The Siren's Piercing Whale.*'

'I'm sorry, is that the time?' said Gordon, retreating as rapidly as dignity would allow.

*

'Can't this be done somewhere else?' Belle asks Gordon, as she attempts to indicate, without turning her head, towards the remains of Lester Mannidge on the carpet behind them.

Gordon, who has placed his handheld on the room's ornamental plastirosewood writing table, turns to Belle and explains, 'We have to secure the crime scene.'

'Can't you just lock the door behind you?' Belle asks. 'I mean, I've seen some pretty gruesome things in the line of my employ – that blanket bath I had to give to the visiting Jovian dignitary last year springs to mind, oh, and Havmurthy's body of course, but this... are you sure there's supposed to be so much blood?'

'Not on the carpet, no,' he answers. (Captain Kurtz's body on the Dart of Harkness last year was a worse mess, he thinks, but does not say out loud. At least, he hopes he has not said it out loud.) 'You don't have to stay for this,' he tells her.

'I feel I ought to,' she says. 'I am the acting module manager, after all, with Luke off-shift.' She sighs again. 'Never thought that this was what I'd be signing up for, I must say.'

The handheld beeps, startling both of them in the process, and Gordon picks it up and slowly passes it across the scene of the crime, as though Mannidge is some kind of grim theremin. It beeps again, and Gordon flips it over to inspect the readout on the unit's screen.

'What's it say?' Belle asks, a morbid fascination evident in her tone.

'Several essential components currently offline, or untraceable. Recommended action: return to manufacturer for reassembly.'

'Hell of a time for your handheld to glitch,' she says. 'I presume it is a glitch?'

'Freeware,' says Gordon. 'Your guess is as good as mine.'

'What I don't understand,' said Rube Greenhorn, 'is why we still need elevators.'

'It's because,' Gordon began, and then realised that he didn't actually know. The three employees – Rube, Gordon himself, and Sue Sheff – were seated in the module's restaurant, taste-testing the new replicator's Danish pastry offerings prior to their inclusion on tomorrow's breakfast menu.

While Gordon feigned fullness of mouth, Sue stepped into the conversational gap.

'It's a long-range order thing,' she replied.

'What, you mean like Lunashop Online?' asked Rube, through a filter of custard and pastry. He wiped his mouth on what he presumably thought was a napkin.

'Uh… no,' said Sue, eyes flicking pointedly between Rube's face and the marks newly smudged onto the tablecloth. 'I mean it's a side effect of operating a hyperdrive within the confines of an appreciable gravity well. Either on the transition into hyperspace, or out of it, there are slight discrepancies in the material order of substances, the way their atoms sit in relation to each other. Gravity's a weak force, so there's only a small discrepancy, but it's enough to ensure that substances for which long-range order is crucial – like human brains – get measurably scrambled.'

'I don't see the connection,' said Rube.

'The almond one is rather good,' declared Gordon. 'And the berry swirl wasn't bad either. These all came out of the replicator?'

Sue nodded, and turned her attention back to Rube. 'So it means that the initial promise of the Saturn Propulsions hyperdrive, as a method for getting around near-instantaneously within the inner solar system, turned out to be a bit of a fizzer. After the compensation payouts Saturn Prop had to put through to the families of their first few test pilots, it rapidly became apparent that it wasn't going to work for passenger craft. Which is lucky for us, because it means people travelling to Earth are still willing to pay for the three-day transit between the surface and geostationary orbit, and for the long voyages to other planets that depart from Skytop Plaza. If the hyperdrive did what they'd been hoping, we'd all be out of work.'

'Yeah,' said Rube. 'That's what I don't understand.'

'So how does it work again? The replicator I mean,' said Gordon.

'Gordon, I *showed* you this earlier,' Sue complained.

'Sorry, I think I missed some of the details.'

Sue sighed. 'You place a food or beverage sample on the left, a beam of photons is shone through it and passes through a lens assembly to a detector fitted into the right-hand-side wall. It builds up an atom-level model of the sample, and then constructs this through high-precision 3D printing in the right-hand compartment. The whole process only takes seconds, and it's remarkably versatile.'

'So the sample gets destroyed in the process?' asked Gordon.

'No, the sample's unharmed. It's a *replicator*. There wouldn't be a lot of point otherwise.'

'Cool,' said Rube. 'But about the hyperdrive, and us not being out of work—'

'Do they come out ready-baked?' asked Gordon.

'Well, yes,' said Sue. 'There wouldn't be a lot of point if they came out raw, and then had to be cooked. It'd kind of defeat the whole food-on-demand idea of the thing.'

'But are they hot? Or does it make a cooled-down version of the baked item?'

'Hot,' said Sue.

'Really? Because these are pretty cold,' said Gordon. 'I mean, they're very good, but they're not what I'd call warm.'

'They're not supposed to be warm,' said Sue. 'I replicated them a few hours ago.'

'Oh. You don't think they'd be better warmed up a little?'

'There's the microwave, if you'd like,' said Sue, getting a quite discernible hint of steel in her voice. 'But they're a dish best served cold. Reuben, did you have a question?'

'It's just Rube. And I was just wondering what you mean about us being out of work.'

'Our salaries,' said Sue, 'depend on the fact that, as it turns out, the Saturn hyperdrive isn't practical for passenger transport within the inner solar system. Nor for haulage of foodstuffs, medical supplies and sensitive electronics... which is a bit problematic for Saturn, really, because it also makes the hyperdrive pretty useless for unmanned vessels too, in most cases. It's great for terraforming, though.'

'For terraforming. Is that because it doesn't matter if the engine survives, because it's designed to crash?' Gordon, sensing a degree of pressure to come out of this demonstrating that he knew more than his protege Rube, and discerning also that he had just about bled dry the topic of fabricated breakfast pastries, felt on sure enough ground to ask what he hoped was an intelligent question.

'Well, partly that,' explained Sue, pausing to take the corner off an apple and pecan danish. 'And with things like ice and minerals for terraforming, the long-range order really isn't crucial: it's just the bulk of, of the *stuff* that you want, for the biosphere or whatever for a particular planet.'

'You're talking about the Mars thing, right?' asked Rube.

'Pretty much. At least, that's the one that's getting all the press at the moment, what with the whole North-versus-South dispute.'

'It sounds like fun,' said Rube. 'I hope it goes ahead. I mean, I *like* oceans. They're cool.'

Gordon's handheld, which he'd placed on 'silent' mode in deference to the lateness of hour, deftly tasered him to alert him to an urgent incoming message.

He introduces himself when she opens the door. 'Ms Yamayne-Fraim?' he asks.

She's tall. She's skinny. Her tee shirt and jeans are black. Her sneakers, too, are black. (Is she quick to adopt mourning clothes, Gordon wonders, or is this just how she'd normally be clad?) Her hair is black (straight, and shoulder-length), as is one of her eyes. It's mostly with the other one that she fixes a Gordon-centred stare. 'I didn't order any…' she begins, but then realisation hits. Her voice is a distinct contralto. 'Oh. Right, of course. You're the dick.'

'I find 'detective' both less pejorative and less subject to misinterpretation,' he replies, allowing himself a glance at her blackened eye. 'Ms Yamayne-Fraim?' he repeats.

'Call me Jacinta,' she offers, and stands aside from the door to permit him entrance.

'You're the North Mars delegation's computer specialist?' he asks, stepping into the room and, without invitation, taking his seat in the room's sole plastileather-upholstered armchair.

'That's me,' she says, glowering briefly at him before deciding to sit on one of the plastichrome dining chairs. 'I gather you've already spoken to Steph and Barry?'

Gordon requires a few seconds to parse the 'Steph and Barry' to which she's referring, and is a little discomfited that Jacinta Yamayne-Fraim knows as much as she does about his interview schedule, and the opportunity such knowledge might present for collusion, or at least for getting one's story straight. He's also, of course, puzzled as to how she came by that shiner. 'As it happens,' he says, crossing his legs, 'I have indeed met with Ms Risolve and Mr Vahatchett. But I'd just like to get this in your own words, if you don't mind.'

'Of course. I'm just wondering how you found them. I mean, Steph's so full-on severe, and Barry is so goddamn flexible. They're one hell of a double act. When I signed up with Lester – with Mr Mannidge – I could never see why he'd taken them both on as political advisers, when the two of them couldn't agree on any one course of action. I always saw them as those cartoon conscience figures, you know, the angel and the devil, standing on opposite shoulders. But I guess Lester found that useful, somehow. And of course there was more to it than that.'

'More to it than that?' Gordon echoes, seeking clarification.

'They were an item.' She coughs, raises an eyebrow over the unblackened eye. 'They were lovers.'

'Mr Mannidge and Ms Risolve?' Gordon asks. 'Or Mr Mannidge and Mr Vahatchett?'

'Yes,' she replies.

Nose still stinging with the tang of ozone, one hand still clutching a half-eaten blueberry danish, Gordon knocked on the door of room 302.

There was no immediate response. 'Ms Notid?' he called through the door's plastimahogany veneer. An answering thump and clatter suggested to Gordon, who was well accustomed to the sound, that the unfortunate guest had managed to get their foot stuck in the room's actively-camouflaged wastepaper bin. While a succession of clomps marked the guest's evident subsequent progress towards the door, Gordon wondered at the nature of the crisis that had led the South Mars team's legal expert to summon emergency assistance. It was, presumably, something pretty substantial – Ms Notid had struck him, from the start, as a very serious-minded, even a driven young woman.

But to Gordon's surprise, it was not Julie Notid who opened room 302's door.

'Sorry for the hold-up,' said Paul E Ritton, grinning awkwardly. 'Got something stuck on my foot—'

Gordon quickly peered past the would-be *auteur* to inspect what was visible of the room, which appeared entirely devoid of Notids and rather too well-equipped with camouflaged-wastepaper-bin-shackled Rittons. The room was also, to his relief, free of indications of flood, famine, fire, or other evident markings of hazard. 'There is some kind of emergency, Mr Ritton?'

'Yes – well, no, I mean, after a… why is your sleeve singed, Mr Mellotron?'

'That's not really impor—'

'Is that a *blueberry danish*?' Ritton asked. 'Where'd you get it?'

'It's from the replicator, down in the restaurant. But perhaps if you could—'

'So it's artificial? The danish?'

'I think the preferred term is "replicated". But really, Mr Ritton—'

'Does it taste as good as it looks?'

'Pretty much so, but… But this is beside the point. You signalled an emergency in – well, *someone* signalled an emergency in Ms No— in this room, which is occupied by one of the other guests.'

'Ah.'

'Could you please clarify what you mean by "ah"?' asked Gordon.

'Ah. Well, that's the thing, isn't it? It's not. Not anymore.'

'Not what?'

'Occupied by another guest, I mean. See, I met the woman who was in this room, in the vid lounge downstairs, and she let on that she'd been having trouble getting to sleep, on account of the guy was in the room nextdoor was snoring so loud. She – can I ask if you snore, Mr Marmalade?'

'I am not known,' Gordon replied, with all the chilled discipline he could muster, 'for the sonorousness of my somnolent episodes. But would you please return to the point?'

'Ah. Yes. Splendid. See, process of elimination. I knew it couldn't be the dictionarian, because he's in Whurd's old room, and I knew it couldn't be your offsider—'

'My what?'

'Your sidekick, your deputy, your what's-the-word?'

'Apprentice?'

'Apprentice, yes, I knew it couldn't be your apprentice, because I already found his room when I was knocking on doors at random, hoping to—'

'Mr Ritton. I must point out that hotel policy strongly discourages disruptive behaviour of that nature. No matter how keen you are to locate your publisher quarry.'

'And he gave me to understand that that was the case, too, your apprentice I mean. But it's alright, because I don't need to. Process of elimination, it has to be Whurd in 301. Because all the other guests are ladies, of the female persuasion. And their snores would be less bison-pitched.'

'Regrettably, Mr Ritton, I'm not at liberty to confirm nor deny your speculation,' replied Gordon. 'And I would take pains to point out that Mycroft Whurd is a *guest*, and as such is thus entitled to *certain standards of privacy*, which include but are most certainly not limited to the right to expect *a good night's sleep*, free of unwarranted interruption.'

'Oh, no problem there, Mr Murraine. I just thought I'd let you know that I'd switched rooms with the woman who'd been in here.'

'Notid.'

'Good, I thought you'd want a record.'

What I would want, Gordon thought, *is a lack of taserings and a bit of peace and quiet*. 'And the emergency is?' he asked.

'Well, not so much an emergency, more a notification, about the room change. I mean, it's the sort of thing you hotel people need to know, isn't it? I mean, in case there was an evacuation, or something like that.'

'Can I request,' said Gordon, rubbing the singed patch on his sleeve, 'that if you have any further notifications you need to bring to our attention, that you use the hotel's internal text-messaging service, rather than press the red 'Emergency' button?'

'Oh. Yes, I suppose that would be alright, Mr Marine.'

'Good. Now, was there anything else, Mr Ritton?'

'Not really. Except, where'd you say you got that blueberry danish, again?'

'Was that...' Gordon pauses to ensure he's got the right words for the task, those that best fit the puzzle. 'Was that an arrangement that was associated with any animosity, in any direction?' While he awaits her response, he wonders why it is that neither Steph Risolve nor Barry Vahatchett had seen fit to inform him of this feature of their relationship with the recently-departed Mannidge.

He wonders, too, at how he managed to miss any signs of multiple entangelement in his interviews with the other two North Mars delegates. Had one of them – or perhaps both – actively sought to deceive him? How had he not noticed?

'It wasn't all sweetness and light,' Jacinta replies. 'There were, I guess you'd say, differences of opinion that emerged from time to time. But no more, I'd say, than would be typical in any on-the-whole harmonious relationship. I don't pretend to be an expert in such matters, but—'

'Would you say that there'd been any recent increase in tension between the three of them?'

'I don't like being led on, Mr Mailman,' Jacinta says, a little sharply. 'No. I wouldn't say that there was any indication of… trouble in the area you speak of.'

'In other areas?'

Ms Yamayne-Fraim gives him a piercing glance. 'Of course, the negotiations are something that was preying on their minds. Lester's most of all.'

'The South's intention for a northern ocean, you mean? Was he out of his depth?'

'No,' she replies. 'But he was, of course, deeply concerned at the proposal, as you might imagine. Quite aside from the very real threat that that much flooding would present for our hemisphere, it cuts across his whole political ethos. I mean, this is a massive, massive intervention the South is trying to push through, and Lester Mannidge has based his entire political career on the ideal of smaller government.'

'And Ms Resolve and Mr Vahatchett were – are on board with this perspective?' asks Gordon.

'They had some differences in detail. I think that's what made them… useful to Lester. As advisers, I mean. But overall, yeah, they were in agreement with what he was trying to achieve.'

'Any, uh, further ambitions that might have pushed them to desperate measures, here? My apologies, Ms Yamay – Jacinta, but I do need to explore these details. There has been a death, and foul play is indicated.'

'I wouldn't say that either of them sought the limelight the way Lester did. He was very good at that stuff, the public debates, the advocacy, the outreach; whereas it wasn't what motivated them, not directly at any rate. I'd say they were happy to be powers behind the throne, as it were.'

'So in your opinion, neither Mr Vahatchett nor Ms Resolve would have had motivation to… remove Lester Mannidge from the equation?'

'No. No, I'd say he gave them both a strong sense of purpose. And besides that, they adored him.'

'And you, Ms Yamayne-Fraim?'

'Oh, they weren't too fond of me.'

'I mean,' clarifies Gordon, 'what were your own attitudes towards Lester Mannidge?'

'He's – he was – my employer, Mr Mantis. Lester was good to work for. And he may have gone overboard on some issues, everyone in politics does. But I fundamentally agreed with what he was seeking to do. I wouldn't have been able to work with him otherwise.' She pauses, gives Gordon a meaningful stare, sighs. 'He was a good man, and I'll miss him. And to answer the question you're skirting around, no, I didn't kill him. I had absolutely no reason to do so.'

'And your whereabouts…'

'We'd been holding a strategy meeting in the module's conference room. Planning for the mediation session with the Southies next week.'

'We?' He raises an eyebrow at her.

'Barry, Steph, and I. And Lester, although he'd left to – haven't Steph and Barry already filled you in on all this?'

'I'd prefer to get your version of events uncontaminated by any consideration of what I might already have been told, thanks,' Gordon remarks. 'So when was this, exactly?'

'The meeting would've started at about 22120 km. At – let me see – 21900 the sprinklers went off, briefly, then they did it again at around 21858 km. At 21855 Lester said he was just going to his room to get something – I think he was upset at the water damage to his paper business suit, and—'

'His what?' Gordon asks.

'His paper business suit. It was part of his schtick, his political persona, a statement that North Mars is sufficiently advanced to have clothing industries other than just synthetic. Nice suits, too... Pierre's of Arcadia. But not, as it turns out, showerproof. Not even colourfast.'

'Did Mr Mannidge say what he was seeking from his room?'

'No idea, sorry. I don't think he'd packed an umbrella.'

'And the rest of you? When did you leave the meeting, Ms Yamayne-Fraim?'

'We waited for another ten kilometres' descent or so, then we called a recess at about 21845 km.'

Gordon breathes in through his teeth. The timing matches the statements of Risolve and Vahatchett quite closely, and it tallies also with Belle's recollection of events, but it doesn't serve as ironclad alibi: Mannidge had been found dead, at 21835 km. 'Can I ask, how did you acquire that black eye?'

'Does it matter?' Jacinta asks, and there's something – a spark, a hesitancy – that catches Gordon's suspicions. Something to hide?

'It's best that I have all the facts at my disposal,' says Gordon.

'It's rather embarrassing,' confesses Jacinta. 'A while ago, I made a personal comment to Barry. Told him he'd need to harden up for the negotiations, or the South Mars delegates would wipe the floor with him.' She looks away, colour visibly rising to her cheeks. 'I was out of line, and I also used a couple of adjectives that – ah – elicited a certain... quenching response from the fittings; I guess I deserved what I got. But I was angry, and I guess I was feeling vulnerable about what had happened.'

'You felt that after the attack on Mannidge, that your life was in danger too?'

'No, I don't actually think that ever occurred to me, though perhaps it should. It was more a concern for my employment – you see, Steph and Barry, they're bona fide delegates in their own right, so assuming there's any kind of continuance to the political movement, their positions are assured, but mine was a direct appointment through Lester, and so with him now gone... I was angry, I said something I shouldn't have, and so this.' She points to the black eye.

'*So Mr Vahatchett struck you?*' Gordon probes, alert to the indication of a quick temper.

'*Not his style,*' remarks Jacinta. '*No, Mr Marimba, Barry didn't hit me. Steph did.*'

'*Would you say that was in character?*'

'*Wouldn't be the first time she's flared up.*' There's a gurgle from somewhere above her, and Ms Yamayne-Fraim peers up at the ceiling. '*Shit.*'

Taking the rampway back down to the lobby level, Gordon was struck with the recollection of how flavoursome had been the blueberry danish of recent memory, and how incompletely it had, in fact, sated his hunger. While he had no wish to descend full-tilt into gourmandry, there was, he judged, a quality-control case that could be made for repeating the important duty of sampling. The pastries had been replicated, rather than genuinely baked, which meant that there should be none of the variability, none of the human fallibility normally associated with the cooking process. A new one should, therefore, be as like its culinary template as would a clone; and while the human palate was not necessarily best-suited to the task of assessing verisimilitude, Gordon fancied that his own taste buds were, at least in the category of sweet pastries, equal to the challenge.

Besides, he quite fancied one.

The restaurant was still lit, but empty; a sign on the entrance, "Open Till Late", caught Gordon's eye, and he registered an "Aha!" moment at the sight of it, hoping he'd manage to retain it long enough to attempt to find that clue in the handheld's crossword.

Sue, it seemed, was not in residence for the moment, nor were the remaining breakfast pastries in evidence. He was reluctant to attempt to unlock the kitchen cupboards and pantries in search of them; and then, as he turned to depart, his eyes fell upon the replicator, stationed midway along the restaurant's longest wall. Tricked out in plastichrome, plastibakelite, and something that looked like it was supposed to look like wood but didn't, the device had a form somewhat suggestive of an illicit coupling between a 1950s-style jukebox and a jeweller's display cabinet, with a hint of high-voltage substation thrown in for good measure. Gordon remembered from Sue's demonstration of the device that the left-hand side of the cabinet was the "template" compartment and the right-hand side the "copy" compartment: a sample placed on the left would result – on the flick of a switch, the passage of a quarter-minute or so, and the generation of a series of frankly disturbing noises – in the apparently spontaneous generation of a replicated and ready-to-eat item in the right-hand section. There was also a mechanism for reproducing edibles from designs stored in the device's memory, but Gordon could not recollect with sufficient precision the algorithm ('Easy as,' she'd assured him) by which Sue had coaxed the device into producing a taster plate of potatoes *au gratin*, peppermint swirl ice cream, and Thai green curry chicken. Nor did he feel confident of his ability to extrapolate towards the invocation of a blueberry danish by this method. Unless the last user of the device had chosen to leave the item in question in one of the replicator's compartments, his quest for second supper would appear to be doomed.

He opened the left-hand compartment. Empty, save for a promisingly-suggestive but ultimately unsustaining dusting of pastry flakes on the compartment's plastichrome floor. Within the right-hand section, however, he had considerably more success: a tall plastiglass tumbler filled almost to the brim with water, and a sweet pastry item that would appear, on the visible evidence, to include berry among its constituents. He reached in, appreciative of his good fortune, then was struck with hesitancy.

If this was meant for someone else, he thought, *then it's inappropriate for me to take it.*

But this is a replicator, so... He lifted out the danish, placed it in the left-hand compartment, and then pressed the short sequence of buttons that he recollected from Sue's demonstration of the unit. There followed a short burst of awkward remorse, courtesy of Desiato's Law – *at night, all noises are louder* – but he was then rewarded with a blinking blue light and the materialisation of a duplicate danish in the right-hand compartment, some centimetres to the right of the tumbler of water.

It's a pity it doesn't replicate serving-plates as well, Gordon thought, lifting the newborn danish out onto his waiting palm before raising it to his mouth for a test bite.

Raspberry. He registered a momentary disappointment.

Dimly aware, in the darkness, that something was not as it should be, he tried turning over. Sometimes turning over helped.

Extra backstrap. (5,5)

No, turning over hadn't helped. Nor had staying up late on that puzzle. Sometimes, the things that were supposed to unwind just resulted in one getting more and more distracted. But was it actually obsessing over those crossword clues that had disturbed his sleep?

No, it wasn't. The afterimage on the inside of his eyelids, and the sharp smell of singed hair and ozone, could only mean that his handheld had tried to alert him to an incoming call. He'd really have to disable that taser setting on it. 'Lights,' he mumbled, and blinked blearily before sitting up and pressing the handheld's "call" button. Pushing his deerstalker nightcap to one side, he gingerly lifted the unit to his ear.

'Gordon?' Rube Greenhorn's voice sounded alarmed.

'Spare parts,' Gordon announced. *Must make a note of that one before I forget it again*, he told himself. 'Yes?'

'Beg pardon?' asked Greenhorn, in something of the tone of one who had requested a kitten and had just been presented, instead, with an aerosol deodorant and a receipt for repair of a ukuleke. 'Mr Gordon, sir? Are you awake?'

Probably, thought Gordon. *At least my brain must be working on some level, even if the escalators are out of order.* 'What's up?'

*

No answer.

He knocked again on the doorframe, louder, while Greenhorn stood behind him, still holding the tray bearing an empty glass and plate, which he'd been carrying when Gordon had arrived at the door.

Still no response.

Having pressed his ear against the door's slight opening and hearing nothing, he pushed gently and peered in. 'Mr Ritton?' he asked, at the threshold.

Still no answer. Gordon flicked a glance at Greenhorn, who looked stunned, perhaps even intimidated. *Has my reputation preceded me?* Gordon wondered. Then he slipped into the room.

He could never say just what it was that marked an area as "crime scene", but Ritton's room had it: that indefinable air of a room in which someone had sought to tidy up, so as to remove evidence, but in so doing had betrayed some fact of their presence. There was, for example, the neat stack of pen-scrawled sheets of paper, placed on the room's writing desk beside a very dog-eared copy of *5000 Useful Synonyms For "Say"*. There was the lack of any discarded clothing in the bathroom, or of any sense of disarray whatsoever in the room... other than Ritton himself, at any rate. The would-be novelist was slumped, dead, in a chair facing the curtain-shrouded window.

Or, no, not in fact dead: the man had a pulse. But he was quite fully unconscious, and could not be roused.

First aid was in Sue's purview. He gave her a call.

'Poisoned,' said Sue.

'Are you sure?' Gordon asked.

'Well, no,' she admitted. 'But it has all the hallmarks. I'll need to wait for the results of the tox scan – Gordon, why would anyone want to do this? *Who* would want to do this?'

'I have my suspicions,' he replied.

*

Seated in the cramped confines of his office, staring at his handheld, Gordon was faced with the unpalatable realisation that he had perhaps taken on something that he could not best.

184 Other: Allowance of false corrosion. (11)

Second letter "R", fifth "T", and tenth "O". At least, those were their identities assuming that his answers to 7 Across, 838 Down, and 3491 Through were correct. It wasn't the inherent difficulty of any of the individual clues, which were not harder than a standard cryptic (at least, that was his perception so far), nor their sheer number. He'd done jumbo-sized crosswords before, sometimes running into a couple of thousand words, but in those instances the spatial relationship between answers had always been readily apparent, even when the crossword grid itself was too large to be fully displayed on the modest screen of his handheld: it was simply a matter of scrolling down or across the grid to get to the next area one wished to work on. But the present puzzle... his device might have been up to the task of displaying the desired active layer of the 13 × 13 × 13 × 13 hypercube, but he was unequal to the exercise of visualising the interrelationship between the hundreds of clued layers. Which meant, among other things, that an error in any one of the almost ten thousand word-answers required for the puzzle's eventual completion might be almost impossible to find. Gordon was having serious doubts about one of the answers he had entered yesterday, and could not even remember where in the four-dimensional crossword puzzle it fitted.

Frustration. He rapped his stylus repeatedly against his forehead, ground his molars against each other, and stared blankly at the currently-active layer of the puzzle.

Murder mysteries might sometimes have too few clues. But perhaps that was better than having too many.

The handheld vibrated so vigorously against his palm that he dropped it in startlement. *I suppose it's better than the taser setting*, he conceded, bending to pick it up. *But still...*

On the screen, the myriad layers of the hypercubic crossword puzzle proceeded to dissolve into a misty grey (Gordon hoped he'd remembered to save his recent progress) which then segued into a dark blue background on which the number "401" flashed persistently.

401? But there's nobody in 401, Gordon thought. 401 had been Ritton's original room, before he'd relocated, thrice, in his pursuit of Whurd. Gordon wondered whether it was worthwhile trying to call up the module's guest listing, but decided against it. *Rube's still learning the ropes on front desk. If I haven't been able to stay current with all the to-ings and fro-ings from room to room, it's parsecs to picometres that the system hasn't kept track either. Which is going to make billing interesting...* He stood up, hesitantly picked up his handheld, and walked out towards the rampway.

At 401, he was met by the depressingly familiar tweed-encased sight of Mycroft Whurd, standing and waiting with all of the florid, out-of-breath confusion of a boiler-suited marathon runner looking to learn what his time had been, and whether there was any prospect of being able to claim it as a personal best.

Whurd certainly looked far from his personal best. His trousers were rumpled, his boots were unlaced, his normally oil-sheened hair unruly, and his old school tie was so askew that its ringed-planet tiepin was only hanging on by the most tentative of fabric margins. 'Been... looking... everywhere... for... you,' he explained, between desperate gulps of air.

Everywhere? wondered Gordon. *It's not that big a module.* 'Mr Whurd?' Gordon asked. 'Do you require some assistance?'

'Indeed... I do. I seem... to be locked... out of my room, and the biometrics... aren't recognising me.'

'And your room would be...?'

'This one. I was in here... just before, and—'

'There's sometimes a delay before the biometric recognition kicks in,' Gordon explained. 'When guests change their rooms repeatedly—'

'Mr Macrame,' Whurd protested, his eyes wide with the enormity of his perceived predicament. 'Every ruddy minute we are standing here...

outside my room… is another minute during which… He Who Should Never Have Been Taught To Write… might chance upon us here in the corridor, and then this blasted relocation… would be all for nought. Please, I urge you—'

Not actually much chance of that, Gordon told himself, *with Ritton currently comatose and under observation in the sick bay.* But he pulled the prosthetic thumb and plastic eyeball from his pocket nonetheless.

I hope Sue gets back to me soon with that tox scan, he thought. *Is it poisoning, or something more benign like merely an infectious disease? I need to know whether I should be treating Whurd as a suspect.*

The door's biometric sensibilities satisfied, he pushed the door open for the book magnate and made his escape before Whurd could inflict on him any further tales of the unsolicited-submission-related atrocities the publisher had suffered at the hands of the now-indisposed Ritton.

He had made perhaps eight steps down the rampway, towards the lobby, when his handheld started to shake disturbingly within the confines of his jacket pocket.

He pulled it out. 'Gordon,' he announced.

'We've got a problem,' Belle informed him. She sounded breathless, and rather strained.

'Are the sprinklers still acting up?' he asked.

'I'm afraid it's a bit worse than that,' she said.

It was, indeed, a bit worse than that.

2

What was worst about Gordon's immediate surroundings, in the hotel module's underbasement area wherein were stowed all the unglamorous items of heavy machinery associated with the module's climate control, artificial gravity, and disaster-response systems, was the stricken, stunned-rabbit expression on the face of Rube Greenhorn, who stood off to one side holding an utterly irrelevant length of plasticopper tubing.

Gordon, wrestling with the inflexible encasements of a spacesuit which he swore had shrunk since the last time he'd worn it, wished he had a better calibre of advice than 'Just don't touch anything until I get back' to offer Rube, whom he was about to leave as acting second-in-command under Sue's supervision, while he himself made the awkward transit up-cable to Belle's module, 271, which was currently between fourteen and fifteen kilometres above Module 270. Gordon wished, also, that he had more trust in the apprentice's ability to cope with the situation, and to make the right decisions. *Not his fault,* Gordon told himself. *It's only his second day on the job. I daresay any of us would have felt as out of our depth in such circumstance.* But he didn't have complete faith in the youngster's capabilities, and he couldn't help that. Not at the moment.

Was he deserting Module 270 to the attentions of a would-be killer, while he was off investigating the apparent murder in Module 271? It did not sit right with him, by any means, and yet the options available, mid-descent like this, were extremely limited. There was no-one else qualified, aboard any of the modules 265 to 275, nor were any of those other modules sufficiently generously staffed that any crew could be migrated to Module 270 to make up the shortfall that his departure would necessitate. *Personnel run the duty rosters too tight; it's been inevitable for months that something like this would happen. Well, well, well.* It was an impasse; it was a mess; it was a sow's ear.

He completed the check of seals on his suit's ankles, wrists, and crotch, then, exhaling heavily, he lifted the helmet over his head and lowered it into place. Just as he was fastening the heavy neck-flange that connected helmet to torso, Rube rapped on his visor.

'What?' he asked, the word reverberating so splendidly within the helmet's confines that he could not make out any of Rube's short reply. He loosened the flange and removed the helmet. 'What?' he asked again.

'How long do you expect to be off-module?' Rube asked.

'I honestly don't know,' replied Gordon. 'It's one of those piece-of-string situations.'

Rube stared at him blankly.

'I mean, it's like asking how long is a piece of string,' Gordon explained.

'What do I need string for?' Rube asked.

'It's a – look, forget it. I mean, I don't know how long this will take. Hopefully not too long. But it does sound as though there's been a serious incident on 271, so it will require investigation. And the sooner I get over there, the sooner it's done.' He pulled the helmet on again. It was almost fastened when Rube again knocked on the visor.

'What?' Gordon asked, then pulled the visor off. 'What?'

'It's just, I was reading the Skyward Health and Safety guidelines last night, and—'

'Yes. Quite right. In a situation where there are more than eight guests on board, module staffing numbers must not fall below three employees at any one time.'

'And we've got nine guests, the six delegates and the others, 'cause Mr Ritton's still alive.' Rube sounded as though he were unhappy about the last part of that statement.

'Rube,' said Gordon, with slow seriousness, 'this is an *emergency*. There is scope for some discretion in emergency situations, provided that all reasonable efforts are made to ensure the safety of our valued guests at all times. Investigating the murder – apparent murder – on 271 is part of the process of ensuring the safety of Skyward's guests.'

'Remaining guests,' noted Rube.

'*Remaining* guests,' Gordon echoed. 'Yes. Naturally, if there are any problems that arise during my absence'—*and I hope to hell there will not be*—'then please, in the first instance, act in accordance with Sue's instructions. Beyond that, I can of course be contacted in an emergency.' He pulled his helmet on again and set about fastening it.

Rube rapped on the visor.

'*What?*' Gordon asked, at such volume that the reverb almost gave him tinnitus. He pulled the helmet off. 'What, Rube?'

'Sorry, Mr Gordon,' Rube replied. 'I just thought – you'll need your handheld, won't you? Have you got it with you?'

Gordon tapped the hip pouch on his suit, with sufficient force that he was momentarily concerned that he might have traumatised the enclosed handheld's touchscreen. 'Yes, Rube. I've got my handheld. Now, please, I need to go.' He pulled his helmet back on, and gave Greenhorn a meaningful stare through the visor before cinching it down. This time he got as far as commencing the suit's airtightness test before he was once again interrupted by the hesitant clump of Rube's fingers lightly knocking on the helmet.

'Oh, for heaven's sake, Rube,' Gordon snapped, allowing the helmet to drop with an impact-testing clatter to the underbasement's plasticrete decking. '*What?*'

Rube, who looked both shocked and a little intimidated by Gordon's outburst, stammered in reply. 'I – I – sorry, I just thought – I need… uh, when you said "emergency"…'

'Yes?'

'Would that include if Mr Ritton were to – uh, become dead? Even though that would mean we only had eight guests left, and would then not be in breach of the module staffing guidelines?'

Gordon closed his eyes, took the longest breath he could, and willed himself calm. 'Mr Greenhorn,' he said carefully. 'I cannot emphasise strongly enough that Mr Ritton's death, indeed the death of *any* guest, would constitute not only an emergency, but also a *very bad thing* for at least three important reasons.'

'Oh,' said Rube, smaller-voiced than Gordon had ever heard him before. 'Of course, I didn't mean—'

'I'm sure you didn't,' said Gordon. *I hope you didn't.* 'For reference, those reasons are, one, that it would obviously cause considerable grief, torment and anguish to our other guests, and to Mr Ritton's family, friends, and associates once they learnt of his demise. And two, that such a circumstance would engender substantial and severe reputational damage to Skyward Transorbital Enterprises as a whole, and to Module 270 and its staff in particular. Are you clear on that?'

'Y-yes, Mr Gordon, quite clear. But—'

'But what?'

'You said three,' complained Rube. 'And you only gave two.'

Gordon picked his helmet up and eyed the airlock forlornly before turning back to the apprentice. 'Paperwork,' he explained.

The task of transferring from one module to another, mid-descent, was inherently difficult and not a little dangerous. It could, in Gordon's humble estimation, have been made a little *less* dangerous had Skyward's health and safety experts, in all their deskbound wisdom, not forbidden the use of the escape pods for module-to-module transit. It was, therefore, accordingly with sullen disgruntlement that Gordon, standing five minutes ago in what now, in hindsight, could be acknowledged as the comparative security of the module airlock, had activated the switch which would automatically fire off the guywire missile. But wishing the transfer protocol were different would not change the fact that he was currently tethered to the roof of a steadily-falling module while he waited for the missile to intercept its target docking port on the base of Module 271, fourteen kilometres above him. A well-worn one-size-fits-all spacesuit, of the exact model for which McGuffin Spaceready had issued a system-wide recall notice last year because of ongoing problems with the airtightness of the knee joints, was all that protected him from hard vacuum; a thoroughly inadequate plastilastic tether was all that anchored him to the roof of the lift module; he wasn't even sure what was currently safeguarding him against the hazardous radiation and high magnetic field strength that pertained at this altitude, but he hoped *something* was.

The hotel's guests, he suspected, would have been horrified at the state of the module's roof surface: repeated re-entry, even the carefully constrained re-entry of a space elevator module through Earth's oxidising and reactive atmosphere, was not kind towards exposed surfaces of metal, glass, and ceramic. Superficially-smooth panels on the module's roof were pitted and stained; the structural ribs and framework were scored, scarred, space-corroded. The metre-wide collar at the centre of the roof, fitting snugly around the tens-of-thousands-of-kilometres-tall central column of the space elevator cable itself, was friction-burned and blackened by oxidation, against which some enterprising soul had been inspired to etch a line of graffiti which would not have been out of place in a gentleman's restroom of less than elegant repute.

The module's exterior, of course, was not subject to the artificially-generated gravity fields which facilitated normal human hotel-ish operations on the floors contained within. This meant that when Gordon saw fit to check, on his glove's wristpatch, the time elapsed since the guywire missile deployment, with his other glove holding the lightweight compressed-gas sled which would propel him precariously from module 270 to 271, there was nothing to stop him bungeeing to the tether's maximum extension while the module beneath him experienced a transitory burst of downward acceleration. It took all his composure to maintain a grip on the precious sled, rather than to ditch it in what his hindbrain assured him was an essential desperate grab for some last-ditch fasthold. Though he was fairly sure module 270 carried one or two spare sleds, he was also sure that he didn't know where they were right now.

The tether started to pull back, and it dawned on Gordon that getting flung off into space by a snapped plastilastic cable might not be so much worse a fate than getting flung back towards a roof surface composed exclusively of unremittingly hard material, while one was encased in a threadbare spacesuit that, he could now see, had already been vacuum-patched in at least three places. He braced for impact, hoping desperately that nothing would rip when he slammed into the roof. He bounced painfully, his left side cushioning the blow, and without thinking flung his arm out to grab hold of the thin guywire which would, when the missile struck home, form the connection between the two modules. *Idiot*, he told himself, even as his subconscious willed his gloved fingers to close on the shining thread. *The wire's still being drawn out, you'll either get your gloves cut or it'll yank so fast the tether snaps.* But his grip on the guywire caused neither of these calamities, and after some careful testing he concluded that the missile must have reached its destination: the wire was no longer spooling out, it was stationary, taut, and was presumably ready to use.

Weird, he thought. *The missile's supposed to send a "target achieved" notification when it gets there. And it hasn't been that long since it was fired off...* He could check on his handheld, but he couldn't keep hold of the wire, the handheld, *and* the sled all at once. But there seemed little harm in fastening the sled to the wire, so he did this. (The "fastening" process, deceptively simple according to the description offered in the Skyward EVA procedures manual, took a few minutes of zero-gravity confusion and panic: conservation of momentum still held, apparently, as did its little brother, conservation of angular momentum. Gordon was sweating and breathing heavily, his heart racing, by the time he had completed the manoeuvre.) Then he buckled himself loosely to the sled and pulled the handheld out of his suit's hip pouch, stabbing at it bluntly with gloved fingers. After inadvertently ordering a gluten-free pizza and accidentally opting in to Skyward's "Adopt-an-Interstellar-Guest" home billetting scheme, he succeeded in confirming that the guywire did indeed completely span the gulf between modules 270 and 271. He was ready to go. He tightened the sled's buckles, adopted the suggested optimum posture for safe transit (which largely involved wrapping one's limbs around the casing that surrounded the guywire's narrow thread, in what he always thought of as the "minimum dignity posture", so as to keep the assembly's centre of mass aligned with the wire) and announced 'Engage!'

The sled slid upward, slowly to begin with but at steadily gathering velocity. The disc outline of Module 270's roof dwindled at alarming speed, and Gordon was newly conscious of being a small and imperfectly coccooned entity in a very big and uncaring environment.

The sled was fully capable of hitting a speed of two hundred kilometres an hour relative to the falling modules, sufficient to traverse the required distance in just a few minutes. But the trick, he knew from bitter experience that owed equally to those twinned concepts of "hitting" and "speed", was to ensure that sufficient reserves of propellant remained to brake safely before he reached his destination. Though 271's ablation-resistant underside would stop him very effectively, it would not do so gently.

Below him, still so far below him that the Earth was very obviously just a planet, of which he could see virtually a complete hemisphere from pole to pole, it was night. A thousand cities shone, all those points of light so close together. So brilliant. So beautiful. So many, many people. Such a large expanse of rock, so much gravity, waiting for him, if he fell.

Gordon wasn't good with heights. He forced himself to look away, ahead along the thread that carried him to Module 271.

It might be a lapse of itself. (9)

Risolve was solidly-built, tall, and dark-skinned, with a curly nimbus of bright orange hair surrounding a rounded, green-eyed face;

Vahatchett was even taller (it was a Martian-gravity thing, Gordon knew; those who had been born on the planet, with genes still programmed to fight against Earth's gravity, shot up like beanpoles when they hit puberty), but spare, stooped, and with quite the slenderest head Gordon had seen on any human.

Both looked like they'd been through the wringer.

He had reservations about interviewing them together, but they were a couple (they had been, with Mannidge, a triple); they had individually succeeded in concealing from Gordon, in his earlier interviews with them, the possibly-salient fact of their relationship; and he was well aware that (1) he was running out of time to solve the murder before they reached ground level and (2) he had left Module 270 shortstaffed.

'Are you any closer to finding the killer?' Steph Risolve asked him, her voice brittle, hoarse. She was leaning across the table in a manner that suggested she'd prefer to be the one conducting the interview.

'No,' said Gordon, who'd spent several hours on various activities, all of them fruitless. He'd perused the security-cam footage from the corridor outside Mannidge's hotel room (the repeated sprinkler activations seemed to have permanently fogged up the security-cam lenses all through 271). He'd interviewed the two guests not affiliated with the North Mars political delegation – to whit, the sentimental balladeer Aretha Durchiroma and the avant-garde composer Mustapha Wynd-Masheen, a task which had been rendered all the more unpleasant through the ever-present aural background, during the latter interview, of the interviewee's hauntingly evocative *Dirge Inspired By A Three-Hour Primary School Brass Band Recital*. And he'd swotted up, via his handheld, on all things Mannidge, hoping to get a sense for the man, his politics, the battles he might have fought in public and private life; hoping to learn *something* of why someone, here, now, had wanted him dead. 'No, I've learnt nothing,' he confessed. Durchiroma and Wynd-Masheen had apparently been rehearsing together at the time of Mannidge's death and in any case did not, he thought, have the temperament for murder; and if there were hints in Mannidge's history as to who might be his personal – rather than purely political – enemies, such hints had eluded Gordon. 'I'm clueless.'

'I wouldn't say that,' offered Vahatchett kindly, reaching across the table to take Risolve's hand. 'A little obtuse, certainly, but…'

'But this is beside the point,' Gordon noted, seeking to strike as sympathetic a tone as he could in the circumstances. 'I need to ask you to review your earlier statements, so we can ascertain whether there's something important within this investigation that I've missed. Something as important, for example, as *a romantic entanglement between several of the principals.*'

'But Mr Mansion,' protested Vahatchett. 'You surely aren't suggesting that Steph or myself were somehow involved in poor Lester's tragic end?'

'I'm not *suggesting* anything in particular,' Gordon replied carefully. 'But just as your own relationship never figured in our earlier discussion, there may well have been other… details… which you neglected to mention. I've no wish to be playing with fi— ahem, that is, I fully understand that the Martian terraforming debate is a high-stakes matter—'

'You're telling *me*,' Risolve snapped, her anger palpable. She was speaking at town-meeting volume, almost a shout. 'The South's proposal gets up, my home town's going to be five kilometres underwater. You can't tell me that's equitable!'

Gordon exhaled, steepled his fingers, looked methodically towards both Risolve and Vahatchett before saying, 'Leaving aside the obvious complexities and capacity for injustice, I still need to ask: who would want Lester Mannidge dead? I asked you this before; I'm having to ask it again, out of concern I've overlooked something. *Someone* wanted him dead. I mean, there's no smoke without fi— um. So who would profit from his… removal?'

'Nobody in politics,' Vahatchett ventured meekly.

'You mean nobody within the – uh – sphere of Northern hemisphere politics, I presume,' said Gordon.

'No, I don't think there'd be anyone anywhere on Mars,' explained Vahatchett, 'who would have profited from his death.'

'But he had *plenty* of enemies in the South,' Gordon noted. 'I've got a module full of them, just fifteen kilometres below us. I'm sure they'd all be keen to add fuel to the fi—'

In the gurgling pipes above the ceiling, it sounded very much as though something was growing tetchy.

'True,' conceded Risolve, now sounding somewhat calmer. 'But the geographic divide on this issue is remarkably clear. Everyone in the Northern hemisphere backs a low-sea-level Mars; everyone in the Southern hemisphere wants the high sea level. But Lester is – was – an astute advocate for the Northern case, and his death has effectively made him a martyr, damn near a saint. That's automatically made it harder for the South to get the outcome they want, and they know it. They're stubborn, they're one-eyed, they often seem incapable of listening to reason; but I can't believe anyone within Southern politics would have been foolish enough to have expected that eliminating Lester would aid their cause. It hasn't; it won't; and Barry and I won't let it.' She flicked a deep, sad smile towards Vahatchett. 'Now, Mr Maudlin, if there's nothing else you have to ask us, we all have work to do. You have a killer to catch, and we have a political case to prosecute.'

Barry Vahatchett stood. 'You *will* catch him, or her, will you not, Mr Mayhem?' he asked.

'I'd better,' Gordon replied. 'Else he or she may strike again, and then we really will be out of the frying pan and into the fire.'

'GORDON!' Belle yelled, from what must have been at least two floors up.

The module, Gordon decided a short time later, could really have done with better drainage.

*

There had been seven people, not counting Mannidge, on Module 271 at the time of the victim's death. Of those seven, Luke Owtbellow, the ingenious but butterfingered liftmodule maintenance worker, had been offshift and asleep; Aretha Durchiroma and Mustapha Wynd-Masheen had been audibly rehearsing two floors up from Mannidge's room; Belle Hopp had been in reception, tallying the restaurant receipts; Steph Resolve and Barry Vahatchett were presumably the two smudges just visible through the sprinkler-fogged security telemetry, as they walked along the corridor towards the connecting rooms that they shared. Only Jacinta Yamayne-Fraim could not be adequately accounted for; but Gordon couldn't believe that Yamayne-Fraim was the killer. The security-cam footage of Mannidge's corridor might be hopelessly indistinct for identification purposes, but it was enough to show that the silhouetted killer was someone reasonably stocky, and Yamayne-Fraim was rake-thin, and half a head taller. And why would someone murder their employer, if it then meant they'd be out of work? Jacinta had not sounded unhappy about her employment, far from it…

It had occurred to Gordon that the rationale which Risolve and Vahatchett had given – for why Mannidge's assassination made no political sense – worked from a South-Mars but not from a North-Mars perspective. If Mannidge became a martyr to the cause, this almost automatically furthered the interests of the North-Mars team… so why *not* bump him off? It might technically be possible that either Risolve or Vahatchett were playing a duplicitous game of lovestruck grief, when one or other of them was in fact the murderer. But was either of them a sufficiently skilled actor to fool not only Gordon, but their surviving partner and Yamayne-Fraim as well? Gordon had thought the indications of affection between the two of them, in his recent interview, genuine and unforced… and the security-cam footage did appear to show the two of them entering their rooms together shortly before Mannidge's death. So *that* seemed not to tally.

If the *who* of it was proving vexatious, at least the *how* of it had met with some signs of progress. In an episode of lucidity, Gordon's handheld had identified the means of death as a close-range blast beam, probably from a distance of two metres or less. The weapon indicated, from the pattern of gore, energy profile, etc, was the Callahan Daymaker. (Gordon had heard of the Daymaker, and did not need to follow the handheld's indicated link to learn of its infamy: it was a byword in overengineered deadliness, and was the preferred stock-in-trade of such notorious underworld figures as Robert Gunpoynt and Phil M Fuller-Hoals.) Although the evidence for the deployment of such weaponry in Mannidge's hotel room was almost irrefutable (leaving unanswered only the question of how many blasts had been discharged), a full security sweep of the module, encompassing all internal and external surfaces, in the hours since Gordon had initiated his investigation, had uncovered no such device.

Mannidge was dead, and Gordon was missing something. He fired up his handheld again.

7328 Across. Harbour a paper size, all in stock. (9)

He had been sitting for hours, reviewing the same short bit of fogged-up security footage, on which the handheld had been attempting a myriad variations of image enhancement – and overheating alarmingly in the process. All the while, he had been subjected to the same short piece of repeated music; for Mustapha Wynd-Masheen had persuaded Luke of the need to cheer up the module's bereaved guests, and what better way to effect such cheer than through the high-rotation performance of Wynd-Masheen's perhaps-unjustly-maligned one-note erotic tone poem for snare drum, trombone, and excessively amplified kazoo, *The Bare Minim*? ("Almost any other way" would have been Gordon's strong recommendation, but he had not been consulted.) Contemporaneously with these visual and aural repetitions, his mind had been looping of its own accord over a couple of the more problematic of the many clues within the four-dimensional crossword puzzle that was one of his current vexations. He was on the cusp of deciding that there was something on which he had nearly almost made an important realisation, something crucial, or just possibly of falling asleep, when the handheld beeped.

'Gordon,' he answered.

'Mr Gordon?' asked the caller.

From the information available, Gordon deduced that the appellant was Rube Greenhorn. 'Rube? What's up? Is everything alright?'

'It's Mr Ritton,' Rube said. He sounded worried. 'And no, he's not alright. The tox tests have come through, and Sue said to tell you, it was definitely poisoning.'

'Poisoning? Is he still... with us?'

'He's in the sick bay,' said Rube. 'Which is located next to the restaurant, on the lobby lev—'

'I mean,' said Gordon, dreading the worst, 'is he still alive?'

'Yes,' said Rube. 'So we're still technically short staffed. But you said not to worry about that so much?'

'I did say that,' replied Gordon. 'Did Sue say what kind of poison had been used?'

'She doesn't know, exactly,' said Rube. 'Something weird and botanical, she thinks.'

'How is Mr Ritton?'

'He's bedridden, he seems very weak. But he's conscious now, though he's not making much sense actually. Said he's got an idea that's sure to get him the prize for the second-best science fiction novel of the year.'

'*Is* there a prize for the second-best science fiction novel of the year?'

'He reckons there is. Says it's the Constellation Prize.'

'Has he been able to shed any light on the circumstances of his poisoning?'

'Like I said, he's not making much sense. He's been rabbitting on about this disaster novel of his, after the koi apocalypse has occurred.'

'Coy apocalypse?' Gordon asked, bamboozled.

'It's when the goldfish have risen up and taken over, apparently,' Rube explained. 'Paul calls it *Sturgeon's Law: Ninety Percent of Every Fish is Carp*. Uh, maybe it'd help if you interviewed him?'

'Rube, I'm in the middle of a murder investigation here, I—' Gordon stared at the hopelessly-indistinct image on the screen. *It's all the fault of that water in the way. All those little water droplets, each one its own little lens...* 'Oh. Yes, maybe you're right. Maybe that's why the blue light was on.'

'Huh? Mr Gordon, what d'you mean?'

'When I find out,' Gordon replied, more portentously than he had intended, 'I'll let you know.'

Oversight. Of course. But then ... what was 7328 across?

Belle came down to the 271 underbasement with him to see him off.

'I do not feel comfortable just scurrying off like this,' he confessed.

'Oh, nonsense!' she replied. 'You've got a poisoning to investigate.'

'And I'm leaving you with an unsolved murder. And therefore, by implication,' he said, throwing his arms wide, in a spacesuit which would persist in squeaking in a most undignified fashion, 'with a murderer still at large.'

'*Gordon,*' she said, staring earnestly into his eyes, 'it's alright. You have to go. I'll cope. *You'll* cope. I'm more worried about you than I am about me, to be honest. You seem to attract murderers the way email attracts spam.'

'Yes, well,' he said. 'Please let me know if there are any developments I need to know about.'

'*Of course,*' she replied. 'Say, you're sure you want to get back to module 270 by sled? Luke has that tightrope-walking contraption he cobbled together, it's a bit, uh, idiosyncratic but I'm sure you'd get the hang of it...'

'Well – no, look, please thank him on my behalf, for the generous offer, but I've seen some of his earlier freelancing engineering projects, so I think it's better that I take the sled again, rather than Luke's guywalker.'

Gordon stepped into the airlock and unclipped the sled from its charging station, holding it awkwardly in gloved hands while he strived to find something to say to close out the conversation.

Belle was staring at the sled. 'Is that the one you came over on?' she asked.

'Think so,' said Gordon. 'Yes, I'm sure. This is exactly where I fastened it when I arrived yesterday. Why?'

'Don't you see?'

'No. What?'

'Turn it over.'

He did. On the inner surface of the sled, a set of prominent identification digits were emblazoned: 271.

'This is not the sled that Module 270 began its descent with.'

'So what the hell does that mean?'

'Belle, I think I've just spent a day interviewing the wrong group of suspects.'

3

Gordon had much to think about on the sled traversal back to Module 270, not all of it concerned with the likelihood of his probable cremation in the event of failure of the guywire's structural integrity, nor with the terrible beauty of the burgeoning day/night landscape on display beneath him, in far too disturbingly clear a panorama for one so troubled with altitudinous concerns. Forcing himself to ignore the fact that he was currently hurtling Earthwards at an uncomfortably high velocity (for all that said Earth was still several thousand kilometres distant beneath him), he tried to mull over the ramifications of Mannidge's murder, in light of the revelation (as it now appeared) that someone had journeyed, before Gordon had himself, from 270 to 271 – presumably using the module 270 sled – had then murdered Mannidge, and had then, for reasons known only to themselves, returned to 270 using the 271 sled. *Why?* And who?

And what was Mannidge's murder intended to achieve? As Risolve and Verhatchett had noted, the death actually played quite neatly into the North's hands... so, while the switched sled gave the South Mars delegation on Module 270 a new lease of life as suspects in terms of opportunity, it really put them no further ahead in terms of motive... but if not the South Mars contingent, who else? Surely none of the bookish crowd (particularly since Ritton at least was already himself incapacitated by that point), Sue was above reproach, and he was almost certain it wasn't the sort of thing Rube Greenhorn would do either. Which left him where he was on Module 271: with a murder that nobody could have committed.

At least with Ritton's poisoning he was fairly sure he knew who the culprit was. Which, he supposed, was something to be thankful for.

Distracted, he left his sled-braking run too late, with the result that two things hit him simultaneously, and with considerable (though fortunately not crippling) force.

One was the final, the crucial clue: *7328 Across. Harbour a paper size, all in stock. (9).* Portfolio.

The other was the roof of Module 270.

Gordon's primary concern, after ensuring that his suit had not sprung a leak, was to hope that his handheld had not been damaged in the impact.

'Sue, I've solved the Ritton thing. I'll fill you in shortly – don't let anyone touch the replicator in the meantime. But first I need you to run some background checks for me, please. On our passengers.'

'It's really good to see you again too, Gordon,' replied Sue, in an aren't-you-forgetting-an-anniversary tone of voice, while she wiped clean a benchful of plasticrystal goblets in the restaurant.

'Sorry. I've had a rough twenty-four hours, and travel by sled doesn't agree with me at the best of times. Look, I know background checks on guests aren't exactly by-the-book—'

'That's putting it mildly, if you're asking what I think you're asking. I could lose my job for a violation of passenger privacy like that, Gordon.'

'I *know* that, Sue, and if I could think of a way around this, I would. But we're due to reach Earth within the next day, and whoever killed Lester Mannidge could well escape for lack of evidence unless I can find the motive. Someone on board this module had some reason to kill him, and I want to know what it is. I don't know it; my handheld doesn't know it. Sue, you're my last hope. Will you do it?'

'Let me think it over. I don't put my arse on the line lightly, you know. But why don't you tell me about who poisoned Ritton?'

Gordon told her of his suspicions, and her eyes widened. 'That is really bloody tricky,' she said.

*

Sue had said that Ritton was well enough to receive visitors, so Gordon had called into the sick bay with some carefully-replicated grapes, a "Get Well Soon" card, and a copy of *Success In Writing Isn't Everything* that he, Sue, and Rube had all signed. Sue and Rube had tagged along.

'How are you feeling?' Gordon asked, handing over the offerings, which were dutifully placed on the bedside table. Gordon couldn't help noticing that the book (into whose selection he'd placed some considerable thought before asking for Sue's assistance in dialling it up via the replicator) hadn't received a second glance since being unwrapped.

'I'm feeling a bit better,' croaked Paul E Ritton. 'I'm really keen to get back into writing. You know, a few years back, I wrote a couple of adventure-fantasy books called *Ear of Krypton* and *Nose of Xenon*, and I'm feeling motivated to write the prequel, but I can't work out what it should be called. Any suggestions?'

'I'm just glad you're feeling better,' said Sue.

'No, that wouldn't—' began Ritton.

'There seems to be some bally confusion over the lunch menu,' announced Mycroft Whurd, who pushed his way into the gathering of hotel employees and then, catching sight of Ritton, sought to backpedal his way out.

'No, please stay, Mr Whurd,' said Gordon. 'We were just about to explain to Mr Ritton the nature of his... illness, and I'm afraid it's almost unavoidable that suspicion very quickly fell upon yourself in that matter. Actually... Rube, if you would be so kind?'

'Mr Gordon?'

'Could you please go and check whether Dr Bayson is currently available? I'm feeling versatile at the moment, I'd like to have a go at settling the poisoning and the murder in one fell swoop, and we may as well have all the protagonists gathered together.'

Rube dashed off.

'Sue, can you connect this through to Belle in 271?' Gordon asked.

'Sure, but transmission between modules is still rather patchy at these altitudes.'

'Just do the best you can.'

'I have a meeting with Alexei Kograffa in half an hour,' warned Whurd.

'I'm hoping it won't be necessary to detain you that long,' said Gordon, as Greenhorn returned with a somewhat confused-looking Phillippa Bayson in tow.

'What's this all about?' Dr Bayson asked.

'In large part,' Gordon replied, 'I've requested your presence as a representative of the South Mars delegation, because this concerns the murder of representative Lester Mannidge of the North Mars delegation—'

'Surely you don't think any of *us* would be capable of such a callous, despicable act! Why, Lester was – was—'

'We'll come to that, all in good time. But first I wish to canvas the fate of our poor novelist, Mr Ritton—'

'He *is* a dashed poor novelist, at that,' interjected Whurd.

'I'm not sure you're helping your case,' replied Gordon. 'Fortunately for you, while you may well have had ample motive for wishing Paul E Ritton ill, yours appears not to have been the hand – or, indeed, hands – which did him in. Indeed, it would appear that I played my own small part in his near demise, and had I chosen differently, his fate might well have instead been my own.'

'You what?' asked Rube.

'Quite unintentionally, of course. It was the replicator,' explained Gordon. 'It uses a collimated photon beam to interrogate the precise atomic structure of any foodstuff – I'm not completely sure what that means myself, but it's what it says in the brochure and it sounds as though it ought to make sense – so the crucial thing is that the beam has to get through the foodstuff to the detector. When I went down to the restaurant for a… uh, late-night snack a couple of nights ago, I found that someone had left a raspberry danish and a glass of water in the replicator side of the device. The glass of water is the crucial bit – it acted as a lens, thus ensuring that what got replicated wasn't the raspberry danish that had been on the sample side, but what was, through a coincidence of optics, *its mirror image* – and the mirror image of one of the artificial flavourings in the danish was actually a very harmful, though fortunately not quite fatal, additive in the looking-glass danish. I unknowingly replicated, and then ate, a mirror image of the mirror image, which was safe, and incidentally quite delicious; Mr Ritton, who I gather visited the replicator some few minutes after me, found the toxic mirror image, and consumed it with the results which are evident now before us. The offending glass of water, which Mr Ritton also carried off and which Rube Greenhorn here had found in Ritton's room when he notified me of Mr Ritton's unfortunate condition was, I gather, called into existence by yourself, Dr Bayson.'

'Was it?' she asked. 'Oh. Oh. Oh, my goodness, you're right. I'd just dialled it up, and then I got a message from Marsha Notions that I simply had to respond to then and there, so I forgot – I am *so* sorry, Mr Ritton. Please believe me, this was never intentional, in the slightest extent.'

'I don't believe anyone's suggesting it was,' said Gordon. 'And it does appear that Mr Ritton is well on the way to a recovery, which is a substantial relief to all concerned, though it does suggest Skyward needs to ensure the device is appropriately labelled, so guests can be alerted to the hazards associated with its use. But now we come to the murder.'

'I really must be getting to that ruddy appointment with Alexei,' said Whurd.

'*Stay*,' said Gordon, and motioned for Rube to block the doorway.

'What confused me for the past day and a half was that I couldn't see who stood to gain from Lester Mannidge's death,' explained Gordon. 'There are certainly people here present who are opposed to the political movement he represented, but the nature of political representation in society is such that assassination does not normally advance the opponent's cause. Nor, in this case, were any of his allies likely to improve their own situations through engineering his demise. Which left me with a quandary that remained unresolvable until I struck upon a possible solution this morning. I had been asking the wrong question: not *who stood to gain from his death?*, but *who stood to lose out from him remaining alive?*'

'But aren't those the same questions, really?' asked Rube.

'They sound like they are, don't they?' replied Gordon. 'But no, they're not. There are plenty of people who would refuse to act, on principle, out of greed, but who would nonetheless take a stand out of preservation, and that, in a sense, is the motivation that drove our killer. Or so, I believe, he would have told himself.'

'Can we wrap this up please, Mr Mansplain?' asked Ritton. 'I'd like to have a discussion with Mr Whurd about my dinosaur/zombie romance.'

'I'll try to be as brief as I can,' said Gordon. 'The answer, as it so often happens in such matters, comes down to money, and the difference in outcomes between the North Mars and South Mars proposals. The South Mars proposal requires a very large amount of cometary ice, which means a large number of hyperspace thruster engines to bring that ice in from the Oort cloud, which means good news for anyone holding substantial quantities of stock in Saturn Propulsions, seeing as the Martian terraforming project is pretty much the only large-scale infrastructure project for which the hyperspace drives are applicable. The North Mars proposal would involve a much smaller amount of cometary ice – not so good for Saturn Propulsions, nor for their stockholders. So it's natural – although I have to say, in light of the political situation, thoroughly misguided – for an outsider to assume that bumping off the North's chief advocate on the eve of talks to decide the outcome of the Martian terraforming project might well help sway things in the South's favour, and keep the share price sweet. Arrange for a bug to render the liftmodule's camera surveillance and airlock operations log systems essentially useless for a couple of hours, leave the weapon and the spacesuit in the airlock and cycle it open once he'd returned, to remove all trace of his passage from 270 to 271.

The only mistake he made was a rookie one – the guywire sleds only pack enough compressed gas for one-way, and he didn't know to load it to the charging station when he arrived in 271, so when he needed to make his escape, the sled he'd brought from 270 was useless – he either had to conceal it somewhere, or more probably he spaced it like the weapon and the suit. And he took a 271 sled, which he left on the airlock bracket of 270, to recharge properly this time, hoping it'd go unnoticed. It very nearly did.'

'Alexei was expecting me ten bally minutes ago,' noted Whurd.

'It might be prudent if you let him know you may be delayed somewhat,' replied Gordon. 'If not to say detained. I was just wondering if you had anything to say in response to what I've just outlined.'

'As you might appreciate, Mr Modicum, I am a very busy man, and while I'm sure the death of this blasted Martian fellow is of some concern to his fellow citizens, I really—'

'Stay,' said Gordon, in a tone that brooked no disagreement. 'I was hoping you might have seen fit to voluntarily declare your financial interests.'

'My financial interests are no bloody concern of yours!' thundered Whurd, growing more purple of face than Gordon would have thought humanly possible.

'I would have said otherwise,' said Gordon. 'Strike one: within hours of embarkation onto the lift-module, you had expressed an interest in the location of the emergency spacesuits, something which I was inclined to overlook at the time, but which I now see was significant. Strike two: your reaction to my suggestion that you might be interested in a non-fiction item by Ritton on the Martian terraforming imbroglio was extreme, and involved threats of physical harm against a fellow passenger, thus demonstrating something of a violent mindset. I also misinterpreted the nature of your reaction to my suggestion, for I judge now that you were not so primarily offended by the suggestion that you *work with Ritton* but that you *be seen to be associated with something which you were hoping to influence through force of persuasion.*

Strike three: an examination of your stock portfolio indicates that you have considerable shareholdings not only in Saturn Propulsions, the corporation which you erroneously hoped would obtain a substantial bounce were Lester Mannidge to be eliminated, but you also hold stock in Callahan Rapid Dispute Settling, Inc, the makers of the weapon that killed Mannidge. Finally, if I were you, I might have gone with different cufflinks and tiepins. Mycroft Whurd, where were you between the altitudes of 22000 and 21500 kilometres?'

'I was... let me think just a dashed minute... wait, did you say his death *isn't* going to make the South Mars plan more likely?'

'You utter, utter, *utter* jerk,' said Phillippa Bayson, staring at Whurd with a look of absolute loathing.

It was just an hour before Module 270 would touch down on terra firma, at the base of the elevator cable, and Gordon would have to very shortly be busying himself with the thousand-and-one tasks that needed tending to in the minutes preceding re-entry and arrival, and ensuring that Rube didn't do anything untoward like letting the lack-of-an-atmosphere in. But there were some minutes available before he absolutely *had* to be thus engaged, and he thought to check in on the sick bay, and Paul E Ritton.

Ritton was much improved, and had filled several sheets of office plastipaper (and the top hem of his bedsheet) with the almost illegible scrawl of his penmanship. He looked up from his bed as Gordon entered. They nodded a silent greeting to each other.

'It's a pity Mr Whurd turned out to be such a murderer, isn't it?' Ritton asked.

'People often get led astray by poor choices,' remarked Gordon, busily trying to determine whether he had sufficient memory space on his handheld to download a five-dimensional jumbo crossword. 'Whurd panicked; he saw Lester Mannidge space-suited, he assumed Mannidge was dressed for an EVA rather than just to try to keep his business suit dry, so Whurd's plan to attempt to reason with him – admittedly backed up with the threat of lethal force – went up in smoke. All of which is no excuse at all, of course.'

'I mean, clearly it's terrible what happened to that Mr Mannidge, but I always felt that Burdester-Whurd were the publishing house I wanted to end up working with, so I was really looking forward to this descent. I idolised Mycroft Whurd,' said Ritton.

'Feet of clay,' said Gordon.

'You what?'

'Doesn't matter.'

'And – I mean, this seems really petty of me, and I suppose it is, but I was really hoping that I was going to have more of a chance to try to sell my stuff to Whurd. I didn't even get the chance to run my best story by him.'

'What's your best story?' Gordon asked.

'It's this weird thing, been working on for ages. Realist magicalism, I think they call it. Guy that's spent his whole life in an elevator, scenic elevator, glass-sided, he's trapped. It's got a door open, but the door faces out onto a chasm, and across the chasm he can see another elevator, also has an open side facing towards him. The other elevator has a much younger passenger, also trapped. So these two guys, they just go up and down, up and down, sometimes in synch, sometimes out of synch with each other – they can wave, but they're too far away to talk properly. But what they do have, is one of them has a baseball. So the book is about how they build a relationship, a friendship, a philosophy, by repeatedly throwing this baseball from one elevator to the other.'

'And this is a book?'

'At the moment, yeah. But I'm thinking of going the full Jackson on it, in which case it might end up, even, as three books.'

'You know, I think you ought to tell Whurd about this book of yours,' said Gordon.

'But isn't the descent about to finish in the next three-quarters of an hour?' asked Ritton.

'I get the feeling that, if you can stick around, Whurd might be what you'd call a captive audience.'

'Oh. Cool. I still have one problem with this story idea, though.'

'What's that?'

'I'm completely stuck for a title,' said Ritton.

'You'll think of something,' said Gordon.

This Guy's The Limit

1

Sue's spike-haired head popped around his office door. 'Got a minute?' she asked.

Gordon glanced up from the crossword puzzle on his handheld. 'What could "five-barred gate, from the sound of it" be? Two words, six and ten letters, second letter—'

The sharp look that Sue directed his way wiped all contemplation of word-puzzles from Gordon's mind. From long experience, he knew her frown could only mean one of two things: either she had uncovered fresh evidence that he'd been quality-control sampling the danishes she'd prepared for the guests' breakfast, or there was a problem. And since he hadn't been anywhere near Module 270's cafeteria in the last few hours, and since Sue Sheff's skill set ranged from food preparation to heavy droid repair with precious few gaps in between, it followed that any problem which she was unable to completely resolve herself, and was therefore motivated to bring to his attention, was likely to be a particularly... problematic problem.

Problematic problems weren't ideal in any situation, and particularly not in the situation of a somewhat run-down hotel lift-module clinging, as though for dear life, to the thirty-six-thousand-kilometre-tall cable of a space elevator. Hopefully, the issue was some kind of dilemma involving a guest rather than something more distressingly technical. When all was said and done, altitude sickness was vastly less disturbing, at umpteen thousand kilometres up, than was metal fatigue...

He stood up with a reluctance only partly reflective of his bodily uncertainty as to the exact gravitational field they were under at this altitude. Technically, there were still twenty minutes until he was due to replace Belle on duty, but he knew Sue was not one to trouble her colleagues unnecessarily with ephemera. 'So, what's up?' he asked as they moved up the hotel liftmodule's rampway.

'It's Münz,' she replied.

'Münz?'

'Sheppard Münz, the rocket guy. In room 204.'

'Oh? And what's up with him?'

'He's a bit dead, Gordon. That's what's up. It looks as though he's been electroplated.'

'That's terrible, Sue. Though I presume you mean electrocuted.'

'No, Gordon,' replied Sue wistfully. 'No, actually, I don't.'

The scene in room 204's bathtub was nothing out of the ordinary, provided one was prepared to overlook the lifesize chromed human figure lying in the plastimarble bathtub. Gordon's natural inclination was to so overlook, but his job dictated otherwise.

Münz's unclothed and metallised body was accompanied within the tub by an electroplated loofah, a chrome-encased rubber duck, and, down by his feet, what appeared to be a metal-sheened cake of Skyward's in-house soap. Around the insides of the tub, only a mirror-stained tidemark indicated the erstwhile presence of water or of some other liquid.

Münz looked to be at peace, Gordon thought, if not particularly comfortable. It was a relief, at least, to be surveying a murder scene in which there was no visible blood, and where all bodily organs were satisfactorily contained within their original dermal wrapping… even if said wrapping was now on the incongruously shiny side.

What had Münz seen, in those last precious moments of life? What had passed through his mind?

Gordon's reverie was interrupted by Sue. 'You need my help on any of this?' she asked, with a broad sweep of her arm as though there could possibly be any doubt as to which "this" she was referring. 'I mean, I hate to cut and run, but I've still got things I need to tend to in the galley, I should try and repair that faulty airlock control panel, and now that you're investigatoring'—she applied a distinct emphasis on the final word—'someone else will have to replace Belle on front desk and room-service. Unless you want me to wake Rube for that?'

'Uh, no,' Gordon replied hastily, pulling a handipack of disposable plasticotton gloves from the pocket of his Skyward uniform jacket and opening it with a noisy flourish. A vision of Module 270's well-intentioned but noteworthily clumsy apprentice attempting high-altitude airlock repair flickered vividly through his mind, and he shuddered involuntarily as he donned the gloves. 'But if you could send Rube up here, I've got just the job for him.'

'Right you are, Gordo. Let me know if you need anything.' She stepped out of room 204's cramped bathroom and was soon off down the corridor.

Gordon returned to the task at hand, which for the most part involved thereminning his handheld over the body in the tub.

If Münz had been having a bath when this happened, Gordon mused, *then somebody let the water out. Presumably the same somebody who did this to him.*

He glanced at the handheld's display, which showed the verdict *Poorly Executed.* This judgment seemed unduly acerbic, even for his handheld, and Gordon scowled when he noticed that he'd inadvertently switched it to its "Art Appreciation" mode rather than "Autopsy". Having rectified this, he re-scanned the bathtub's vista and waited several seconds. Then, having determined that its onboard forensics package hadn't yet concluded anything useful, he backgrounded the ongoing analysis and put a call through to Sue.

'Gordon?' She sounded harried and seemed to be surrounded by clanking and rumbling machinery.

'Sorry, I don't mean to interrupt your airlock repair work. I just—'

'I haven't started the repair work,' she explained, then swore as something fell to the floor. 'This is dessert I'm getting ready. What d'you want?'

'Just checking. When you found Münz, was there water in the tub?'

'No, there wasn't. It looked like someone had drained it.'

'That's what I thought,' said Gordon. 'By the way, what alerted you to him?'

'The climate control had gone into overdrive again. You know how the Level Two heating has had a bit of a hair trigger the past couple of months, you only have to keep the minibar-fridge door open for longer than two seconds in any of those rooms and it decides it needs to singlehandedly stave off the next ice age – and Systems Engineering has been making threatening noises about power load in recent weeks, saying that the older modules' fusion units can go critical if there's too heavy a drain on their output—'

'Wait. When you say "fusion units can go critical", in what exact sense are you using the word?'

'The word "fusion"?'

'No, the word "critical".'

'Oh, Gordon, I don't know. They're engineers. Groundside. They might simply be referring to a standard critical failure, a failsafe, rendering the unit harmlessly inoperative. In fact I'm sure that's what they *do* mean. Mostly sure. Like, ninety-nine percent sure. Ninety-five at least. Definitely more than, say, eighty. I think. But you'd have to ask—'

'So it might mean something different. Something more uncontrolled and... catastrophic?'

'No,' said Sue. 'Well, yes, it might. But probably not. Maybe. Look, Gordon, I just try to do my job.'

'I know, Sue,' said Gordon. 'And you don't *think* they're saying "could go critical" in a catastrophic sense, but—'

'But better safe than sorry,' said Sue. 'So I've been making a point of responding promptly whenever the control board shows any kind of problem. To minimise load on the module's power systems. Just in case.'

'Does this also explain why salads and cold cuts have featured so heavily on the cafeteria's menu lately?' Gordon asked.

'It might do,' Sue conceded.

'And why the lighting has been at honeymoon levels across the entire structure for the last few ascents?'

'Well, yes,' allowed Sue. 'And why the solarium is locked, and why I've disabled the hot water setting on the laundry machines, and why I've switched the room-service transporter setting to "econo". But the point is, I thought I should stop by room 204 to show Münz how to disable the heating – I mean it's in the video advice to guests, but nobody ever watches that thing because the lipsynching is so unconvincing – and when I got there, there was no answer when I knocked.'

'The room door was open, or closed?'

'Closed but unlocked. And he didn't answer. I opened the door a crack, called out "Housekeeping" a couple of times, and went in. And found him as you see him.'

'Okay, thanks Sue. Sorry to have disturbed you. I'll be in touch if there's anything else I need.'

Gordon returned to his perusal of the body.

The figure's mouth was open, though whether in mid-scream or mid-song Gordon had no way of determining. And he was disconcerted to note that the body's chrome coating extended into the visible reaches of Münz's mouth. Teeth, tongue, tonsils… *In all probability, he was just trying desperately to breathe,* thought Gordon. He shuddered.

It was as though the man had been transfixed by the stare of some postmodern Medusa. Gordon didn't imagine it could have been a pleasant way to die. But then again, presumably, not many were.

He left the metal-encased figure to its own devices – such as they might be – and returned to the suite's main room. His initial impression had been that Münz's belongings – a suitcase, opened but hardly unpacked; a jacket draped across the armchair's arm; a pair of shoes beneath the bedside table on which stood a closed vid-reader, a datastick, an expensively-branded handheld, and a wallet – did not appear to have been disturbed: they were, taken as an ensemble, too neatly arrayed. He thumbed the wallet open. It contained a not-insignificant amount of pseudocash, three credit cards, a current aircar licence, and business cards for a rare-isotopes supply specialist, for a public events weather-cancellation service, and for a well-known jetpack repair franchise whose logo was sufficient to spark in Gordon's mind a singularly irritating earworm.

It was probably never going to be possible to be sure that the killer had taken nothing from the suite except Münz's life, but the personal items in plain view suggested that the murderer had not felt bothered to acquire either the deceased's money or his data. *So he was most likely killed for personal reasons, then.* But who among the module's inhabitants could have committed such an act? Gordon stared, deep in what he supposed was thought, at the shoes, the suitcase, the jacket.

He moved back through to the bathroom. Münz's clothing was piled, reasonably neatly, on the vanity unit's benchtop, beside an unopened bag of what Gordon presumed were toiletries. The bathmat was down; the towels still hung neatly folded on the towel rail. *How had it happened?*

Rube turned up, outsized and cheerful. 'Ms Sheff told me you required my assist—' he announced, only belatedly noticing the shiny figure in the bathtub. 'Baths aren't good for robots,' he announced, seriously. 'Except for the waterproof ones, and that one doesn't—'

'Rube,' said Gordon, 'this isn't a robot.' He glanced in some frustration at the elaborately animated "please-hold-for-diagnosis" popup now displayed by the handheld's forensics program and wondered idly how much of the handheld's processing power was thereby diverted from diagnosis to animation.

'Oh,' replied Rube. 'Then why's there a mannequin in the bath?'

'It's not a mannequin. Rube, I need you to help with something.'

'Sure thing, Mr Gordon, sir. What d'you need?'

'Just stand at the door,' said Gordon, ushering Rube out towards the corridor. 'Not the bathroom door, the main door. This door. I need to check something with Belle.'

'Just stand at the door?' Rube asked, sounding – not, it must be confessed, without some justification – as though this were not an entirely adequate use of his considerable talents.

'Stand at the door, and don't let anyone in,' said Gordon. He took a couple of steps away, paused, and then returned. 'Except me, when I get back.'

2

Gordon strolled down the rampway towards the reception desk, making an unsuccessful attempt as he did so to contact Skytop Policing on his handheld. Reaching the foyer, he gave a wide berth to the rack of interactive tourist brochures, then chatted briefly with Belle while she printed off the seven names on this ascent's guest list for him. He tried again to connect to the police on Skytop: he knew, from experience, that (1) they expected to be kept informed of all matters that fell under the heading of "assisted curtailment of passenger vitality" and (2) the likelihood of them being able to contribute to the case in any meaningful way, particularly so early into the module's ascent, was vanishingly slender. Then he spent fifteen minutes rummaging through his office/cupboard in search of his roll of "Crime Scene – Do Not Enter" tape, which he eventually found next to the emergency breathing apparatus.

On his return to the room 204 doorway (barely managing, en route, to avoid collision with the autonomous linen trolley, when he stumbled as the artificial gravity suddenly kicked in), he found that Rube had placed a "Do Not Disturb" sign on the doorhandle.

Actually, he conceded to himself, attempting to stuff the Crime Scene tape roll into the insufficiently-generous pocket of his Skyward uniform jacket, *that works better*. Rube might well still lack the experience required to safely operate a lift module, but his ad hoc solutions were sometimes very effective.

'Do you need me for anything more, Mr Gordon, sir?' Rube asked.

Gordon was just about to reply in the negative, but found himself instead asking a question of the apprentice. 'You've brushed up on the module's plumbing recently, haven't you?'

'Polished it, you mean?'

'No, I mean… you've familiarised itself with it, as part of your training.'

'I guess so,' said Rube. 'Why?'

'I'm just trying to remember which holding-tank room 204's wastewater feeds into.'

'It's Tank Three, in the sub-basement,' said Rube. 'But don't worry, I've already vented it.'

'Vented it? Why?' Gordon asked, more sharply than he'd intended.

Rube looked flushed, as was, Gordon supposed, appropriate in the circumstances. 'Mass minimisation,' the apprentice explained. 'It was one of the recommendations in the memo that came through from Accounting last week. You know, this big economy drive the corporation's on.' Rube blew his nose on what looked, to Gordon's trained eye, suspiciously like a Skyward face towel, then asked, 'Did I do something wrong, Mr Gordon, sir?'

That water was evidence. But Gordon bit his tongue, said instead, 'No, if Head Office in all their wisdom directs us to throw out a recoverable resource, who are we to act otherwise? It just would've been useful to have that water to analyse.'

'To find out if he was using too much soap?'

Gordon sighed. 'No, Rube. To determine how he got plated. Whatever it was, it seems to have coated everything within the tub. In any event, unless you've anything further to add, I'd better start interviewing the other guests. One of them has to be behind this.'

'No, I've nothing further. Where are you going to interview them?'

Gordon glanced down the corridor. 'Room 203's free.' *And considerably more spacious than my office. Not to say better appointed.*

To interview the guests, Gordon first had to find them. None of the room doors he knocked on evoked any form of reply. For a moment he had a vision of each guest lying fatally chromed in his, her, or their room's bathtub – which would, he supposed, have the silver lining that meal preparation for this ascent would be substantially simplified –

but then he reflected that, since it was still comparatively early in the evening, the guests were most likely in the module's cafeteria (which was, in the evenings, converted to a "restaurant" by changing the signage, Frenching the menu, doubling the prices, and dimming the lights). On his way down the rampway, he further reflected that "silver lining" might be, in the circumstances, a distinctly callous metaphor. As, itself, might the act of reflection.

The restaurant was steeped in atmosphere, if one's concept of "atmosphere" meshed with the ideal of Stygian gloom – Sue evidently took this business of dimming the lights very seriously – and Gordon made his way through it, by a combination of echolocation and percussive navigation, to the service counter upon which stood an artfully flickering hologram of a glowing candle.

He unfolded the flimsy which Belle had printed off for him. 'Can I have your attention, please?' he began, in a slow and authoritative voice sufficiently loud to make its way to the room's extremities. Then he belatedly realised that telling a dimly-lit room full of passengers all confined, for the next fifty-eight hours, to the same small lift module that one among their number was, it seemed, a murderer – and furthermore one who was not content to rest on the laurels of any past death-dealing accomplishments but who had shown a continuing commitment to his, her, or their craft by having very recently dispatched a fellow passenger – might be a recipe for mayhem and panic. (Or if not the full recipe, then at least one of the crucial ingredients, like baking soda or egg white.) He'd need to dissemble a little, so as not to spark a riot. 'There's been a— well, I suppose you could call it a complaint, and I just need to ask each of you some questions, in confidence, dealing with your experience of the ascent so far. I'll call out your names, in turn – I'd appreciate if you'd each just wait here until the process is complete, it shouldn't take long – and I'll take each of you for an interro— interview in one of the vacant rooms.'

'What's an entero interview?' asked a woman's voice from towards the back corner. Brassy. Confident. A little loud.

'It's an interview,' said Gordon. 'Just an interview.'

'Then why,' asked the woman, 'did you call it an entero interview?'

'I didn't,' Gordon explained, somewhat testily.

'You most certainly did,' said the woman, whose voice carried across the darkened room with a clarity that would be the envy of any professional orator, drill sergeant, or heckler.

'Madam,' said Gordon, deploying his best the-terms-of-my-employment-sadly-do-not-allow-me-to-be-rude-to-our-passengers-but-I-am-well-practised-in-weaponising-my-courtesy voice, 'we could spend the time debating the intricacies of language, or you could allow me to do my job.' He peered at the passenger list and addressed the room at large. 'Ms Player.'

Silence.

'Ms Player?' he echoed, louder. Perused the list again, holding it directly against the holographic candle's eerily cold flame, which he suspected of being rated in millilumens. 'My apologies. Ms Slayer?'

Silence.

He inspected the list once more, frowned, and pulled out his handheld, activating its "torch" function and directing the brilliant white beam at the flimsy. 'My apologies again. Uh, Ms Slater?'

Silen— 'I think that's meant to be "Layta",' said the woman with the brassy voice. 'First name Sia.'

'Room number?' Gordon asked.

'One oh two.'

He peered closely at the flimsy. 'Yes, that appears to be correct. Follow me, please.' He pocketed his handheld, turned, and walked into a barstool.

Following in Gordon's wake, Ms Layta muttered darkly. She was aggrieved, he sensed, that he had misnamed her; but it plainly had not been personal on his part. And clearly there were much worse names than "Layta" to which one could append an errant prefatory sibilant: Trumpet. Ewermouth. Phyllis…

'Please,' he said, ushering her into room 203, 'take a seat.' He turned up the lighting, offering a silent prayer to the presumably-nonexistent gods who protect against criticality. The illumination, provided principally by a standard lamp which clearly wished to be somewhere else, revealed a room in which no one aspect of the decor – muted green walls, earth-brown ceiling, a carpet resembling nothing so much as congealed butterscotch, rust-toned skirting boards and doorframes – could be said to be in blatant disagreement with any other aspect; nor could they be described, either, as constituting any kind of harmony. It was a room in which to unpack one's suitcase rapidly before heading for the bar; a room in which to close one's eyes tightly and hope sleep came quickly; a room in which, by and large, guests did not bother to tarry sufficiently to check whether anything had been left under the bed, or in the wardrobe, or on the nightstand. Even the furniture looked as though it had been assembled for a quest through uncharted and hostile terrain, rather than chosen to blend in with any part of its surroundings. The room's focal point was a large and not particularly expertly-painted streetscape of what appeared to be the largely uneventful nightlife of a nondescript sidewalk in a city best honoured through the honest application of anonymity. The artwork seemed, on first glance, to have been designed to depress the humanoid spirit, a consideration rendered yet more emphatic on perusal of the explanatory text on the small art-exhibit-style placard mounted beside the picture, which declared the image to be one of a range of mood-sensitive artworks on display around the module (and available for purchase from the Skytop souvenir shop, should the guest so desire).

Gordon stared at the picture for no more than four seconds, but that was ample time for light rain to begin to fall on the depicted streetscape. He turned hurriedly away.

Ms Layta opted for the room's plastileather-coated armchair. Gordon sat on a slender chair that seemed to have been handcrafted – or, more probably, mass-printed – for optimal discomfort, beside the room's plastimahogany writing desk. Setting his handheld to "record" and placing it on the desk – angled, he hoped, so as to catch as little as possible of the sound of drizzle emanating from the artwork – he turned to his guest and cleared his throat.

Ms Layta was clear of skin, fair of face, medium of height, moderate of girth, stern of expression, and businesslike of outfit. She gave Gordon the distinct impression that she took no nonsense from anything, whether "anything" was her pageboyed strawberry-blond hairstyle, the law of gravity, or the lift attendant / part-time hotel detective she sat facing. She started speaking at the exact moment Gordon uttered the words "Ms Layta".

'—hope this won't take long,' she imprecated.

'That would be my aspiration also,' Gordon assured her. 'I'm just hoping to get a sense of your whereabouts over the last four hours.'

'To what end?' she asked. 'I must say, this doesn't sound like a customer-service questionnaire. If you've lured me here under false pretenses, Mr Mandrax—'

'Not in the sense you imply,' he replied. 'But you're correct, this is unorthodox. I did not wish to panic the guests as a group, but you look severe enough – I mean, of course, sensible enough – to be apprised of the facts. There has been an incident involving one of the guests.'

'What sort of incident?'

'I'm afraid I can't disclose that.'

'Why not?'

'I'm afraid I can't disclose that, either.'

'Why not?'

'If I were to disclose that, then that, almost by definition, would also necessitate disclosing *that*. The other that, if you see what I mean. The first that, contingent on and pursuant to the second that. Or words to that effect.'

'Please tell me when we get to the bit about this not needing to take long,' she said, pulling a nailfile from the recesses of her bag and pointedly tending to her cuticles.

'If you can just brief me on your whereabouts over the last four hours,' said Gordon. 'Please.' Within the painting behind him, the rain had audibly intensified.

'I've been confined in a badly-staffed hotel module, ostensibly crewed by idiots,' she replied. 'Though when I say "badly-staffed" and "idiots", the women have been competent enough, I suppose.'

'Ms Slay— Ms Layta,' said Gordon, allowing some steel to replace the lighter, more malleable alloys in his voice, 'I am merely trying to do my job.'

The look his interviewee directed at him spoke volumes, and those volumes would have been best shelved in the "Content Advisory: Contains Implied Strong Violence" section of the library, within a locked glass-fronted cabinet to which only the most austere of librarians would be entrusted with the key. '"Trying" seems accurate,' she said, slow and cold, and paused while she inspected her nails. 'I would have thought,' she continued in the same chilled drawl, 'that after eighteen years you might have got the hang of it.'

'Your whereabouts,' Gordon prompted. 'If you please.' *How does she know it's been eighteen years?*

She looked as though she was about to say something, but didn't. Then she did. 'I admired the smog from the observation deck. I returned to my room for a rest, a shower, and a change of clothes. I checked on my work messages. Then I went down to the restaurant for a drink before dinner.'

'Can anyone vouch for those movements?' Gordon asked.

'There was someone else up on the observation deck while I was there,' she replied. 'A ballasty sort of man, red-faced, wearing a uniform like yours, though with more singe marks. He was cleaning the panoramic window with the dirtiest cloth I think I've ever seen. And pressing rather too enthusiastically on the plastiglass while he was cleaning it. I was concerned for its structural integrity, given the altitude and associated conditions.'

Rube, thought Gordon. Well, that would be straightforward enough to check. 'How long did you stay on the obs deck?'

'Ten minutes, maybe,' Layta replied. 'I'm not brilliant with heights. Nor with ostensibly-breakable transparent surfaces.'

Gordon made a note on his handheld, then replaced it on the table. 'And after that?'

'I saw several of the other guests in the restaurant.' She paused. 'Well, when I say "saw", I mean more that I sensed their presence, as bodies in the room. I presume some of them can say the same about me. Certainly I'd been there about an hour and a half when you barged in.'

'So to sum up, your whereabouts can be confirmed for perhaps the first ten minutes and the last several minutes of a four-hour window of interest, with the intervening time spent either solely in your own company or in the company of people who, under ambient lighting conditions, would have had difficulty seeing even the cutlery in front of them.' Gordon sighed. 'Did you chance to see anything suspicious in that time?'

Ms Layta snorted, markedly enough to suggest that something might have gone down the wrong way in the process. 'See anything suspicious in my room? Or in the sensory-deprivation dining area?'

Gordon sighed again. 'Quite.' He reached for his handheld, about to terminate the interview, then reconsidered. 'I realise I haven't yet asked you what it is you do, Ms Layta, nor your purpose for making this ascent.'

'No, you haven't,' she observed.

'I'm asking it now.'

'Is it relevant? What I do?'

'It might be.'

'I'm travelling for my work,' she replied.

'And what's the nature of that work?' Gordon asked.

'HR,' she said. 'I specialise in retrenchments.' She gave him a challenging glare, then reached into her handbag and extracted a business card, which she passed to him. 'Was that everything?'

'For the moment,' he replied, pocketing the card just as the unmistakable sound of thunder issued from the painting on the wall. 'Thank you. I shall be in touch if there are further questions I need to ask you.'

'For this… customer-service questionnaire,' she said with exaggerated precision as she stood up.

'For, as you rightly observe, this customer-service questionnaire,' agreed Gordon, showing her to the door.

3

'Mr Kinnerbarth,' Gordon began, eyeing the man whom Rube had sent up to room 203 and abandoning, for now, his effort to drape a spare blanket over the painted streetscape along which an ostensibly cold wind was currently scudding a dented and tarnished smartbeer can.

Kinnerbarth was a lean, balding, pale-skinned man of middle years, with hands that would not have looked out of place on a loris and with, it seemed, a fondness for faded black denim. Gordon suppressed as uncharitable the half-formed thought that the man looked as though he might well have stepped out of the artwork on the wall.

'Call me Alonzo,' the other replied.

Gordon gave the suggestion due consideration. 'Mr Kinnerbarth,' he began again. 'Can I start by asking if this is your first ascent with Skyward?'

'Well, now, yes.' Kinnerbarth paused and used the fingernail on his index finger to remove some irritant from behind his thumbnail. 'Though I've been in lifts before.'

'Other transorbitals, you mean?' Gordon asked.

'No, just lifts like this. Though this one seems to be taking a while.'

'That's why we provide accommodation, Mr Kinnerbarth.' Gordon lifted his hand to his chin and scratched at its underside in a thoughtful manner. *Is it just the lighting*, he wondered, *or are Kinnerbarth's fingernails distinctly metallic in appearance?* 'And what is it that brings you here?'

'Well, now, I caught a sky-taxi,' said Kinnerbarth. 'Though it—'

'No, I meant your visiting Skytop.'

'Skytop?'

'The hotel,' Gordon explained, 'at the top of the space elevator.' He flinched at a sudden noise over his shoulder, which he at first mistook as a cascade of space debris particles hitting the elevator module's casing. Hail.

He really needed to find a way to drape a cover over that thing.

'Space elevator?' asked Kinnerbarth.

'Yes,' replied Gordon, regretting almost at once the testiness with which he had deployed the syllable. Management was very forthright in insisting on the importance of adhesion to the creed that "the customer is always right". Gordon's personal view, informed by almost two decades of employment, was that the staff member was, purely by virtue of experience, more often right than the customer, though he would at least concede that the customer was more often right than was Management.

'This is the first I've heard of any Skytop,' said Kinnerbarth. 'I was just told that the person I needed to see could be found on the top floor of the hotel. I must say, this lift is taking a while.'

'And who was the person you needed to see?'

'It's a Mr Niedwoshing. They said he was the person I'd have to talk to about the baths.'

'Which baths?'

'The spas for the hotel,' Kinnerbarth said, speaking as though he were explaining the simplest of ratcatching principles to the slowest of terriers. 'They said they were looking at replacing them for the top floors, said the zero-gravity showers they had – rather gimmicky if you ask me – weren't popular with guests, so they're looking to replace them with spa baths. I'm an agent, you see, for Hoot Spa Bath & Tub, and my manager suggested, after the fire—'

'Fire?'

'Yes,' replied Kinnerbarth. 'There was a fire destroyed our warehouse, and I didn't find out until it was too late to stop it.'

'You were elsewhere at the time?'

'Well, no, I was there, but I didn't realise, with all that smoke...' Kinnerbarth sighed heavily. 'I'd thought that I was merely witnessing the selection of an unusually large number of popes.'

'Popes?' asked Gordon.

'Well, yes, popes. They have quite a number of them in Italy somewhere, apparently. I'd been watching this doco the night before, about Catholicism, see, and—'

'Fascinating though this is,' said Gordon, 'perhaps we could return to your reasons for making this ascent? You said you were here about replacing the bathroom fittings on Skytop—'

'Well, now, yes. And the person I spoke to said I'd need to see Hansel Niedwoshing, on the top floor, because he was the hotel sub-manager for bathroom fixtures and such. But if I'd known this lift was going to be so slow, I might have been better off taking the stairs.'

'No,' replied Gordon. 'No, you wouldn't be.'

'I don't see how you can be so sure about that,' replied the guest.

'Mr Kinnerbarth,' said Gordon, pausing to draw a deep breath, 'do you have any idea how many steps you'd need to climb to get to the hotel at the top?'

'Well, now, no. I'm guessing rather more than a hundred, though? Still, I'm quite fit, if I do say so myself—'

'Distinctly more than a hundred,' said Gordon. 'Very substantially more than that, in fact. But if I may return to recent events... can anybody vouch for your whereabouts over the past, let's see, five hours?'

'Well, I've been in this lift, now, haven't I? So that's where I've been. Mainly in the cafeteria, I suppose, though why a lift should need a cafeteria is a bit beyond me. Still, rather lucky that it does, wouldn't you say? I mean, given how long this trip to the top floor is taking...'

'Did anyone else see you in the cafeteria? Someone who can vouch for the time you spent there? And since you said "mainly", can I ask where else you've been during that time?'

'Well, now, that young man with the bright red face and the jacket that's been in harm's way a few too many times, he found me down in the cafeteria. Bit of luck he had a head-lamp, it's quite dark in there – I mean I could sort of tell other people were there, from the voices and such, but I don't think I ever saw any of them that clearly. And before that, I went to the gents, had to answer the call of nature... and I must say, it's a bit odd having a gents in the lift, isn't it? Probably just as well, though, given how—'

'Mr Kinnerbarth,' said Gordon. 'Can I just verify that you cannot identify anyone, apart from my fellow employee young Mr Greenhorn, to whom I believe you've alluded, who can substantiate your whereabouts at any time during the past five hours?'

'Well, now, there was that receptionist at the check-in desk, just before the lift started going up – though why a lift should need a check-in desk, I mean; and she asked me what room I was booked in. And I said "well, now, what room am I booked in?" And she said, that's right, what room—'

'And what room are you booked in?' Gordon asked. On the wall behind him, the hailstorm had intensified. Gordon wondered if the artist had seen fit to incorporate a volume control on the piece.

'Well, I didn't get one, now, did I? Didn't see the point. Though if I'd known how long this trip to the top fl—'

'Mr Kinnerbarth,' said Gordon. 'Leaving aside, for the moment, the question of your non-existent alibi—'

'Alibi? Like, you mean, I could be accused of something?'

'Let's leave that for now. Might I enquire how your nails came to acquire that metallic coating?'

'Well, now, that's my daughter. She's landed a part in a student production, playing a robot. It's all very minimalist, sets and costumes and stuff, but she felt if she was supposed to be a robot there should be some part of her that was metal, and she thought the fingernails. So she was trying out a few different varieties of metallic nail polish.'

'And she lent you her fingernails?' Gordon asked.

'Well, no, she didn't. Hers are smaller than mine, see, and rather pointy. And attached to her fingers. But she wanted to see what each type of polish looked like from a distance, such as the audience would be seeing them, and she couldn't get that effect from her own hands. Well, I suppose she could have amputa—'

'So they're nail polish?' asked Gordon.

'Well, now, yes,' said Kinnerbarth, holding up the middle finger of his right hand. 'This is the one she decided to go with. It's called... it's called... actually I can't remember what it's called.'

'Do you mind,' Gordon asked, lifting his handheld out of his jacket pocket, 'if I scan it?'

Gordon had time, before Rube escorted the next guest up, to establish that room 202 was also free, and so he relocated there for the remaining interviews. While the decor in room 202 was a dispiritingly close match to that of 203, its sole artwork – an especially garish example of that style of paintball-gun portraiture which had been inexplicably popular for a couple of years in the previous decade – was, importantly, non-interactive.

He was eyeing, with considerable disfavour, an unpleasantly silvery-looking glass of water that he had just dispensed from the bathroom faucet when Rube showed the guest in.

'Rube,' said Gordon, glancing once again at the glass of alleged water in his hand, 'can you please wait here with the guest? I'll be back shortly – I've remembered something I need to check with Sue.'

'I'm supposed to be helping her with room service,' the apprentice replied.

'This won't take long, and it's'—Gordon caught himself on the cusp of saying "urgent", which was one of those horse-spooking words that, from the passengers' perspective, seemed to grow more ominous with altitude—'important that I check this with her.'

Rube mumbled his agreement – or so Gordon chose to interpret it, though it could equally well have been a *sotto voce* complaint at the injustice of having too many masters – and Gordon offered a brief nod and set off down the rampway.

Sue, in the kitchen, was in the act of placing a room-service tray on the transporter pad. She looked up at his approach. 'Everything okay, Gordo?' she asked.

'No further fatalities, so far as I know,' he replied. 'But I wanted your opinion about this.'

'It's a glass of water,' she informed him.

'Is it, though?' he asked. 'Because I'm wondering if it's perhaps a bit too shiny. I mean, I know water in a glass generally looks shiny, but—'

'Hm,' she said, as he passed the glass to her. She lifted it to eye level, twisted her hand, studied it. Sniffed it.

'Don't drink it,' Gordon cautioned.

'I wasn't going to,' she replied, putting the glass down on the counter. She picked up a slim breadstick from an adjacent tray and dipped the end in the glass.

The breadstick's tip was noticeably silvered.

'Well, that's not good,' said Sue. 'This from room 204?'

'No,' said Gordon. 'It's from 202. Which means that at least the whole second level… we're going to have to shut off the water supply to the rooms. I'll get Rube on that, but can you notify the guests that the water's off?'

'And tell them what? That it's off because we found a dead spacepigeon in the tank? Gordon, it's *water*. We're going to have to give them a reason. Preferably without unnerving them.'

'We can tell them…' Gordon paused in thought. 'Tell them this ascent's water has been sponsored by whoever-our-bottled-water-supplier-is, and hand out the bottled water.'

'That would be a transparently terrible act of sponsorship,' she replied. 'How are they supposed to flush the loo, or wash their hands? And it's not going to work if any of them want showers.'

'Neither is letting any more of them get chromed, either externally or internally.'

'We don't actually have that much bottled water to hand.'

'I thought we had caseloads of the stuff,' he said.

'We do,' she said, 'but most of it's in long-term storage, which is a bit inaccessible at the mo, if you recall.'

'Just do the best you can. Is the piped-water supply on this level okay?'

'It better be,' she replied. 'I used enough of it in preparing dinner.'

Gordon placed a hand on his stomach in response to the sudden stabbing pains of an attack of acute hypochondria. 'Can you check?'

Sue rolled her eyes. 'Yes, Gordon, I'll check. Though given how rapid Münz's transformation seems to have been, I'd say the water on this level is probably okay if none of the diners have turned into cyberpeople on us.'

'You're probably right. Look, I'd better be getting back to that interview. I'll send Rube down to help you sort out the logistics of the water cut-off.'

'Unless he's had a swig in the interim,' Sue replied, her smile dying on her lips as she saw the expression on Gordon's face.

'Please, take a seat,' he said to the guest waiting in room 202, having dispatched Rube to liaise with Sue on the water business. 'And you are…?'

'Planitz,' she replied, in a gravelly contralto. 'Myna Planitz.' She was short, broad-shouldered, with enough ash-blonde hair gathered atop her head as to constitute not so much a bun as a complete baker's dozen. She was dressed in a yellow-and-black garment that owed something to the muu-muu, something rather more to the sari, something more again to the shower curtain and something else entirely to the radiation hazard symbol. Her glasses were so chunky that Gordon feared for the structural stress they must be placing on her nose and ears. As if sensing his concern, she lifted them (the spectacles, that is, not the aforenamed facial features) with a practised flick to rest within the superstructure of her hairstyle. 'I don't suppose you've seen Sheppard?' she asked. 'He's not answering his comm. If you do see him, could you tell him that if he wants to swap rooms with me, I'm okay with that, but I don't see what difference it could make, however scared of heights he might be.'

'You know the deceas— I mean, you know Mr Münz?' Gordon asked.

'Who's this Mr Münz? I don't know any *Mister*, but I am well acquainted with *Doctor* Sheppard Münz,' Planitz replied.

'And how's that?' asked Gordon.

'We're colleagues,' she explained.

'Colleagues where? That is, what is it that you do?'

'Why don't you just ask him yourself?' Planitz asked. 'And where is he, anyway?'

'That is, respectively, difficult and complicated. Mr Münz is— Doctor Münz is... no longer with us.'

'What, he got a transfer?'

'Not exactly. He has – how can I put this delicately? – he has attained his final state.'

Planitz seemed to ponder this a few moments. 'He already had tenure,' she deliberated. 'So I'm guessing you must mean... he's retired?'

'Not exactly. Ms Planitz—'

'Professor Planitz.'

'Professor Planitz. Perhaps you should be sitting down.'

'I *am* sitting down. So what is this that's happened to Shep?'

'He's dead, Ms Planitz.'

'Professor Planitz.' Some animation seemed to go out of her face, as if a skilled cartoonist had just at that moment handed this and subsequent frames over to a less-talented junior artist. 'Dead?' The brief question was posed in fluting and uncertain tones that seemed quite out of keeping with her earlier professional confidence. 'Shep is... dead?'

'I'm afraid so.'

'But this is terrible!'

'I sympathise with your loss, Professor.'

'My loss? No, it's not *me* who has lost anything, Mr Maglev, it's poor Shep. He hadn't co-signed the form.'

'Form, Professor Planitz?'

'Acknowledging acceptance of grant funding,' she explained. 'We'd put in an application for a major grant, new equipment, research assistants, press officer et cetera, and it came through. We both needed to sign off on the acceptance, but Shep went off on a tangent, and never got to co-sign. So all that money will just go—'

'To waste?' suggested Gordon.

'To *me*, Mr Momentum,' she corrected.

'How large a grant application are we talking about?' Gordon asked.

'A4; they're always a standard size, for administrative reasons, I guess. But it was for a lot of money, seventy megacredits all up.'

Gordon whistled. Seventy megacredits was indeed a very substantial sum. 'Perhaps you should tell me, Professor, just what it is that you and Dr Münz have been researching?'

'Propulsion, Mr Muon. We're— we were – hoping to perfect a dark-matter drive for interplanetary travel. It would offer no material improvement in efficiency over matter/antimatter annihilation, but it would be inordinately safer, since neither dark matter nor dark antimatter – which Shep always kept wanting to call 'antidark matter', but I told him, Shep, just *no* – interact with normal matter. So you can use normal-matter containment, and then when you need them to combine and go kaboom, just like they do in those prototype unclear reactors, you simply—'

'I presumably don't need the full lecture on the process, Professor. I'm just trying to determine the circumstances of Shep— of Dr Münz's death.'

'Are you saying,' Professor Planitz asked hesitantly, 'that his death may not have been natural causes?'

Gordon thought back to the scene in Room 204's bathroom. 'I don't think I've yet seen an instance of a cause more unnatural. So anything you can tell me that might shed light on who might want him dead would be of value. As well as, of course, a summary of your whereabouts since commencement of our ascent.'

'I've been in my room, mainly. Asleep, until probably an hour or so ago. Or trying to sleep. I must say that bedding is not at all comfortable.'

'We recommend the velcro sheets and pyjamas so as to guard against problems of artificial gravity failure,' said Gordon. 'But if you would prefer, I can have some regular plastilinen bedding sent up to your room, provided you're willing to sign the standard waiver against accidental falls.'

'Falls? From what height?' she asked, glancing either towards the floor or towards the distant Earth it obscured.

'Generally no more than a few centimetres,' Gordon reassured her. 'Though there have been two recorded incidents from ceiling height, but when I think about it both of those individuals were helium salespersons. Uh, which room—'

'One-oh-four,' said Planitz.

Gordon noted the room number on his handheld and held the screen towards her for her signature. 'So there's no one able to corroborate your whereabouts?'

'I suppose no, not real— wait, does this mean I'm a suspect?'

'At this stage,' replied Gordon, 'I'm just seeking to get a sense of everybody's movements. But I have to say that a seventy megacredit grant is certainly a sizeable consideration.'

'But that's ridiculous!' she exclaimed. 'Shep and I, we enjoyed a long and very fruitful collaboration! We've had papers together in the *Annals of Speculative Engineering*, in *Spooky Action at a Distance Quarterly*, and in *Properties of Obscure Materials*. We've got a major review coming out in the *Journal of Cryptophysics*. We've both held important honorary positions on the editorial board of *Monthly Notices of the Quasiatom Appreciation Society*, and last year we organised a very successful interplanetary conference on the safe detection, confinement, and handling of covertly massive objects. And there was plenty more we still hoped to achieve – I've lost much more through Sheppard's death than any measly thirty-five megacredits can compensate for.'

'And your reasons for making this ascent to Skytop with Dr Münz?'

'We're – we were – to attend the third Farside Colloquium on the Measurement of Pseudoproperties of Clandestine Matter. Shep was down to give one of the keynote addresses.'

'Nonetheless,' said Gordon, still struggling to parse the concept "measly thirty-five megacredits", 'it's clear that someone on board saw some reason to dispose of Dr Münz. In the absence of information to the contrary – and I have to confess, at this stage of the investigation, information to the contrary is in very short supply – it's inevitable that suspicion regarding the death of a noted academic is most strongly going to concentrate around any other noted academics who happen to have been nearby at the time of the death, particularly if financial gain is indicated. I'm not saying that this formally elevates you to the dubious privilege of the title "suspect", but it does, as I'm sure you will concede, represent reasonably accurately the circumstances in which we find ourselves.'

'I see,' said Planitz, adopting a distinctly cautious tone.

'I'm merely summarising the situation for you,' said Gordon, who had been watching closely the researcher's reaction to an informal declaration of suspicion. She didn't seem overly confronted by the notion, which puzzled him and didn't really help him. Nor, for that matter, did she seem particularly afflicted by the news of an ostensibly close colleague's unpleasant death: surely someone, on learning of the untimely demise of a longstanding co-worker (and not being themselves responsible for said co-worker's untimely demise), would display at least a modicum of sorrow at the news? And in the circumstance that they *were* responsible in the untimely-co-worker-demise department, would not someone as assuredly astute as a professor have at least the nous to fake same? Perhaps it would have been better to be conducting these interviews with Belle at his side: she was much better at reading people than was he, with a much keener sense for what he thought of as emotional snake-oil in a guest's behaviour. But to co-opt a second person to the investigation would be to inflict a crippling staff shortage on the module, with Sue and Rube left striving to manage all the multitudinous hotel duties between themselves. It would not be fair on them, nor on the guests. Nor, really, on Belle, who would naturally feel a strong sense of responsibility for any uncompleted or mishandled tasks in her absence. 'There is, though, something with which you can almost certainly help me,' he added.

'Oh?' asked Planitz, now decidedly frontloading the caution.

'I need a sense of what Dr Münz was like, as a person; what he was like to work with; whether anyone might have had a reason to wish him ill. I can possibly get some idea of that through a search on my handheld, but it's often true that individual sources are a more reliable guide than the great online continuum of unfiltered knowledge in matters of this kind. And you're presumably the person onboard this module who's best able to provide that information.'

'Ah,' said Planitz. Then she paused. It was a lengthy pause, accompanied by several changes in breathing mode, three indistinct noises that sounded as though they might have been words trying to escape, and the kind of rapid eyelid movements one otherwise sees only in sleeping Schnauzers who are under the momentary misapprehension that the squirrel they are chasing is real. 'I'm not sure there's anything to tell, really,' she said finally.

'I'm not asking for a detailed character assessment,' reassured Gordon, though in fact he was if he could get it. 'Just a sense.'

'We have been collaborating together for the past twelve years now,' Professor Planitz began. 'I suppose I took quite a shine to Sheppard when he first joined my group as a junior research associate. He had the kind of highly-reflective attitude that's more or less essential for a career in research, and the setbacks our research suffered in those early years certainly tested his mettle. We had an unalloyed respect for each other, I think. He— it feels very odd, I must say, to be using the past tense in reference to him.'

'I imagine it must,' prompted Gordon. 'Was he gregarious? Private? Outspoken? Introspective? Abrasive? Easygoing?'

'Yes,' said Planitz. 'Yes, that describes him very well.'

Gordon raised a quizzical eyebrow. 'Enemies?'

'No, I don't think that would describe them so accurately.'

'I mean,' said Gordon, deploying a frown which quite quashed the eyebrow's hard-won quizzicality, '*did he have* any enemies?'

'He had plenty of adversaries,' said Planitz, 'and several rivals, and a few staunch opponents. But enemies? No, I wouldn't call any of them that.'

'Nobody willing to kill him for his research, then?' asked Gordon.

'Mr Manflu,' Planitz replied slowly, affecting a quizzical eyebrow of her own. 'Academics never seek to kill each other. They prefer to humiliate: it's generally more damaging.'

He should, he thought, push through with the interviews – there were three guests yet to speak to – but Gordon strongly felt the need for a brief reprieve. He picked up his handheld, preparing to return to the crossword of recent vexation, but decided instead that a stroll would be both more recuperative and more prosocial. He locked room 202's door behind him.

Dinner was long finished and Gordon was mildly surprised to see that the restaurant had been converted to a dancefloor, with all the furniture pushed back around the walls. An unexpectedly bright array of ceiling-mounted, colour-changing lamps swivelled and pirouetted in time to the music, one of those jangly, irritatingly simple tunes that had allegedly been popular during Gordon's childhood, and which he felt strongly lost any semblance of charm when played at such a high volume. Beneath the light show, three or four dancers – he recognised Ms Layta and Mr Kinnerbarth – also swivelled and pirouetted, in somewhat indifferent synchronisation. Gordon, thinking wistfully of a missed crossword opportunity, sidled over to Sue, who was watching from the sidelines like an exceptionally disaffected soccer coach.

'I'm surprised the lights are so bright,' he yelled at her.

'Can hardly hear you,' she replied. 'The kitchen'll be quieter.'

It was, although the thin plastiboard walls did little to deaden the music's bass thump.

'I'm surprised the lights are so bright,' he repeated. 'You know, what with the power concerns.'

'Oh, we're on auxiliary,' she said.

'That reminds me,' said Gordon. 'Or actually it doesn't, but I've remembered something nevertheless. I've been trying to contact Skytop police, and I haven't had any joy.'

'I'm not particularly surprised,' said Sue. 'The concepts "joy" and "Skytop police" don't really go together.'

'I mean I haven't been able to contact them. About Münz.'

'Oh, Gordo, I realised that's what you meant. It was a joke. A jo— oh, never mind.'

'I thought this new high-bandwidth connection they've intertwined into the elevator cable was supposed to ensure good connectivity. Especially in emergencies. Even if a standard call can't get through.'

'Yes,' said Sue, 'it's supposed to. And it seems to. But I think I saw that they were wargaming a cyber-attack on Skytop's police HQ, and my guess would be that it's had some unintended consequences.'

'Right. I'm not too fussed, I mean there's not a lot of help they can offer down here, just that they'll expect me to have crossed the eyes and dotted the tees.'

'They can't blame you if they've made themselves accidentally unreachable,' Sue opined.

'I guess not.'

Sue flinched and frowned. 'Damn – it's started the next song. I was intending to shut it down after the previous one.'

'The guests seem to be enjoying themselves. Another song shouldn't hurt.'

'Rube might think differently,' replied Sue. As if on cue, the lights dimmed and the music slowed erratically, taking on, as it dwindled to a merciful close, something of the tonal qualities of a drunken bagpiper urinating on an electric fence.

Sue led Gordon back into the restaurant. 'Sorry folks,' she announced. 'Curfew.'

The guests grumbled but headed towards the rampway.

'I'd better follow that one,' Gordon said, suppressing a yawn and pointing to the wheeled device which had accompanied the other dancing guests. He found his way briefly blocked by a tall, perspiring wall of radiant heat which he subsequently identified as a sweat-soaked Rube, face glowing like a furnace and panting like a bellows.

'Sorry, Sue,' said Rube, in between laboured breaths. 'I couldn't last another minute on that exercycle.' He looked around and, spying a solitary bottle of water on one of the room's peripheral tables, paced over and downed its contents in two gulps.

'Hey!' Sue exclaimed. 'I was keeping that, it was the last one. Now we'll need to get more from the store. Gordon?'

'Sue, I need to conduct this interview. Can't you do the storeroom run? Or Rube?'

'I'm still working on the setup for breakfast tomorrow,' said Sue. 'Plus there's the airlock repair that I need to get to. And I don't think Rube is in shape right now to do any kind of run.'

'I'll do this interview first,' said Gordon. 'I can do the store bit after that.'

'What do I do if anyone else asks for water in the interim? Give them vodka?'

Gordon's response, as he headed back up the rampway, was inaudible.

4

Staring (and, of course, trying not to stare) at the device stationed in front of him in room 202, Gordon reflected that he really didn't like surros. He disapproved of them in some dark recess of the reptilian hindbrain that has been tasked, since prehistoric times, with overseeing the standard hominid response to autonomous mechanised surrogates. He distrusted them, in much the same way that he detested interactive advertising and self-motivated furniture. He realised, of course, that for some people – bedridden, incapacitated, otherwise confined – the surro was the most accessible, most immersive way to experience an actual, rather than a virtual, voyage, and for this reason he conceded that the devices certainly had their place. But the fact remained that most who travelled by surro were not genuinely in *need* of the technology, but merely *wanted* it, and were possessed of the funds to make it so. A hired surro – or, more often, a suite of surros hired in parallel – made it possible, in the same fortnight, for some overly-wealth-burdened individual to effectively spend two weeks in a seafloor theme park, fourteen days on the Moon (or, indeed, on some arbitrary other moon), a fortnight lounging around in a circumnavigating solar-powered zeppelin, and two weeks living paleo-rough in a Caveman Experience Camp on the Siberian veldt, complete with robomammoths and sabertooth tigerdroids, all without ever, in fact, leaving the creature comforts of one's own fully-automated self-aware five-star three-storey heritage-listed Belgian Riviera mansion, and it was all too often this class of passenger whom Gordon encountered through the impersonal vehicular medium of the surro. Of course, as a hotel employee, he was inured to the inevitability of dealing, on a day-to-day basis, with guests bothered by vastly more in the way of material assets than himself, but he infinitely preferred it when such guests did not take on the appearance of multilimbed, articulated waste receptacles on wheels.

When it came down to it, what he really wanted was for things to show their own identity: to seem as they were. And if there was one thing a surro did not look like, it was a wealthy and aggressively entitled businessperson of any gender who expected service with a smile, and probably substantially more subservience than Gordon was constitutionally capable of displaying. It was the same problem he had with personal avatars, or with artificial gas lighting, or – if you got right down to it – with interactive artwork. Why did people who did not need the service use surros? Why could they not just be what they were?

It was what it was.

This pair, now – this pair of Culture Group representatives, whatever *that* was, and he understood it to be something tangentially associated with banks – they surely had no real need of the services of a surro, and if they had might have decently hired two rather than simply opting to timeshare the one unit. Thankfully their hire evidently included tone-accurate vocalisation, so that the surro's governing intelligences could straightforwardly be distinguished, male from female. But it was undeniably unsettling to have addressed the apparatus in response to a remark uttered in a bright if overly girlish soprano to receive, in turn, from the same apparatus not three seconds later an answer in a clearly masculine tenor. Two minutes into the interview, and Gordon felt the middle of a headache without having yet had the saving grace of experiencing its beginnings.

He really did not like surros.

Of course, he was determined not to let that show. And, of course, it would. However one might feel obliged to dissemble otherwise – and the surro paradigm more-or-less insisted on such pretense – the surro form was not that of the human body, and so one's body-language interactions with a surrogated guest were, both consciously and unconsciously, markedly different than they would be with any guest who was genuinely, personally, physically present. Gordon knew this; the pair of guests (who might equally well be sitting adjacent to each other as might they be as many thousands of kilometres apart as they were, in truth, from him) doubtless also knew it; yet they would all try to pretend otherwise. The surro social contract depended on it. He had already forced himself to shake its awkward, inhuman, rubber-gloved hand, and was relieved to note that the unit's grip was less vice-like than he had expected. He took a seat, wondering whether he should remain standing: the surro, of course, was neither visibly standing nor seated, it just *was*. This, too, the structurall-imposed ambiguity of the thing, was something that irked him about it.

'Thank you for making yourself – yourselves – available,' he said again, automatically attempting to make eye contact with the things he actually knew to be speakers. 'But I think that in the interests of clarity, I will need to speak to each of you in turn, not both at once. So as to be clear as to who saw what, if indeed either of you saw anything. If that does not present you with any difficulties.'

'Of course, Mr Mainstream,' said the woman's voice. Her age, he judged from her voice, might have been anywhere from twenty-five to fifty. Nothing about the surro's appearance offered any hope of refining this estimate, though its chestfront display screen helpfully displayed the minimalistic pictogram of woman-in-dress that was instantly recognisable from gendered bathrooms across the Solar System. (Evidently she had not sprung the extra credits for a full virtutronic screen avatar.) 'Which order do you want us?'

'We may as well start with you, Ms…'

'Fleabass. Conchita Fleabass,' she said.

'Thank you. And what do you remember of the first four hours of the ascent?'

'Not a lot, I have to say; I was sleeping for much of it; then I awoke and had a shower. In real, that is, not in surro. I didn't get handed over to the unit until it was already three hours into the ascent; I took it for a bit of an exploratory trundle up to the obs deck at the top of the module, just to get my space-wheels, as it were, and then I wandered the corridors getting a feel for the place. There didn't seem to be anyone else around;

then I found they were mostly in the restaurant for dinner, so I rolled in there. Dark as, I must say, but I suppose that's the fashion. It took me a while to get the unit's infrared vision working – I had to get Yusuf to help me with that.'

'Yusuf?'

'That would be me,' said the tenor, as the pictogram conveniently switched to trousered-man-of-bathroom-door fame. His own voice fell broadly within the same apparent age range as his companion, though he could feasibly be twenty years older or younger than her. 'Yusuf Weppins.'

'Right,' replied Gordon. 'Returning to you, though, for the moment, Ms Fleabass'—he waited while the pictogram obliged with the appropriate gender-switch—'did you happen to note which of the module's other guests for this ascent were in the restaurant during the interval between, what, three and four hours in?'

'Oh, all of them, I should say,' said Conchita Fleabass. 'Bearing in mind, of course, that I wasn't physically present – actually no not physically, I mean yes not physically, but I don't mean that, I mean not even virtually present, during check-in – because Yusuf was at the helm at that point. So I hadn't actually seen any of them before I saw them in the restaurant, so I suppose I can't be sure if the all of them I saw was the all of them there was to see, or whether there might have been an additional all that I hadn't yet encountered. If that makes sense.'

I'm not sure that it does, thought Gordon, whose headache appeared to have decided that now would be a good time to phone a friend. He rubbed his temple distractedly. 'I believe I see what you're saying,' he conceded. 'So you think you saw all of them, but you can't be sure?'

'Yes,' said Fleabass after a brief pause. 'Yes, I think I saw all of them.'

'For the entirety of the time you were in the restaurant? You didn't see anyone leave during the fourth hour of the ascent?'

'Yes, no, that's correct.'

'You didn't see anyone leave during that hour?'

'Yes,' said Fleabass.

'Is that yes you did, or yes you didn't?' Gordon asked, getting the distinct sense that his headache was developing a headache of its own.

'Yes.'

'Which?'

'Which what?'

'Did you see anyone leave the restaurant during the fourth hour of our ascent?'

'No.'

'Thank you,' said Gordon.

'Actually I don't think that's strictly correct,' said the surro in Weppins' tenor, while the pictogram was still in the process of shuffling genders.

One at a time, please, thought Gordon. *Is that too much to ask?* 'You're saying someone did leave during that time?' he asked.

'Well, no. I think Con's right about that,' said Weppins. 'But if she's saying all the people there were the people there at the start of that hour, then they weren't all there. Not while I was setting the infrared vision on.'

'What do you mean, not all there? Were some of the people there only partially there, somehow?' Gordon pressed his hand to his forehead: it still hurt, but in a different way to his forehead without the hand there, and he decided he disliked the pain-with-hand slightly less than he disliked the pain-without-hand, so he kept the hand there. *My head is impeding my ability to think*, he thought. *Isn't that in contravention of a head's mission statement?*

'No, I don't mean that,' said Weppins. 'I mean there was a guest missing.'

'Can you describe him?' asked Gordon. 'I mean, can you describe the ones that were there, so I can determine by a process of elimination who wasn't?'

'Con can probably do that better than I can,' Weppins replied. 'She was in charge of the surro for most of that time, after all – I was only there enough to get a brief impression at that time. But I can tell you who was missing, if it helps.'

'Yes,' said Gordon. 'That may well help.'

'It was that suit who made such a fuss at reception.'

Gordon's ears pricked up. (In a metaphorical sense, at any rate. Metaphorical not insofar as the ears themselves, which were actual enough, unless you happen to adhere to the belief that all existence is a simulation, in which case do the concepts "real" and "metaphorical" even have any real meaning? Or indeed, any metaphorical meaning, if that isn't, if you see what I mean, the same thing in that circumstance? No, the metaphoricality concerns the "pricked up", which was an action that Gordon's ears were just not biomechanically equipped to perform, except in the metaphorical sense to which I allude.)

Could this "suit" be Münz, or more pedantically what he was wearing at the time? Not that Münz's absence from the restaurant during that last hour was so very remarkable, since his schedule for that hour may well have necessitated him lying dead within the bathtub of his hotel room and therefore would not really have allowed him to partake of dinner in the restaurant with his fellow guests; but Weppins' comment intimated at a possible earlier sighting of the deceased which might illuminate his final (or at least semi-final) movements. 'When you say "made such a fuss at reception…"'

'He was making that poor receptionist's life hell, asking on whose authority she was refusing to allow him to check his stowed baggage for twenty grams of vacuum-confined dark matter. She kept telling him the regulations forbade it, and he kept insisting that the dark matter was commercial material vital to the long-term success of a project in which he was importantly involved. But she just point blank refused, and he wasn't at all happy about it.'

I'd missed all that, Gordon thought. It must've happened while he was double-checking that the module's plant room had sufficient oxygen reserves onstream to provide for a three-day ascent with seven guests, five of whom would need to breathe the module's air. 'This gentleman – did you catch his name?'

'No, I didn't.'

'Can you describe him?'

'Obnoxious. Insistent. Somewhat domineering.'

'I mean, can you describe his appearance?'

'A bit on the large side. Silver hair. Does that help?'

Not really, thought Gordon. 'Anything else?'

'Pasty faced – well, once he'd finished going apoplectic, at any rate. And a striped green tie I wouldn't be seen dead in.'

The tie, at least, sounded familiar. There'd been one like that in the pile on room 204's bathroom floor.

'Actually,' said the surro, 'I should be able to show you. Just let me fast forward back through the visual feed.' There was a brief whirring sound, and then the screen switched its display to a slighty-pixellated close-up of a man's face, open-mouthed in the midst of some displeased-looking exhortation.

Gordon leaned forwards. The face was indeed that of Münz. *Now we're getting somewhere*, he thought. 'And this was – when?' he asked.

'An hour into the ascent,' said Weppins.

'Aside from witnessing this front-desk altercation,' said Gordon, 'did you see this gentleman at all? To talk to, or perhaps in conversation with other guests or staff?'

'Me? No. I kept well away.'

'You didn't see him again during the next two hours?'

'Next one-and-a-half hours. I logged off two-and-a-half hours into the ascent, so Con could have a turn.'

His head pounding at the conclusion of the surro interview, Gordon ruefully recalled his commitment to collect the next tranche of bottled water from the module's long-term storage. What he most wanted was a chance to lie down, to close his eyes for a brief spell, and to assess whether his current crossword had grown any more solvable in the interim. But he knew the water couldn't really wait.

Module 270's long-term storage was located, as per standard Skyward lift-module specifications, in a chamber beneath the sub-basement. In happier times it had been accessible through a manhole in the sub-basement floor, but had undergone a refurbishment several months ago, designed to impose upon the storage process the wondrous benefits of automation. The refurbishment had seen the storage chamber fitted out with (1) a transporter pad of the same type as had been installed, for room-service purposes, in the kitchen and in each of the module's bedrooms, and (2) a robot designed to identify items to be brought out of storage and to place them on the transporter pad for rematerialisation on an analogous pad in the basement. Since the new transporter pads meant the manhole was no longer needed, it was inevitably (3) covered over with the type of unidentifiable but probably-essential heavy plant that seems to accumulate within lift-module sub-basements. The system had worked like a dream for three ascent/descent cycles; like a distinctly more poorly-scripted dream, populated by spilled instant-pudding powder and overripe artichokes, for two more; and like a terminally gummed and irreparable storebot, which was to say not at all, for all subsequent cycles, with the result that the chamber was only accessible via (4) an unpleasant spacewalk from the sub-basement airlock, necessitating a rather excessive amount of awkwardly clinging to the module's underside and, almost mandatorily, a not inconsiderable amount of swearing.

The whole process was rendered more exacting by virtue of the fact that the storage chamber, never intended for EVA access and designed solely for ground-level replenishment, featured only a simple (if airtight) door rather than a functioning airlock. This design feature dictated that the chamber needed to be purged of any atmosphere before entering (so as not to be pelted by heavy escaping objects accompanying the explosive outflow of the chamber's air) and also conferred the additional consequence that any substances sealed within containers never designed for exposure to vacuum – which was to say most containers, for the system had never been intended to be accessed from the outside while in transit to geostationary orbit – were, of course, likely to rupture unpredictably.

Gordon could still remember the mess, and the flying shrapnel, that had resulted when most of the bottles in a crate of Saturnian champagne had decided to burst.

Consequent on the above, the spacewalk to retrieve two heavy pallets of bottled water was one fraught with ongoing tension, and not helped by the frequent progress-report requests from Rube who, similarly suited, was standing in the comparative safety of the sub-basement airlock, ready to haul up the cargo net once Gordon had loaded it.

'Are you ready yet, Mr Gordon?' Rube asked, for the seventh or eighth time.

'Rube,' Gordon replied, 'when I'm ready, I will let you know'. He blinked a trickle of sweat away from his eyes, and wished Skyward had seen fit to provide the kind of spacesuits in which it was possible to sneeze, or to cough, or to have one of those creepy but helpful little robotic hands wipe away the sweat from one's face, or scratch one's back, or make any of the other numerous small gestures that one never missed until one was suddenly prevented from implementing. But it hadn't, so one couldn't. 'You do have the other end of that rope securely, anchored, I hope? You're not just holding it, because if you're just holding it then there's a good likelihood that the Earth will suddenly acquire two new artificial satellites, one of which will be Rube-shaped.'

'What will the other one be?' Rube asked.

'Cargo-net-shaped,' replied Gordon. 'Just tell me you've anchored the rope properly within the winch.' He grunted with the effort of manoeuvring a bottled-water pallet around the bulky and immobile storebot bolted, for convenience, to the centre of the chamber's floor. Casting a baleful glance at the transporter pad – which was frustratingly still functional but which, due to an untraceable registry error that had apparently occurred some days before the storebot's demise, would only transport material to the adjacent modules 269 and 271 that were, respectively, several kilometres beneath and above 270 itself – he pushed the pallet past the storebot and onto the cargo net. 'Actually, don't just tell me. Make sure you've done it, and *then* tell me.'

'Yes, Mr Gordon.'

'And make sure the winch is properly anchored to the airlock floor.'

'Yes, Mr Gordon. Are you ready yet, Mr Gordon?'

'Rube, for the umpteenth time, when I'm ready, I will let— yes, alright, I'm ready. Everything securely anchored?'

'Yes, Mr Gordon.'

He pushed the pallet-laden cargo net out into space, stepped back into the storage chamber so as to be out of danger when the heavy pendulum of the cargo load swung back, and watched as it was slowly hauled up towards the airlock. *Great*, he thought, trying as best he could to ignore his headache. *One load down – or rather, up. Now to climb back up to the airlock, get the cargo net back, and do it all again.*

He wondered, not for the first time, why the lift-module didn't just have two cargo nets...

5

While it initially appeared that all of the guests had now retired to bed – for it was now late into the evening – there was one still up, a largish, dark-haired man with what Gordon considered an altogether unhealthy predilection for polyester plaid. He was also decked out in a substantial amount of wearable electronics, sporting a small shoulder-mounted optical device of some description as well as a heavy-looking helmet with an opaque full-face visor. The man was sitting in one of the foyer's bulky plastileather armchairs and the sound effects leaking out from the helmet strongly suggested he was watching a teleplay or movie, most likely one that revolved around the adventures of a technologically-advanced troupe of gibbons. This being the apparent case, Gordon opted not to attempt to interrupt the guest's viewing; instead he identified the individual, from the ascent passenger list, as the only guest with whom he'd not yet spoken. He composed a brief message on his handheld requesting that the guest please see him in room 202 before calling it a night.

Waiting in room 202, Gordon then sought to use the intervening time as wisely as possible, but the crossword refused to reload on his handheld. Ignoring as best he could his still-throbbing head, he ran some searches on the network to see what he could learn of the history of those he'd already interviewed (and of Münz, whom for obvious reasons he hadn't interviewed).

There were, it was fair to say, a few surprises, and he was just beginning to ponder what these new discoveries might mean when—

'Is this room 202?' the voice at the door asked.

*

Gordon's final interviewee was a documentary maker. Wyatt Madders, of large-technohelmet-and-plaid-suit fame, was also possessed of a windswept face, rheumy eyes, and the kind of awkwardly croaky throat that discouraged lengthy conversation.

'So what are your reasons for travelling to Skytop?' Gordon asked.

'The usual,' replied Madders, who had concocted a rectangular frame from forefingers and thumbs and was now steering it across his forward vision, as though seeking the perfect vista in a room patently lacking in such an attribute.

'And that is …?'

'A documentary. I make documentaries, you know. You will have seen my critically-acclaimed dinosaurs-were-actually-birds doco, *Flight of the Brontosaur*, no?'

'No,' agreed Gordon. 'So you're making a documentary? On Skytop?'

'Well, no, on the Moon,' said Madders. 'There's some big conference on dark stuff—'

'Dark matter?' Gordon felt his ears do the metaphorical thing again.

'That's the one, yeah. I'm hoping to get the lowdown on all the ethical violations associated with the dark stu— dark matter trade.'

'*Are* there ethical violations?' Gordon asked.

'Bound to be,' said Madders, who was now pointing a light-meter in ostensibly-random directions. 'I'm going to call this one *Shady Secrets*, it'll have some famous he-man like Carsten Brons as the narrator, it's going to be big as.'

'Fascinating,' said Gordon, pressing his fingers hard against his forehead. 'But what I'm really interested in is whether, during your time aboard—'

'You're going to ask what I've been up to, aren't you? I can tell. A filmmaker knows these things.'

'Indeed. So how have you spent your time aboard thus far? Particularly during the first four hours or so of the ascent.'

'I've been in my room, mostly, haven't I? Writing up curly questions to ask at the conference. Well, and then in the restaurant. Though that was a bit eventful.'

'Eventful in what way?'

'I'd just come out of my room, at the same time as this other guy left his room. So of course I introduced myself to him, explained I was hoping to expose the dark underbelly of dark matter, and he threatened to deck me there and then. Outrageous! And also tragic, because I didn't have my shoulder-cam switched on.' He nodded to the side, indicating the small searchlight-shaped device perched like a pirate captain's parrot on the shoulder of his jacket.

'Why tragic?'

'Getting roughed up by the subjects, on film, is what makes a doco,' Madders explained. 'The main selling point of *Flight of the Brontosaur* was me getting mauled by a Komodo dragon when it inexplicably objected to me trying to attach wings to its back.'

'Indeed,' said Gordon, demurring for this occasion on displaying a burgeoning respect for the Komodo dragon. 'And this gentleman – did you catch his name?'

'Well, no.'

'Can you at least describe him for me, please?'

'Pugnacious, obviously. Middle-aged, a bit paunchy, medium height; I don't really remember much else about him. But chickenhawk, I guess, because he didn't follow through; just went back into his room, so I went down to the restaurant to catch Happy Hour. I must say, the lighting in that restaurant is useless for filming.'

'Quite. Do you at least remember his room number?'

'In fact, yes. Two-oh-four.'

'And when did this ... abortive altercation occur?'

'Would've been about two hours into the ascent.'

'Did you see this guest again?' Gordon asked.

'In *that* restaurant? I couldn't even see my way to a table without barking my shin on the barstools. Say, are we done here? I think I hear supper calling my name.'

6

Gordon checked his handheld. He'd been interviewing the module's passengers for almost four hours in total, plus a couple of additional hours of decidedly unrestful activity. The morass of ostensibly well-intended testimony (piled atop the muscle fatigue of a lengthy and fraught EVA) was threatening to swamp him, if that was indeed something morasses did. He would normally know such things – the swampable properties of morasses and the like – but the combination of an extensive sequence of interviews and an increasingly recursive cluster of headaches (they were now, he thought, nested four deep like Russian dolls or like stackable measuring cups, or possibly like both, all within the confines of his pounding skull) seemed to have dulled him quite severely. He needed a tall glass – or rather, in the circumstances, bottle – of water; he needed a derm-patch for his headache; he needed a break. He paid a visit to the now-deserted restaurant for the first; stopped by the first-aid cabinet for the second; and locked himself within the cramped confines of his office for the third, leaning as far back in his chair as the room's geometry would permit, his eyes closed, waiting for sleep or something akin to it.

Sleep was off somewhere else, apparently. His thoughts whirled around in his head like the sort of pesty and bitey things that might whirl above morasses, if morasses had things that whirled above them like that. For the moment he didn't know whether morasses did, but he allowed the thoughts free rein, not making the time nor the effort to think them himself. Gradually, however, as the medication made inroads into first the nebulous fringes and then the more substantial core of his primary headache, the thoughts became more distinct, more intrinsically pertinent. Which didn't necessarily help, because the thoughts merely underscored how much was not known of the relevant details of Münz's murder.

Someone, between the first and the fourth hour of Module 270's ascent, had apparently entered Münz's room, had interrupted Münz mid-bath, had in some as yet undetermined manner caused an electrochemical reaction in said bath that had left the victim, presumably, unable to breathe. Did the killer watch and wait for Münz's death throes to play out? Someone had certainly either stayed, or returned, so as to drain the tainted water from the tub… which Rube had then unthinkingly caused to be sluiced from the module, thereby destroying potentially useful evidence. That couldn't be helped; but it did constitute an additional difficulty for the investigation.

Who had done it? Almost certainly not Münz himself: even if it were possible that the man's final act was to pull the plug on the tub of his own mortality, the act of electroplating oneself just did not seem credible as a last desperate gesture. Münz might well have been in the advanced stages of a terminal illness – according to the information Gordon had gleaned from his handheld search, the scientist was thought to have mere weeks to live – but there were surely less intrinsically painful ways to make an end, had he been so inclined. Plus, no note. No useful clues of any kind, really: while some minor scuffing on the bathroom floor appeared to be recent, the only fingerprints that Gordon's handheld had been able to detect within the bathroom were those of Sheppard Münz himself, Sue's, on the doorhandle and light switch, and Rube's, on the vanity. Sue had discovered the body; Rube had cleaned the rooms in preparation for ascent. The killer had left no prints.

And none of the guests had an alibi worth a damn, when it came down to it: the abysmal lighting in the restaurant, where all had apparently congregated, had seen to that. (Or, more pertinently, *not* seen.)

Layta? He hadn't yet had time to properly search out her background, but, while the HR flack presumably had form in removing people from her workforce, Gordon strongly imagined her methods were generally less final than those employed here. And electroplating just did not seem to fit: it was a highly technical method, with which he had no reason to believe she could be in any way familiar. He didn't like the woman – and he was fairly sure there was mutuality to that feeling – but he didn't believe her capable of murdering someone with whom she had no visible connection.

Kinnerbarth? Well, there was certainly a "tub" connection with Münz's demise, and Gordon supposed the spa specialist might have some familiarity with chroming treatments and the like, but what possible motive could the man have for killing a researcher in an abstruse and unconnected field? Plus, while Gordon had accompanied thousands of guests on previous ascents to geostationary orbit, he'd never before encountered anyone who seemed to have embarked on such an ascent unwittingly. Put simply, he didn't believe Kinnerbarth to be equipped for anything as challenging as premeditated murder, and it was difficult to envisage a situation in which Münz's demise could be at all inadvertent. But, he supposed, if there were any way in which the death *was* an accident, it would most likely have been at the hands of someone like Kinnerbarth.

Fleabass and / or Weppins? He ought possibly to consider these two separately, but it was difficult to do so when they were, in effect, so obviously bundled together within the one physical presence of the surro, and the background searches on his handheld confirmed that they were closely linked as colleagues in the financial services industry, specialising in the processing of funds to the education / research sector. It was distinctly possible, therefore, that they may have had some involvement in the dispersal of grant funding to Münz and Planitz, and if so their silence on the matter, during the interview, might well be incriminating. Or, equally well, it might not. There was, as yet, no smoking gun: while they were involved in grant funding, there'd been nothing from the interview or Gordon's subsequent preliminary background research to suggest they had any direct connection with Münz or his work. It was probably worth searching more deeply on that score, nonetheless. Plus there was a troubling thirty-minute gap in the surro's occupation by first Weppins and then Fleabass: in all likelihood, the device had merely returned to its charging station to maintain power reserves, but that would need to be double-checked.

Madders? There appeared to be no love lost between the filmmaker and the academic, and presumably the suspicious death of a key player in dark-matter research, particularly in such a visually arresting manner, could be a drawcard of sorts for the planned documentary. But would Wyatt Madders have gone to such extreme lengths, given that he did not appear to know who Münz was? Besides, Gordon doubted that the documentarist would have been sufficiently foolish as to self-incriminate by filming Münz's demise, while a death off-camera would not carry nearly so much pathos or marketability.

Which left Planitz... who clearly had much to gain from Münz's demise. Thirty-five megacredits in grant funding, as Münz's share of the joint total they had been awarded. It was a staggeringly large sum, easily enough to kill someone over, if one were even slightly motivated by such things. But was it, in truth, such a magnetic incentive? Because on the face of it, Münz and Planitz had been close collaborators for more than a decade, had apparently pooled their resources in the furtherance of common goals. Wasn't it rather like deciding to kill one's husband so as to be able to afford, on his estate, to buy the house that the pair of you were always going to purchase anyway? The only way in which the admittedly towering pile of credit could be seen as an impetus for provoking Planitz to kill her colleague was if she had disapproved of Münz's plans for his share of the funding and wished, instead, to expend it on something substantially different; and this Gordon had no way of knowing, nor could think of any satisfactory means of interrogating. While he could ask, she could easily dissemble on the subject, if necessary, and he would likely never realise. But a superficial search for images containing the duo returned scenes in which the pair seemed genuinely comfortable in each other's presence: if Planitz harboured animosity towards the deceased, she concealed it well. Still, there could be information to the contrary that he hadn't yet uncovered, either in the public record or in the finer details of their shared academic output. Gordon didn't fancy his chances on that last possibility: the research world of Planitz and Münz was a highly specialised one, in which he was completely at sea. Perhaps Sue, who was distinctly more cluey about matters technical, might be better equipped to form a judgement one way or another as to whether the pair's research history hinted at any important difference of opinion between the chrome-clad doctor and his bereaved colleague and former mentor? But Sue was always rushed off her feet as it was, and Gordon had the distinct sense that forming a reliable opinion on the shape of the Planitz/Münz collaboration might well take substantially longer than just the one ascent cycle, even if pursued with a single-minded intent during that time.

Had he succeeded in eliminating any of the guests from consideration as a possible culprit? Hardly.

Had he made significant inroads into a motive for Münz's murder? Not really.

Had he been able to move anyone front-and-centre as chief suspect for the killing? No.

Had he managed to decipher the vexatious 35 across: *five-barred gate, from the sound of it (6, 10)*? Not even close.

Was he really going to need to interview all of these people again tomorrow, to follow up on questions he hadn't previously known he needed to ask? He didn't want to have to answer that one just now…

And he was still waiting on completion of his handheld's forensic analysis of the crime scene; but for now, there was nothing that could be considered a clue, or a pointer, or a breakthrough.

Sleep was drawing closer; though he sensed that it would be the sleep of the futile and the disillusioned, which was never a rewarding sleep. He decided, by way of forestalling it, to see if Belle was back on shift yet. He could at least ask her about the argument that Münz had had with her.

'Argument? No, Gordon. In fact, I don't even remember this Münz at all,' said Belle, who was indeed ensconced behind the module's reception desk. 'The only interaction I've had that could be classified as any form of argument was with that trashcan-on-wheels, who saw fit to complain about the gradient on the rampway leading to its room. I told it – sorry, him – that none of the earlier surros had ever had any difficulties with the slope of the ramps. Other than that, it's all been sweetness and light. Oh, and the murder, of course.'

Shiny happy people, thought Gordon distractedly. 'But the trashc— but Mr Weppins was quite clear about having seen you *in flagrante argumento* with Sheppard Münz, here, in this very foyer. About dark matter, he said. About an hour into the ascent.' Was it possible that Yusuf Weppins had been seeking to misinform him for some shady purpose?

'Well, all I can say is that it wasn't me,' replied Belle. 'So it must've happened after I'd signed off for the evening. The timing sounds right for that.'

'In which case it would have been Sue,' said Gordon. She'd been due to take over following Belle's shift, hadn't she? *Odd that she didn't mention any earlier run-in with Münz, though, when she told me he'd been found dead.*

'You mean Sia,' said Belle.

'Sue,' insisted Gordon.

'No, Gordon,' explained Belle. 'Sia took over from me, because Sue had to repair something-or-other and to prepare something-or-other else. You know how it is, she always has a hundred and one things that need her attention.'

'Sia?' asked Gordon.

'Yes.'

'Sia *Layta*?'

'Yes, Gordon.'

'On reception?'

'*Yes*, Gordon.'

'But she's not— do you mean to tell me she's *staff*?'

'Yes, Gordon. Surely you knew that already. Didn't you interview her?'

'Well, yes, but I don't think she saw fit to mention…' And then he remembered the business card Layta had given him, which he had pocketed without perusal. He reached into his pocket now and located and extracted the card.

It was blank, but this turned out to be because he was looking at the back of it. He turned it over. *Sia Layta,* it read, in the kind of fussily cursive script, much favoured by wedding invitationalists, of which he'd never seen the point; below which, in a sensible businesslike font, was printed the single word "Relegator". Beside this was the unmistakeable monogram of Skyward Transorbital Enterprises, Inc. His employer.

Real men didn't faint, of course, but it was surely excusable that a type of semi-conscious miasma, at a time like this—

'Gordon.'

His mother was leaning over him, holding a damp facecloth with which she was preparing, he presumed, to wash his face.

No, not his mother, one of his colleagues. Belle.

'Gordon.'

He made an effort to sit up, an action which caused his head to spin. He wondered, idly, what the gravity was set to at the moment.

Belle brushed his face with the damp cloth. It seemed to help. 'Are you alright?' she asked.

'Ow,' he said, which was both a sidestepping of the question and an answer to it. His headache seemed to have returned with a vengeance, or possibly reinforcements.

'Let's get you to sickbay,' she said, as he hauled himself unsteadily to what he had reason to believe were his feet.

'But I need to—'

'Rest, Gordon. You need to rest. And to keep your fluids up.' She led him towards the module's sickbay, a small and unremittingly white room from which repeated cleaning had never managed to dispel that disconcerting hospital smell of baked beans and ammonia. 'When was the last time you slept? Or ate?'

It wasn't tiredness or hunger that caused me to keel over, he thought, though he conceded he couldn't be entirely sure about that. *It was discovering that the Hostile HR Woman is a Skyward employee. If she's here to rationalise staffing levels...*

And then, of course, there was the murder investigation on top of everything else. But he wouldn't do anyone any favours by pushing himself past his metabolic limits. 'You're right,' he replied, seating himself on the room's three-quarter-length bed. 'A couple of hours rest would certainly help.'

Belle eyed him quizzically. 'Perhaps more than a couple of hours. We're not exactly understaffed this run, after all. With Sia.'

No, he thought. *We're not.*

7

Some decisions are taken with no initial reservations, and go on to brook no regrets; conversely, other choices, even from the outset, may seem shaded, ill-judged, even when entirely unforced. Gordon, staring at the bewildering array presented on his handheld's screen, was beginning to believe that he had allowed himself to be talked into one of the latter.

No, that wasn't quite correct. Because *he himself* had done most of the sales-talking required. All Rowan had had to do was to stand back and watch.

It had all sounded so straightforward – a simple twenty-five by twenty-five grid, quite minor in scale compared to the jumbo-sized offerings that specialists were constructing nowadays. And just two-dimensional, of course: none of this three- or four-dimensional crosswordery which had been all the fad of the last couple of years. (There were rumours, he'd heard, of someone who'd gone to the trouble of constructing a six-dimensional crossword, but mercifully his handheld didn't possess sufficient active memory to run the thing, so he couldn't be tempted even in a moment of abject weakness.) Against such manifest complexity, such excess, the promise of a modest two-D puzzle, comprising barely a hundred clues, offered a return to the classic simplicity of yesteryear's crosswords, married with one exciting, beguiling, up-to-the-minute innovation. *This*, he had been assured by Rowan Khollum, the proprietor and chief salesperson of Gordon's favourite boutique crossword-speciality store, One Down, on his last-but-third descent Earthside, was where the future of crosswordage most assuredly was to be found.

And Gordon had fallen for it. He'd duped himself, persuading himself that there was no harm in it, that the twinges he felt, even at the moment he'd handed over his hard-earned virtucash, were just premonitions of excited anticipation. Not a warning signal of any kind. After all, he'd even trialled the puzzle instore, and the clues on the demo were not that fiendish. A one-hundred-and-twenty-three clue puzzle; so what if it was self-aware? What was the worst that could happen?

Now, in Module 270's sickbay, having managed (a) four or so hours of sleep, (b) a replicated snack from the cafeteria (two mueslibars that may or may not have provided his recommended daily intake of extruded plastic), and (c) to outlive his headache of the night before, all he wanted to do was (d) to unwind, and his preference for unwinding was via the medium of the crossword puzzle. But the sentientpuzzle was time-critical, which meant in practice that relaxation went out the window. Already Gordon suspected that his answer to 13 down, which half an hour ago had borne the clue "problematic rhyme with past combat" (7) but now read "horse pulling a pint?" (7), was no longer correct; and it definitely didn't help that the grid was too large for the handheld's small screen to display the whole puzzle at once. (And there had been a helpful menu which allowed you to select the rate of "mutation" which you were willing to experience, with a speed scale ranging from "three-toed sloth" to "overstimulated scramjet test pilot". Gordon had opted for a setting just to the left of the median, a decision which – like the purchase of the puzzle itself – he was now regretting. But could this helpful menu be located in-game? Well, no... it had gone 15 down: "outback perimeter on foot". *Walkabout.*)

As he watched, the clue for 14 across (7 letters) changed from "trodden for delivery" to "confoundedly sawn-off".

He put his fingers to his temples, closed his eyes, and inhaled deeply.

He could quit the puzzle, but he couldn't restart it, nor could he find any way, now, to slow down the mutation rate.

He'd been working on the crossword for the past two weeks, and in all that time the closest he'd been to completing the puzzle was to have just five unsolved clues. He was further behind than that, now, because of the slow but mercilessly unceasing invalidation rate.

Great, he thought. *So my respite, my light relief from a crime I can't solve... is a puzzle I can't solve.*

*

While Gordon had been spinning his metaphorical wheels, his handheld had been doing double duty. Not only had it been facilitating his crossword compulsion, but it had also been labouring through the forensic analysis of the room 204 crime scene. Elemental analysis of Münz's new metal "skin" was consistent with a readily-available industrial treatment, Kromify E-Z-Kote, described in its promotional literature as "the leading air-activated autoelectrochemical plating process in a can". Kromify was, the handheld informed him, widely used for applications as diverse as (1) the fabrication of perfectly-reflective, precisely-shaped surfaces such as mirrors for telescopes, laser beam research, and the like, (2) the chroming of bathroom fittings, and (3) the tastefully non-taxidermic preservation of deceased pets (excepting axolotls).

Which, apart from the "pet" aspect, could as equally implicate Kinnerbarth as Planitz, thought Gordon despondently. Or, indeed, since Kromify was readily available over the counter (and, according to the handheld, was not difficult to use, provided one deployed rubber gloves while working with it), could almost as straightforwardly be any of the other guests, particularly if the intent was to deflect suspicion.

Though the deflecting of suspicion would only be operative if one had prior knowledge of Module 270's passenger list for this ascent...

Who, among the passengers, would have had – or conceivably could have had – such prior knowledge?

And who could have brought aboard the lift-module a sufficiently large quantity of a chemical treatment that, in accordance with the Civil Space Elevation Authority's restrictions on dangerous goods, was expressly proscribed from interorbital transport?

And even if such a passenger could be identified – and the inkling of something that might, given plenty of sunlight and regular watering, bloom into something that could justifiably be termed a suspicion was starting to spark within Gordon's mind – the question remained: *why?* What purpose did Münz's death serve?

Or, asked another way, what did Münz's death *achieve?*

It enriched Planitz, according to a narrow definition of "enrichment" that didn't necessarily apply, Gordon suspected, to the circumstance of a researcher who had just lost a valued colleague and collaborator who would probably have spent the grant money on the same things she would anyway.

It impeded research into dark-matter propulsion, which would have some knock-on benefit to people with vested interests in other forms of propulsion... he'd need to check whether any guests were in that category.

It left bereaved a small and not-especially-close collection of Münz's family members: neither parents nor siblings, according to Gordon's handheld, and no known descendants.

Other than that... it was a mystery.

Which, perhaps, was the point?

His reverie was interrupted by a call on his handheld.

'Gordon.'

'Mr Gordon?'

'Speaking. What's up, Rube?'

'I think I've found something you need to see.'

Gordon sighed. This had been going on all week. 'Rube, if this is another of those trained walrus holovids—'

'Nothing like that, Mr Gordon. I think this might be important.'

'Okay, tell me what you've found.'

Rube told him. Gordon thanked him for the call, disconnected, and descended once more into contemplation.

A suspicion firmed in his mind. Only one passenger, as he now saw it, had both the means and the opportunity, though motive still eluded him. With mounting apprehension, he called on the passenger's room, but it was empty; he sent an urgent memo to Belle, Sue, and Rube to alert him immediately if they sighted the guest. Then he headed for the plant room, to inspect Rube's find.

8

They argued, as men do when confronted with a more-or-less hardware-related task, over the best, most efficient, most straightforwardly counterintuitive way to decouple the electroplating-solution canister from the module's Level 2 bathroom-water supply. Rube had been of the opinion that simply removing the canister would suffice, while Gordon strongly felt that both the canister, inelegantly spliced into the water supply line, and the main Level 2 water tank, needed to be completely removed, because they had no guarantee that the bulk water supply had not been contaminated by the canister's contents.

'Wait. Isn't all this pipework normally concealed behind panels?' Gordon asked.

'Oh, yes, it was, Mr Gordon, sir, and they weren't easy to remove without the special tool, which wasn't where I'd left it. I'm afraid they got a bit damaged when I took them off.'

'Did they now.' Gordon looked around the plant room. 'So where are these damaged panels?'

Rube's Adam's apple gave a brief jump, like an express lift ascending one floor then coming down again. He flicked a glance at the plant room's airlock. 'Mass minimisation, Mr Gordon.'

Gordon refrained from direct comment, instead offering a brief silent prayer on behalf of the junknauts involved in interception and removal of space debris. 'Well. In any case, the first thing is to detach this canister. So why not just—' He broke off at the sound of small wheels rolling across the plant room's plastinoleum flooring behind him.

He turned.

The surro had compacted down to barely more than one metre in height. *Not a choice I would have made, were I seeking to intimidate,*

Gordon thought. *I'd have opted to go full-height, give it an altogether more ominous appearance.* He was fairly sure 'intimidation' was the intention, nonetheless. Maybe it was the no-nonsense, purposeful directness of the surro's approach. Maybe it was the evident stealth with which it had made its way into the storage bay. Maybe it was the unit's identity pictogram, which now displayed a white skull-and-crossbones on an ink-black background. Or maybe it was the array of weaponry the device deployed in apparent readiness to strike. Affixed to the top of its largely-retracted head was the broad, open-mouthed barrel of a Gigavolto Microwave Bazooka, one of the nastiest pieces of crowd-control weaponry available anywhere within the Solar System. Clasped in its left hand was what Gordon surmised to be a Surestun Haptic Bludgeon, a high-tech pulverising implement known colloquially as the Phrenologist's Friend. And the slim, shinily-lacquered crimson cylinder that the surro wielded in its ungloved and chrome-splashed right hand could only be the new Deadly-Sirius Multimodal Dagger, an upscale and exceptionally versatile cutting weapon that had already earned itself the sobriquet "the Swish Harmy Knife".

The surro stopped rolling, less than two metres from the group. And when it spoke, it wasn't with Fleabass's voice, nor Weppins'.

It wasn't with a recognisably human voice at all.

'Over to the airlock, please,' it intoned. 'Just you,' it clarified, gesturing at Gordon with the knife. 'The lunkus has a job to do for me first.'

It seemed to take Rube several seconds to realise that he was the one identified as "the lunkus". Gordon used the time, which was otherwise spent in shuffling towards the plant room's airlock at a speed that seemed the best compromise between "obedience" and "delay", to scour his surroundings for items with which he could defend himself from the surro. There were plenty of such items, but they were all bolted to the wall. A desperate effort might well prise some makeshift weaponry loose; but there was the slight problem that the prising would very likely rupture the module's outer casing, leading to death for himself, Rube, and, if the module's emergency vac-seal system didn't function perfectly, every other human physically aboard 270. Not the preferred option, then.

He racked his brain, trying to elucidate some technique by which he could outsmart his assailant. But villains weren't like crossword puzzles: they were dangerous to play unless you had such a detailed knowledge of their psychological makeup as to be able to reliably predict their responses to any action, and Gordon didn't have such knowledge. Not yet, not against the foe he currently faced. Unless he could quickly derive such knowledge, or unless he were suddenly the beneficiary of some *deus ex machina* twist of circumstance – and what, realistically, was the chance of that? – he was very likely to die, either from asphyxiation *in vacuo* or at the business end of the surro's weaponry, within minutes. Possibly seconds.

'You,' said the surro, gesturing towards Rube, 'remove that electrolyte canister from the water line. Then lower it carefully to the floor.'

Rube ambled over to the plant-room wall and reached up for the Kromify container, first closing the valve on the main line.

'Aarrrgh!' said the surro. 'You're in the way – move to the side and do it.'

Rube attempted to comply, staring down towards the surro for approval, then reached out again. 'I can't,' he said. 'I can only get leverage if I'm standing straight in front of it.'

'That'll have to do. Just don't take too long about it.'

Gordon, watching this performance, still felt powerless to try anything: though the bulk of the surro's attention, as judged by the orientation of its optical and auditory receptors, seemed to be on Rube, he was keenly aware that the unit's microwave bazooka was firmly trained on himself. *It's not worth trying anything,* he thought. *I just have to hope an opportunity arises. But what's the song-and-dance it's putting Rube through?*

Of course. Footage. And footage can as easily be compiled and shown backwards as forwards. It's going to show Rube in the act of connecting up the solution that killed Münz.

The Kromify canister looked heavy. Presumably it still contained a fair fraction of its original liquid load. Gordon waited until Rube had just uncoupled the connection to the water line, then he called out sharply, 'Don't drop it, Rube!'

Rube, in his surprise at Gordon's interjection, dropped the container. It spilled away from the apprentice, mostly sloshing across the plant room's decking. The surro moved quickly back a couple of paces, out of the silvery tide, and discharged its microwave bazooka towards the airlock. A ripple of concentrated heat surged past Gordon – he'd moved aside barely in time – and struck the airlock's inner hatch. The hatch's plastiminium frame buckled, bubbled, and deformed, congealing into a disturbingly warped (though still unbreached) surface.

It's a good thing that wasn't a more intense blast, thought Gordon, only now realising how injudicious he had been in provoking the surro (or, more to the point, the woman controlling the surro). But it looked as though the airlock wasn't going to be usable any time soon, which suited him well enough in the circumstances.

'I wouldn't try that kind of thing again, Mutton,' the surro intoned. 'Don't make me improvise.'

'No, you wouldn't want that,' suggested Gordon, keenly aware of the bazooka's stare directed straight towards him.

'What's that supposed to mean?' asked the surro.

'I just mean you'll make another mistake,' said Gordon. 'Like the one you made when you killed Münz.' *Where am I going with this?* he asked himself, and waited for an answer to that question. There wasn't one forthcoming, except: *Time. Play for time.*

'The only mistake I've made,' replied the surro, 'was missing you with that maser burst. Stay where you are.' This last statement was directed at Rube, who had taken two steps away from the site of the spillage.

'I'm just going to get a mop,' he protested. 'Spillages need to be dealt with promptly.' He gestured with his hands, in a fashion that Gordon presumed was intended to represent either the form, or the function, or possibly both, of a mop.

'There'll be no need for th—' said the surro, and froze.

'We'd better escape, Mr Gordon, sir,' said Rube, moving past the now-immobile surro towards the door.

'Rube,' said Gordon, 'what just happened?'

'I put a stop on the surro with the safety gesture,' explained Rube.

'And in English?'

'There's an emergency gesture you can use to deactivate a surro,' said Rube. 'It was in last week's training assignment. Mr Gordon, we really should leave the plant room.'

'Yes, of course,' said Gordon, stepping mistrustfully past the surro. He paused, turned, and prised the weapons from its hands, tossing the Haptic Bludgeon to the room's far side and absently pocketing the sheathed knife. '*Why* is there a gesture for deactivating a surro? I mean, I'm not complaining, by any means…'

'It's if they're running amok,' explained a voice from the doorway.

Half-silhouetted against the corridor's blue-white lighting were the forms of Belle Hopp and Sia Layta, connected by the auxiliary form of the gun held in Layta's hand and pointed at the small of Belle's back. Before Gordon or Rube had any time to react – other than, on Gordon's part, to reflect that dropping the Swish Harmy Knife into his pocket, rather than retaining it in his hand, had been a spectacularly unhelpful idea – Layta shoved Belle roughly into the plant room, advanced a step into the room herself, and slid the door closed behind her. She fumbled for the latch while training the gun on Belle, on Rube, and primarily on Gordon. 'So. Let's keep this little staff meeting brief, shall we?' She did something to the gun, which issued a steadily-rising hum that might be construed as either reassuring or unnerving, depending on which end of the weapon was closest to you. 'Over against that wall there, please,' she directed, indicating the section of wall against which the water mains line was mounted. She stepped carefully around the inert form of the surro and positioned herself at the far edge of the shining puddle of chroming solution, facing her three captives who had now reached the wall and were organising themselves very much in the manner of schoolchildren instructed to pose for what, on the face of it, looked likely to qualify as the most dispiriting class photo ever. 'Now, who wants to go first?' The gun, which judging from its appearance was a base-model Zappem & Runn Plasma Jolter – crude, but of undoubted lethality – remained pointed at Gordon.

'If you're acting to terminate us,' said Gordon, a lump in his throat from all this contemplation-of-weaponry-in-unfortunate-circumstances business and the intimations of mortality which went with it, 'aren't you formally obliged to provide us with the grounds for termination?'

'If you think I'm—' Layta began, then allowed an unpleasant smile to work its way across her face. 'Actually, why not? Satisfy the bureaucratic requirements. Basically, Mantra, you've been around too much murder. *Those* are the grounds for termination.'

'You're looking to kill me – kill us – because I've been on hand when other people have committed murder? That doesn't make sense.'

'Oh, it makes perfect sense,' replied Layta. 'One of the benefits of my job is the access it gives to the records of each module's ascent and descent. Hundreds of thousands of journeys through the atmosphere. But when, just out of idle curiosity more than anything else, I looked at the incidence of major crime on those ascents and descents, do you know what I found? All but one of those incidents, Mr Maelstrom, involved you. I ran the numbers on that, and statistically it just does not add up. Blind chance cannot explain Module 270's status as the murder capital of Skyward Transorbital Enterprises. But something else can.'

'Actually,' replied Gordon, 'most of the murders happened elsewhere.'

'Doesn't matter,' said Layta. 'You were involved in all of them, and that's the key.'

'I wasn't *involved* in them. I *solved* them.'

'Exactly,' said Layta. 'And that's the problem.'

'I don't follow.'

'Oh, come now. Surely you've heard of the Marples-Maigret threshold?'

'Actually, no, I haven't.'

'A man in your line of work? I find that difficult to believe. But to update you, the Marples-Maigret threshold is a measure that comes into play in criminology, whenever a statistically improbable concentration of murders or other significant crimes is observed to occur within a localised area, and when said crimes are consistently solved by one independent and notably idiosyncratic individual. Once the threshold is exceeded, this crime-solving individual then spontaneously and unavoidably attracts further major crimes, at a steadily escalating rate, by, as I understand it, some combination of sleuthing reputation and a sort of criminal gravitational attraction. You are one crime-solution away from exceeding that threshold, Mr Mattress, and therefore you need to be stopped. Irreversibly. Before the murders become self-sustaining.'

'This is nonsense!' Gordon expostulated, not even pausing to consider whether "expostulated" was truly the best verb choice in this instance.

'No, it's well-documented. There are numerous lengthy case studies by Christie, Parker, Hammett, Conan Doyle, and Simenon that demonstrate the effect repeatedly. Once enough people meet an unpleasant end, others will continue to do so. You, Marksman, are a liability to Skyward – we're already getting booking requests that specify "please don't put me in the module that people die in", and once the murder rate starts to climb any further, our sales are really going to suffer. So, sorry, Maxipad, it's you or Skyward. And Skyward is too big to fail.'

'But – and this is still utterly ridiculous, but – then why Belle? And Rube?'

'Ms Hopp has been on hand for too many of your escapades; she's probably contaminated by the threshold too. I can't take that chance. Mr Greenhorn just happened to be in the room. Sad, but there you go. You might all want to close your eyes for the next bit.'

'None of this explains why Münz had to die,' complained Gordon.

'Doesn't it? I created the perfect insoluble crime. I rearranged the ascent schedules, during a week when I was covering for a colleague from Ticketing, to ensure that every one of the guests – myself excepted – had a motive and an opportunity for killing Münz, whose days were in any case numbered because of his terminal illness.

Planitz stood to gain financially. Madders would have gained notoriety and therefore a box-office boost for his upcoming doco. Kinnerbarth would be exacting revenge on the man who broke up his marriage. Flea—'

'I didn't know that,' said Gordon.

'You didn't dig deep enough,' replied Layta. 'Fleabass and Weppins had invested heavily – and in my opinion unwisely – in a competing drive technology. With Münz out of the picture, their stock would rise substantially.'

'I didn't know *that* either.'

'Again, you didn't look hard enough. I had thought that by feeding you the perfect crime, you would run aground, and the Marples-Maigret threshold would not be breached. But, as your memo to your colleagues demonstrated – and yes, I have admin privileges on staff comms, so I saw that memo too – you recognised it for the setup it was.'

'I had suspicions,' said Gordon. 'But I hadn't solved any of it. Except for finding the Kromify canister down here – and that was just luck on Rube's part – and figuring how you got into Münz's room to drain the bath without triggering the corridor cams. You used the surro, because the cams are biosensitive; they wouldn't register the surro. And you arranged it so both Fleabass and Weppins would believe the other of them was in control for the time you'd hacked into it. But I didn't know *why*. All of this far-fetched Marples-Maigret stuff—'

'You're filibustering, Mancave,' said Layta. 'Hush now. It's lights out time.'

And indeed it was.

9

Upstairs, in the cafeteria, the overworked Sue Sheff – who had not had any time to check her messages and who was, under her breath, muttering dark things about colleagues who apparently chose to sleep in rather than pitch in on this time-consuming business of keeping a hotel operating – had just switched on the replicator, the dishblaster, and the MIG welding rig all at once, without for once heeding the combined load's impact on Module 270's struggling power supply.

The lighting was off for only five seconds, but that was plenty long enough for a laser blast aimed at the spot where Gordon, Rube, and Belle had been gathered; for a few expertly-chosen swear words and an "oof!" uttered in a brassy female voice; for the thud of a hard object and a human body hitting the plant room floor almost simultaneously; and for Gordon to collide painfully with something so large and so apologetic that he was ninety-nine percent certain it was Rube.

The dim emergency lights came on to the sight of Rube sprawled uncomfortably on the decking, clutching his stomach, and of Belle seated awkwardly on the back of the prone Sia Layta. The latter was fumbling to reach the gun that lay just beyond her outstretched fingertips. Gordon tottered over, almost skidding on the spilt chroming-solution puddle in the process, and kicked the Plasma Jolter well out of reach. Then, seeing that Rube had recovered sufficiently to have offered Belle assistance in restraining the fluently-cursing Layta, he went off in search of tethers to effect a more long-term confinement of the murderous HR rep.

He had reached the midpoint of the rampway leading to the next level when a shrill and mercifully short klaxon note cut through the air, followed by a highly-amplified announcement uttered by one of those annoyingly-calm-and-slow synthesised voices: 'The power supply for module... Two. Seven. Zero... has gone critical. You have... five... seconds to launch the escape pods. Please do not attempt to retrieve your personal belongings. The power supply for module... Two. Seven. Zero... has gone critical. You have... five—'

Then silence.

Then what turned out to be definitely more than five seconds' worth of 'hold' music.

While waiting for his heart to slow, Gordon, who had started retracing his steps to the plant room, stopped and took out his handheld. Made a call. 'Sue?'

'Yeah, sorry 'bout that, Gordo.'

'Sorry about what?'

'Pressed the wrong button. Don't worry, it's just a recording.'

'So we're not imminently in danger of the module exploding around us?'

'Not unless I press another wrong button. But it's okay, I think I know what I'm doing now.'

'What *are* you doing now?'

'Rebooting the power supply. Auxiliary won't last much longer, and if we stop hauling upwards, the module beneath us will ram into us in a few minutes... hold on... dammit... no, I think that's okay. Yep, I think we're good to go. No splody stuff today.'

'Oh, good,' said Gordon.

The module had put several thousand more kilometres below it by the time things aboard Skyward 270 could truly be said to have settled down. Layta was incarcerated within the subbasement dangerous-goods lockup (the dangerous goods themselves having been moved to the lost-property store, which was a less than ideal arrangement but still seemed like the best option for keeping Layta securely confined until the module reached Skytop in another day or so). Gordon had been in touch with Weppins and Fleabass, explaining that a severe technical malfunction in the surro had cut short their shared remote experience of ascent and assuring them that a representative of Skyward Ticketing would contact them to arrange a substitute voyage at no expense. Sue had assisted Gordon with the task of recovering from his handheld the audio recording of the plant-room altercation with the surro and then with Layta – it had been fortunate that he had had the handheld's crossword function set to "verbal instruction" mode, or he would not have had the benefit of a recorded confession from the murderer. Belle had then told Sue, in no uncertain terms, that she was excused for the next eight hours and should get some well-earned rest while the other three of them set about keeping the module ticking over. Rube spent most of that time cleaning up in the plant room, and repairing what damage was amenable to in-transit repair: the melted inner hatch of the plant room airlock, though, would need to wait until they reached Skytop, or perhaps even their next time Earthside. Belle set about ensuring the comfort of the three passengers, Kinnerbarth, Madders, and Planitz, who remained at large, and Gordon spent several hours in conference with the Skytop police (whose wargaming problems had by now been resolved) apprising them of the developments of the past twenty-four hours. Finally, though, he was able to take a seat in the cafeteria with a coffee, a danish, and the Crossword of Ongoing Infuriation active on the handheld in front of him.

12 down: Excessively careful baker's rite of propitiation? (9, 2, 7)

Gordon spent several minutes staring into what would have been the middle distance if the middle distance hadn't been obstructed by the cafeteria wall. He scowled, he sipped his coffee, he chewed a mouthful of danish, and he scowled again, this time more contentedly.

A-bun-dance of caution. He spoke the answer, and the letters filled themselves in on the crossword's matrix.

Just the one left now. 35 across: *Five-barred gate, from the sound of it (6, 10).* He wondered if he should wait for the clue to change to something more comprehensible; but knowing his luck, it would be the other clues, the ones he'd already solved, which morphed first, and unsolved themselves. But this one had him stumped.

Belle came into the cafeteria, followed by Rube. They smiled at Gordon as they approached his table. Both were limping a little, a legacy of the desperate activity in the plantroom. Gordon sympathised; his own gait probably wouldn't look any more graceful at the moment.

Gait, he thought. *I wonder…*

Belle took a seat while Rube went to collect coffees for them. 'Well, this has been an ascent and a half, hasn't it?' she asked.

Gordon narrowly refrained from observing that it hadn't yet been even half an ascent. 'That was a pretty efficient takedown you pulled, of Layta back there,' he remarked instead.

'It didn't seem like I had anything to lose,' she replied. 'And it just goes to show, you never forget those hover-derby skills.'

He made a noncommittal noise in response, but his mind was back elsewhere already. *Gate. Gait. Five: no options there. Barred… baa'd… bard.*

Five baa'd gait?

Five bard gait?

Rube sat down after placing two coffees, a muffin, and a wedge of cheesecake on the table. 'Say, Mr Gordon, did you—'

'Iambic pentameter,' Gordon announced excitedly, and his handheld gave a self-satisfied little trill to announce that he'd successfully completed the crossword. He shut it off quickly before it could decide to escalate the puzzle to the next level. 'Sorry, Rube, you were asking?'

'I was just wondering if you thought there was anything in that Margaret Maple stuff that Ms Layta was going on about. You know, the murders attracting other murders and stuff like that.'

'No, I don't think we need to worry about that,' replied Gordon. 'It'd be a pretty silly world if it operated by such rules.'

'That's what I thought,' said Rube, before biting off a large chunk of muffin.

'Damn,' said Belle, pushing her chair back. 'Just got buzzed for room service. Mr Bigshot Documentary-Maker says he wants to place an order. He's probably just complaining about the lighting again. I'll be back in a few minutes.'

It was just one minute later that she called his handheld. 'Gordon, I was on my way past room one-oh-four, and the door was open. Not quite sure how to put this... but we've got a problem with Prof Planitz.'

'What kind of a problem?' he asked, wondering why his coffee suddenly tasted of trepidation.

'Well, she's not moving at all,' replied Belle. 'Plus she's looking a bit melty.'

Gordon's spirits plummeted. *It begins*, he thought.

DISCLAIMER: Skyward Transorbital Enterprises, Inc., regrets that the lift-module 270 featured in these reports concerning the activities of our former long-serving employee, Lift Operator (3rd Class) Grodon Mammal, is no longer in service as a result of catastrophic and irreparable heat damage to an auxiliary airlock. We apologise to those of our valued customers who have expressed a particular preference for travel within this now-defunct lift-module, and trust that they will find the service on any of our five-hundred-and-fifty-nine other lift-modules, each making the ascent to (and descent from) the Skytop Plaza on a near-weekly basis, just as memorable.

It is the official position of Skyward Transorbital Enterprises, Inc., that the rumoured breaching of the notional Marple-Maigret threshold onboard Module 270, under Mr Mammal's stewardship, is utterly fallacious and without foundation in anything approximating fact.

Mr Mammal is no longer associated with Skyward Transorbital Enterprises, Inc. For reasons utterly unrelated to Skyward's nonexistent concerns over the Marple-Maigret threshold, he is now serving as cleaner / janitor / infotainment officer on board Chastity Cosmic's new faster-than-FTL interstellar passenger vessel, the *Crimea River*.

Small presses depend on word of mouth.

If you've enjoyed this book, please mention it to friends.
Or leave a review on Goodreads, Amazon, LibraryThing, or elsewhere.

Acknowledgements

'Murder on the Zenith Express' was first published in *Andromeda Spaceways Inflight Magazine* 29 (2007), ed. Dirk Flinthart. 'Single Handed' was first published in *Kaleidotrope* 6 (2009), ed. Fred Coppersmith. 'The Fall Guy' was first published in *Masques* (CSFG Publishing: ed. Gillian Polack & Scott Hopkins, 2009). 'The Hunt for Red Leicester' was first published in *Flight 404 / The Hunt for Red Leicester* (Peggy Bright Books: ed. Edwina Harvey, 2012). 'Elevator Pitch' was first published in *Difficult Second Album: more stories of Xenobiology, Space Elevators, and Bats Out Of Hell* (Peggy Bright Books: ed. Edwina Harvey, 2014). 'This Guy's The Limit' is new to this collection.

About the Author

Born and raised in North Canterbury, New Zealand, Simon Petrie now lives in Canberra, Australia, with his books, his occasional ongoing forays into scientific research, and his least-effort plans for galactic domination. His short fiction has appeared in numerous places; much of it has been conveniently corralled into his collection *80,000 Totally Secure Passwords That No Hacker Would Ever Guess*. He has been shortlisted several times for the Sir Julius Vogel, Ditmar, and Aurealis Awards, and he has won the Sir Julius Vogel Award three times: in 2010 for Best New Talent and in 2013 and 2018, with *Flight 404* and *Matters Arising from the Identification of the Body* respectively, for Best Novella. He also scored a coveted Dishonourable Mention in the 2011 Bulwer-Lytton Fiction Contest.

He has edited five issues (numbers 35, 40, 51, 54, and 61) of *Andromeda Spaceways Inflight Magazine*, and has co-edited two anthologies (*Light Touch Paper, Stand Clear* and *Use Only As Directed*, published by Peggy Bright Books) with Edwina Harvey and one (*Next*, published by CSFG Publishing) with Rob Porteous. He's also acted as a typesetter and e-book formatter for several small-press and indie publishers in Australia and North America. He is currently a member of the Canberra Speculative Fiction Guild and SpecFicNZ writers' communities.

Also by Simon Petrie

She took her helmet off.
That's where it starts; that's where it ends.
That's all there is.

Tanja Morgenstein, daughter of a wealthy industrialist and a geochemist, is dead from exposure to Titan's lethal, chilled atmosphere, and Guerline Scarfe must determine why.

This novella blends hard-SF extrapolation with elements of contemporary crime fiction, to envisage a future human society in a hostile environment, in which a young woman's worst enemies may be those around her.

Matters Arising from the Identification of the Body is a Sir Julius Vogel Award winning SF / mystery novella, out now.

Also by Simon Petrie

Light levels are low. It's killingly cold. These conditions are, it transpires, connected.

The icy landscape around you—hillocks, boulders, ravines, foregrounding a hazy, rumpled horizon beneath an opaque, lowering sky—wears a patina that shades from sepia to umber, puddled with drifts of dark sand. The atmosphere, though thick, would permit only a parody of respiration: there is no succour in it. Were it not for the insulating, carefully-regulated containment of your suit, you would be dead within minutes, frozen solid within an hour.

Welcome to Titan.

Wide Brown Land: stories of Titan is a collection of eleven hard-SF short stories set on the same Titan that Guerline Scarfe (*Matters Arising from the Identification of the Body*) calls home.

Also by Simon Petrie

Amorous space squids. Sentient fridges. A derelict alien spacecraft adrift within an interstellar cloud. Speed-dating zombies. The truth behind the extinction of the dinosaurs. A potentially lethal interasteroidal freight consignment. And a planet on which biological diversification has utterly failed to take hold in eight billion years.

80,000 Totally Secure Passwords That No Hacker Would Ever Guess is a misleadingly-named collection of SF short fiction, sometimes humorous and sometimes deadly serious. While several of these stories have previously appeared in the earlier collections *Rare Unsigned Copy* and *Difficult Second Album* (both now out-of-print), this new collection also includes a significant amount of newer fiction.

Also by Simon Petrie

'They're dead. They're all dead.'

The comment, innocent of deeper intent, is on the flowers withering in a glass vase. But there's a flash of panic, in response, that I only perceive on later re-examination.

The search for a missing interstellar passenger vessel brings investigator Charmain Mertz back to the unwelcoming world of her boyhood.

Flight 404 is a Sir Julius Vogel Award winning SF / mystery novella.

www.ingramcontent.com/pod-product-compliance
Lightning Source LLC
Chambersburg PA
CBHW021420110726
47901CB00008B/2237